SLEEPING
GIANTS

SLEEPING GIANTS

BOOK ONE OF THE THEMIS FILES

SYLVAIN NEUVEL

DEL REY
NEW YORK

Copyright © 2016 by Sylvain Neuvel

Published in the United States by Del Rey, an imprint of Random House, a division of Penguin Random House LLC, New York.

DEL REY and the HOUSE colophon are registered trademarks of Penguin Random House LLC.

Library of Congress Cataloging-in-Publication Data
Names: Neuvel, Sylvain.
Title: Sleeping giants / Sylvain Neuvel.
Description: New York : Del Rey, [2016] |
Series: The themis files ; book 1
Identifiers: LCCN 2015040166| ISBN 9781101886694
(hardback : acid-free paper) | ISBN 9781101886700 (ebook)
Subjects: LCSH: Giants—Fiction. | Robots—Fiction. |
Women physicists—Fiction. | Science fiction. | BISAC:
FICTION / Science Fiction / Adventure. | FICTION /
Technological. | FICTION / Action & Adventure.
Classification: LCC PR9199.4.N476 S58 2016 |
DDC 813/.6—dc23
LC record available at
https://lccn.loc.gov/2015040166

Printed in the United States of America on
acid-free paper

randomhousebooks.com

2 4 6 8 9 7 5 3 1

First Edition

Book design by Elizabeth A. D. Eno

À Théodore.
Maintenant, on va t'apprendre
à lire . . . et l'anglais.

SLEEPING GIANTS

PROLOGUE

It was my eleventh birthday. I'd gotten a new bike from my father: white and pink, with tassels on the handles. I really wanted to ride it, but my parents didn't want me to leave while my friends were there. They weren't really my friends though. I was never really good at making friends. I liked reading; I liked walking in the woods; I liked being alone. And I always felt a little out of place with other kids my age. So when birthdays came by, my parents usually invited the neighbors' kids over. There were a lot of them, some whose names I barely knew. They were all very nice, and they all brought gifts. So I stayed. I blew out the candles. I opened the presents. I smiled a lot. I can't remember most of the gifts because all I could think about was getting out and trying that bicycle. It was about dinnertime by the time everyone left and I couldn't wait another minute. It would soon be dark; once it was, my father wouldn't let me leave the house until morning.

I snuck out the back door and pedaled as fast as I could into the woods at the end of the street. It must have been ten minutes before I started slowing down. Perhaps it was getting a little too dark for comfort and I was thinking about going back. Maybe I was just tired. I stopped for a minute, listening to the wind throwing the branches around. Fall had arrived. The forest had turned into a motley landscape and given new depth to the hillsides. The air suddenly got cold and wet, as if it were about to rain. The sun was going down and the sky behind the trees was as pink as those tassels.

I heard a crack behind me. It could have been a hare. Something drew my eye to the bottom of the hill. I left my bicycle on the trail and started slowly making my way down, moving branches out of my way. It was hard to see, as the leaves hadn't fallen yet, but there was this eerie turquoise glow seeping through the branches. I couldn't pinpoint where it came from. It wasn't the river; I could hear that in the distance, and the light was much closer. It seemed to be coming from everything.

I got to the bottom of the hill. Then the ground disappeared from under my feet.

I don't remember much after that. I was out for several hours and the sun was coming up when I came to. My father was standing about fifty feet above me. His lips were moving, but I couldn't hear a sound.

The hole I was in was perfectly square, about the size of our house. The walls were dark and straight with bright, beautiful turquoise light shining out of intricate carvings. There was light coming out of just about everything around me. I moved my hands around a bit. I was lying on a bed of dirt, rocks, and broken branches. Underneath the debris, the surface was slightly curved, smooth to the touch, and cold, like some type of metal.

I hadn't noticed them before, but there were firemen above, yellow jackets buzzing around the hole. A rope fell a few feet from my head. Soon, I was strapped onto a stretcher and hoisted into daylight.

My father didn't want to talk about it afterward. When I asked what I had fallen into, he just found new clever ways of explaining what a hole was. It was about a week later that someone rang the doorbell. I called for my father to go, but I got no answer. I ran down the stairs and opened the door. It was one of the firemen that had gotten me out of the hole. He'd taken some pictures and thought I'd like to see them. He was right. There I was, this tiny little thing at the bottom of the hole, lying on my back in the palm of a giant metal hand.

PART ONE

BODY PARTS

FILE NO. 003

INTERVIEW WITH DR. ROSE FRANKLIN, PH.D., SENIOR SCIENTIST, ENRICO FERMI INSTITUTE

Location: University of Chicago, Chicago, IL

—How big was the hand?

—6.9 meters, about twenty-three feet; though it seemed much larger for an eleven-year-old.

—What did you do after the incident?

—Nothing. We didn't talk about it much after that. I went to school every day like any kid my age. No one in my family had ever been to college, so they insisted I keep going to school. I majored in physics.

I know what you're going to say. I wish I could tell you I went into science because of the hand, but I was always good at it. My parents figured out I had a knack for it early on. I must have been four years old when I got my first science kit for Christmas. One of those electronics kits. You could make a telegraph, or things like that, by squeezing wires into little metal springs. I don't think I would have done anything different had I listened to my father and stayed home that day.

Anyway, I graduated from college and I kept doing the only thing I knew how to do. I went to school. You should have seen my dad when we learned I was accepted at the University of Chicago. I've never seen anyone so proud in my life. He wouldn't have been any happier had he won a million dollars. They hired me at the U of C after I finished my Ph.D.

—When did you find the hand again?

—I didn't. I wasn't looking for it. It took seventeen years, but I guess you could say it found me.

—What happened?

—To the hand? The military took over the site when it was discovered.

—When was that?

—When I fell in. It took about eight hours before the military stepped in. Colonel Hudson—I think that was his name—was put in charge of the project. He was from the area so he knew pretty much everyone. I don't remember ever meeting him, but those who did had only good things to say about the man.

I read what little was left of his notes—most of it was redacted by the military. In the three years he spent in charge, his main focus had always been figuring out what those carvings meant. The hand itself, which is mostly referred to as "the artifact," is mentioned in passing only a few times, evidence that whoever built that room must have had a complex enough religious system. I think he had a fairly precise notion of what he wanted this to be.

—What do you think that was?

—I have no idea. Hudson was career military. He wasn't a physicist. He wasn't an archaeologist. He had never studied anything resembling anthropology, linguistics, anything that would be remotely useful in this situation. Whatever preconceived notion he had, it must have come from popular culture, watching Indiana Jones or something. Fortunately for him, he had competent people surrounding him. Still, it must have been awkward, being in charge and having no idea what's going on most of the time.

What's fascinating is how much effort they put into disproving their own findings. Their first analysis indicated the room was built about three thousand years ago. That made little sense to them, so they tried carbon-dating organic material found on the hand. The tests showed it to be much older, somewhere between five thousand and six thousand years old.

—That was unexpected?

—You could say that. You have to understand that this flies in the face of everything we know about American civilizations. The oldest civilization we're aware of was located in the Norte Chico region of Peru, and the hand appeared to be about a thousand years older. Even if it weren't, it's fairly obvious that no one carried a giant hand from South America all the way to South Dakota, and there were no civilizations as advanced in North America until much, much later.

In the end, Hudson's team blamed the carbon dating on contamination from surrounding material. After a few years of sporadic research, the site was determined to be twelve hundred years old and classified as a worship temple for some offshoot of Mississippian civilization.

I went through the files a dozen times. There is absolutely nothing, no evidence whatsoever to support that theory, other than the fact that it makes more sense than anything the data would suggest. If I had to guess, I would say that Hudson saw no military interest whatsoever in all this. He probably resented seeing his career slowly wither in an underground research lab and was eager to come up with anything, however preposterous, just to get out of there.

—Did he?

—Get out? Yes. It took a little more than three years, but he finally got his wish. He had a stroke while walking his dog and slipped into a coma. He died a few weeks later.

—What happened to the project after he died?

—Nothing. Nothing happened. The hand and panels collected dust in a warehouse for fourteen years until the project was demilitarized. Then the University of Chicago took over the research with NSA funding and somehow I was put in charge of studying the hand I fell in when I was a child. I don't really believe in fate, but somehow "small world" doesn't begin to do this justice.

—Why would the NSA get involved in an archaeological project?

—I asked myself the same question. They fund all kinds of research, but this seems to fall outside their usual fields of interest. Maybe they were interested in the language for cryptology; maybe they had an interest in the material the hand is made of. In any case, they gave us a pretty big budget so I didn't ask too many questions. I was given a small team to handle the hard science before we handed everything over to the anthropology department. The project was still classified as top secret and, just like my predecessor, I was moved into an underground lab. I believe you've read my report, so you know the rest.

—Yes, I have read it. You sent your report after only four months. Some might think it was a little hasty.

—It was a preliminary report, but yes. I don't think it was premature. OK, maybe a little, but I had made significant discoveries and I didn't think I could go much further with the data that I had, so why wait? There is enough in that underground room to keep us guessing for several lifetimes. I just don't think we have the knowledge to get much more out of this without getting more data.

—Who is we?

—Us. Me. You. Mankind. Whatever. There are things in that lab that are just beyond our reach right now.

—Ok, so tell me about what you do understand. Tell me about the panels.

—It's all in my report. There are sixteen of them, approximately ten feet by thirty-two feet each, less than an inch thick. All sixteen panels were made around the same period, approximately three thousand years ago. We . . .

—If I may. I take it you do not subscribe to the cross-contamination theory?

—As far as I'm concerned, there's no real reason not to trust the carbon dating. And to be honest, how old these things are is the least of our problems. Did I mention the symbols have been glowing for the last seventeen years, with no apparent power source?

Each wall is made of four panels and has a dozen rows of eighteen to twenty symbols carved into it. Rows are divided into sequences of six or seven symbols. We counted fifteen distinct symbols in total. Most are used several times, some appear only once. Seven of them are curvy, with a dot in the center, seven are made of straight lines, and one is just a dot. They are simple in design but very elegant.

—Had the previous team been able to interpret any of the markings?

—Actually, one of the few sections of Hudson's report left intact by the military was the linguistic analysis. They had compared the symbols to every known writing system, past or present, but found no interesting correlation. They assumed each sequence of symbols represented a proposition, like an English sentence, but with no frame of reference, they couldn't even speculate as to their interpretation. Their work was thorough enough and documented at every step. I saw no reason to do the same thing twice and I declined the offer to add a linguist to the team. With nothing to compare this to, there was logically no way to arrive at any sort of meaning.

Perhaps I was biased—because I stumbled onto it—but I felt drawn to the hand. I couldn't explain it, but every fiber of my being was telling me the hand was the important piece.

—Quite a contrast from your predecessor. So what can you tell me about it?

—Well, it's absolutely stunning, but I assume you're not that interested in aesthetics. It measures 22.6 feet in length from the wrist to the tip of the middle finger. It seems to be solid, made of the same metallic material as the wall panels, but it's at least two thousand years older. It is dark gray, with some bronze overtones, and it has subtle iridescent properties.

The hand is open, fingers close together, slightly bent, as if holding something very precious, or a handful of sand, trying not to spill it. There are grooves where human skin would normally fold, others that seem purely decorative. All are glowing the same bright turquoise, which brings out the iridescence in the metal. The hand looks strong, but . . . *sophisticated* is the only word that comes to mind. I think it's a woman's hand.

—I am more interested in facts at this point. What is this strong but sophisticated hand made of?

—It proved nearly impossible to cut or otherwise alter by conventional means. It took several attempts to remove even a small sample from one of the wall panels. Mass spectrography showed it to be an alloy of several heavy metals, mostly iridium, with about 10 percent iron and smaller concentrations of osmium, ruthenium, and other metals of the platinum group.

—It must be worth its weight in gold?

—It's funny you should mention that. It doesn't weigh as much as it should so I'd say it's worth a lot more than its weight, in anything.

—How much does it weigh?

—Thirty-two metric tons . . . I know, it's a respectable weight, but it's inexplicably light given its composition. Iridium is one of the densest elements, arguably the densest, and even with some iron content, the hand should easily weigh ten times as much.

—How did you account for that?

—I didn't. I still can't. I couldn't even speculate as to what type of process could be used to achieve this. In truth, the weight didn't bother me nearly as much as the sheer amount of iridium I was looking at. Iridium is not only one of the densest things you can find, it's also one of the rarest.

You see, metals of this group—platinum is one of them—love to bond with iron. That's what most of the iridium on Earth did millions of years ago when the surface was still molten and, because it's so heavy, it sunk to the core, thousands of miles deep. What little is left in the Earth's crust is usually mixed with other metals and it takes a complex chemical process to separate them.

—How rare is it in comparison to other metals?

—It's rare, very rare. Let's put it this way, if you were to put together all the pure iridium produced on the entire planet in a year, you'd probably end up with no more than a couple metric tons. That's about a large suitcaseful. It would take decades, using today's technology, to scrounge up enough to build all this. It's just too scarce on Earth and there simply aren't enough chondrites lying around.

—You lost me.

—Sorry. Meteorites; stony ones. Iridium is so rare in Earth rocks that it is often undetectable. Most of the iridium we mine is extracted from fallen meteorites that didn't completely burn up in the atmosphere. To build this room—and it seems safe to assume that this is not the only thing they would have built—you'd need to find it where there are a lot more than on the Earth's surface.

—Journey to the center of the Earth?

—Jules Verne is one way to go. To get this type of metal in massive quantities, you'd either have to extract it thousands of miles deep or be able to mine in space. With all due respect to Mr. Verne, we haven't come close to mining deep enough. The deepest mines we have would look like potholes next to what you'd need. Space seems much more feasible. There are private companies right now hoping to harvest water and precious minerals in space in the very near future, but all these projects are still in the early planning stages. Nonetheless, if you could harvest meteorites in space, you could get a lot more iridium, a whole lot more.

—What else can you tell me?

—That pretty much sums it up. After a few months of looking at this with every piece of equipment known to man, I felt we were getting nowhere. I knew we were asking the wrong questions, but I didn't know the right ones. I submitted a preliminary report and asked for a leave of absence.

—Refresh my memory. What was the conclusion of that report?

—We didn't build this.

—Interesting. What was their reaction?

—Request granted.

—That was it?

—Yes. I think they were hoping I wouldn't come back. I never used the word "alien," but that's probably all they took out of my report.

—That is not what you meant?

—Not exactly. There might be a much more down-to-earth explanation, one I just didn't think of. As a scientist, all I can say is that humans of today do not have the resources, the knowledge, or the technology to build something like this. It's entirely possible that some ancient civilization's understanding of metallurgy was better than ours, but there wouldn't have been any more iridium around, whether it was five thousand, ten thousand, or twenty thousand years ago. So, to answer your question, no, I don't believe humans built these things. You can draw whatever conclusion you want from that.

I'm not stupid; I knew I was probably putting an end to my career.

I certainly annihilated any credibility I had with the NSA, but what was I going to do? Lie?

—**What did you do after you submitted your report?**

—I went home, to where it all began. I hadn't gone home in nearly four years, not since my father died.

—**Where is home?**

—I come from a small place called Deadwood, about an hour northwest of Rapid City.

—**I am not familiar with that part of the Midwest.**

—It's a small town built during the gold rush. It was a rowdy place, like in the movies. The last brothels were closed when I was a kid. Our claim to fame, besides a short-lived TV show on HBO, is that the murder of Wild Bill Hickok happened in Deadwood. The town survived the end of the gold rush and a few major fires, but the population dwindled to about twelve hundred.

Deadwood sure isn't thriving, but it's still standing. And the landscape is breathtaking. It's sitting right on the edge of the Black Hills National Forest, with its eerie rock formations, beautiful pine forests, barren rock, canyons, and creeks. I can't think of a more beautiful place on Earth. I can understand why someone would want to build something there.

—**You still call it home?**

—Yes. It's part of who I am although my mother would probably disagree. She appeared hesitant when she answered the door. We barely spoke anymore. I could sense that she resented the fact that I never came back, not even for Dad's funeral, that I left her all alone to cope with the loss. We all have our way of dealing with pain, and I suppose that deep down my mother understood that this was just my way, but there was anger in her voice, things she would never dare to speak out loud but that would taint our relationship forever. I was OK with that. She had suffered enough; she was entitled to resentment. We didn't talk much the first few days, but we quickly settled into some form of routine.

Sleeping in my old room brought back memories. When I was a child, I often snuck out of bed at night and sat by the window to watch my dad leave for the mine. He would come to my room before every night shift and have me pick a toy to put in his lunch box. He said he would think of me when he opened it and come spend his lunch break with me in my dreams. He didn't talk much, to me or to my mother, but he knew how important little things can be for a child and he took the time to tuck me in before every shift. How I wished my dad were there so I could talk to him. He wasn't a scientist, but he had a clear view of things. I couldn't talk to my mother about this.

We'd been having short but pleasant discussions for a few days, which was a welcome change from the polite comments about food we'd been exchanging since I arrived. But what I did was classified and I did my best to steer our conversations away from what was on my mind. It got easier with every week that went by, as I found my-self spending more time reminiscing about childhood mistakes than I did thinking about the hand.

It took nearly a month before I hiked to the site where I'd first seen it. The hole had long since been filled. There were small trees starting to grow back through the dirt and rocks. There was nothing left to see. I walked aimlessly until nightfall. Why did I find the hand first? Surely there must be other structures like the one I fell in. Why did no one find them? Why did it happen on that day? The hand had been dormant for millennia. Why did it happen then? What triggered it? What was present twenty years ago that hadn't been for thousands of years?

Then it hit me. *That* was the right question to ask. I had to figure out what turned it on.

FILE NO. 004

INTERVIEW WITH CW3 KARA RESNIK, UNITED STATES ARMY

Location: Coleman Army Airfield, Mannheim, Germany

—Please state your name and rank.

—You already know my name. You're staring at my file.

—I was told you would cooperate with this process. I would like you to state your name for the record.

—Maybe you could start by telling me what this "process" is about.

—I cannot do that. Now, state your name and rank for the record.

—"I cannot do that . . ." Do you overarticulate everything all the time?

—I like to enunciate things. I find it allows me to avoid misunderstandings. If there is one thing I loathe, it is to repeat myself . . .

—Yes. My name. You can say it, if it's so important to you.

—As you wish. You are Chief Warrant Officer 3 Kara Resnik, and you are a helicopter pilot in the United States Army. Is that correct?

—Was. I've been removed from flight status, but you probably know that already.

—I did not. May I ask what happened?

—I have a detached retina. It doesn't hurt, but my vision is affected. I'm scheduled for surgery tomorrow. When I asked, they said there's a reasonable chance I might be able to fly again . . . which sounds suspiciously like "no" to me.

What did you say your name was again?

—I have not.

—Then why don't you? For the record . . .

—There are many reasons why, some more relevant than others. From your perspective, it should suffice to know that you would never be allowed to leave this room alive if I did.

—You could have just said no. Do you really think threatening me will get you anywhere?

—I sincerely apologize if you felt threatened in any way, Chief Resnik. It was never my intention to make you uncomfortable. I simply did not want you to think I was being coy.

—So you were concerned for my safety? How chivalrous. Why am I here?

—You are here to talk about what happened in Turkey.

—Nothing happened in Turkey. Nothing interesting, anyway.

—I will be the judge of that. You know that my clearance is several levels above yours, so start at the beginning.

—I'm not even sure what that means.

—How did you end up in Turkey?

—I was called on NATO duty. I arrived early in the morning and got some sleep. Mission briefing was at 16:00. They introduced me to my second, CW Mitchell, and we went over the mission. We would fly out at 02:00 on a modified stealth UH-60 out of Adana. We were to enter Syrian airspace at very low altitude and collect air samples about twelve miles south of the border, near Ar Raqqah.

—You said you had never met your second-in-command. It is my understanding that the Army likes to keep its crews together. It seems odd for them to break up a team just before a dangerous mission and have you fly with someone you barely know. Why not have your usual co-pilot come with you?

—He was reassigned.

—Why is that?

—You'd have to ask him.

—I did. Would it surprise you to know he asked for any post as long as it was with another pilot? I believe the words he used to describe you were: *obdurate*, *volatile*, and *irascible*. He has quite the vocabulary.

—He plays a lot of Scrabble.

—Is that why you did not get along?

—I never had a problem with him.

—That seems somewhat beside the point. You do not often see people willing to jeopardize their military career simply to avoid having to spend time with another person.

—We disagreed over a lot of things, but I never let it get in the way of our flying. I can't help it if he wasn't able to do the same.

—So it is not your fault if people have a problem with you. That is just who you are.

—Something like that. Look, you want me to say I'm not the easiest person to get along with? I'll give you that. But somehow, I don't think we're here to discuss my charming personality. You want to know how I crashed a twenty-million-dollar helicopter into the middle of a pistachio farm. Is that it?

—We can start with that. You said you were supposed to collect air samples. Do you know why?

—NATO believes that Syria has been pursuing a nuclear weapons program for years and they want to put a stop to it. Israel bombed a suspected nuclear reactor back in 2007, but NATO doesn't want to do anything that drastic on a whim.

—They would prefer to have some hard evidence before they take military action.

—They wanna catch them with their pants down. A source in the Syrian Military Intelligence told the US that underground testing was going on near Ar Raqqah, and since Syria is refusing to allow inspectors to visit suspected nuclear sites, we were to use a more covert approach.

—Did this surreptitious inspection involve anything other than collecting air samples?

—No. We were to fly in and out. They brought in some pretty big equipment with us to detect signs of nuclear activity from the air samples we'd bring back. We left Incirlik Air Base at 02:00 as planned. We went east along the border for about an hour and turned south into Syria. We flew nap-of-the-earth for about twelve minutes with an AGL of eighty feet. We reached the designated coordinates around 03:15, collected air samples, and headed back the way we came.

—Were you nervous?

—You're funny. I get nervous if I forget to pay my phone bill. This is a little different. You're ground-hugging at 160 miles an hour over possibly hostile territory, at night, with night-vision goggles. If that doesn't get your heart pumping, I don't know what will. So yeah, we were both on edge. You can't see anywhere but straight ahead with the NVGs on. It feels like flying through a narrow green-lit tunnel at an incredible speed.

—Did everything go as planned?

—Like clockwork. We were back in Turkish airspace in less than twenty-five minutes. I climbed up to eight hundred feet while we put some distance between us and the border. We were approaching Harran when we noticed some light directly below us. It wasn't city lights. We were over farmland, and the color wasn't right. Then out of nowhere, the engine stopped, and the entire cockpit went dark.

We could hear the rotors slowing down, then nothing. There was this turquoise glow emanating from the fields below. Countless small bush-like trees planted thirty feet apart with nothing but dirt in between. We just sat there, staring. It was surreal, very . . . peaceful. Then we dropped like a rock.

The air bag slammed into my visor and knocked me out when we hit the ground. I woke up a few minutes later. I was alone in the helicopter. An old man in a white cotton tunic was trying to undo my restraints. He must have been at least sixty. He had dark, leathery skin. He looked at me and mumbled something he must have known I couldn't understand. Then he just smiled. Some of his lower teeth were missing, but he had very kind eyes. I regained my composure and helped him unstrap me from the seat.

He helped me out slowly, putting my arm over his shoulder. Someone grabbed my other arm, a young girl, maybe sixteen years old. She was very pretty. She kept looking down, spoke only a little bit when the man addressed her. He could have been her father, maybe her grandfather. They sat me down about a hundred feet from the helicopter and the man gave me some water out of a canteen. The young girl showed me a piece of cloth and gestured toward my forehead. As I didn't object, she put the wet cloth over my right eye. She removed it and quickly put it away, probably hoping I wouldn't notice the blood.

—Where was your co-pilot?

—I didn't know at first. It took a minute or two before I noticed several people gathered a few steps behind the helicopter. I couldn't make out any of their faces, only their shadows against the turquoise light. I got up. The young woman kept repeating the same few words—"don't get up," I suppose. I started walking toward the light. I made it to the edge of this huge crater that defaced the pistachio field. The light was so bright.

Mitchell was there with some locals. He grabbed my arm and put it around his shoulder, then held me to his side. He seemed genuinely happy to see me. I'm not quite sure what we were staring at, but it was the most awe-inspiring thing I've ever seen.

It looked like a whale made of dark metal—maybe a ship, or a submarine, though it seemed a little small. It was sleek and curvy, like the body of a 747, but with no apparent opening, no propeller. It looked more like an Italian work of art than it did anything practical. Turquoise veins were running through the surface at regular intervals forming a weblike pattern.

—How long were you there?

—I don't know. Maybe ten minutes. We were distracted by the sound of other helos and the wind blowing sand in our faces. Four Blackhawks landed around the crater, letting out more Marines than I could count. They brought Mitchell and me to one of the helicopters and we took off immediately. The Marines on the ground were moving people away from the crater. I saw two of them attempting to stop the local police from approaching the site.

—Yes, it was . . . unfortunate . . . that the local authorities got involved. It would have been a lot easier had they arrived a few minutes later. Please go on.

—That's it. There's nothing more to tell. I was taken to the infirmary at the base in Turkey. Then they flew me here for eye surgery an hour ago. How did you even know I was here?

—Does it really matter?

—I'll take that to mean you won't tell me. Can you at least tell me what that thing was?

—The State Department is now asking the Turkish government permission to repatriate wreckage of a secret WWII airplane found by local farmers in the Urfa Province.

—You've got to be kidding. Some old plane wreck didn't bring down my helo. You really expect me to believe that?

—What you believe is not particularly important at this juncture. What is important is what the Turkish government believes. What they need to believe is that we are taking a seventy-year-old US plane wreck back to America.

—So what was it?

—What do you think of Chief Mitchell?

—You're not going to answer my question?

— . . .

—Mitchell's fine. He handled himself well.

—That is not what I meant. What do you think of him personally?

—Look, I nearly died because there's a big shiny thing out there capable of bringing down a fully armed Blackhawk helicopter from a distance in a matter of seconds. You really wanna know what I think of my second on a personal level?

—I do. I am well aware that your helicopter crashed. I would have to be blind not to see that you find it insufferable not to know why. If time were not an issue, we could talk about it for a few hours to validate your feelings, but I have to leave soon.

You may see what I ask as insignificant. What you must understand is that I have access to a tremendous amount of information you are not privy to. Consequently, there is very little you can tell

me that I do not already know. What I do not know, and what I wish
to hear from you, is what you think of Mr. Mitchell.

—What do you want me to say? I was with him for an hour and a
half. We're both from Detroit. He's two years older than me, but we
went to some of the same schools. He thought that was quite a coincidence we ended up on the same bird. He likes country music, which
I can't stand, and neither of us thinks the Lions will make the play-
offs. Is that personal enough for you?

—What is his first name?

—I have no idea. Ryan, I think. Are you going to tell me what that
thing was? Can you tell me if there are more of these things lying
around?

—Thank you very much for your time, Ms. Resnik . . .
    I almost forgot. If it means anything to you, your former co-pilot
also said you were the best pilot he had ever seen.

INTERVIEW WITH DR. ROSE FRANKLIN, PH.D., SENIOR SCIENTIST, ENRICO FERMI INSTITUTE
Location: University of Chicago, Chicago, IL

—Could it be the Davis experiment?

—I do not know. Could it? What is the Davis experiment?

—I'm sorry. I'm talking to myself. It has to be argon! I should have thought of that. My father worked at the mine for so long.

—What mine? I know what argon is, but I am obviously missing whatever point you are trying to make.

—In the late sixties, a couple of astrophysicists devised an experiment to collect and count neutrino particles emanating from the sun. I remember reading about it when I was a kid. They built a big pool of dry-cleaning fluid almost five thousand feet belowground to shield it from other solar phenomena and basically just waited for neutrinos to hit it. When a chlorine atom is hit by a neutrino, it turns into a radioactive isotope of argon—argon-37, to be precise. Every once in a while, they would bubble up helium to collect the argon and they were able to count the atoms that were hit. Beautiful science, they took something purely theoretical and managed to turn it into something concrete. They ran this experiment for nearly twenty-five years at the Homestake mine where my father worked, a couple miles from where I fell onto the hand. I'm willing to bet these things react in proximity to the argon.

—I am not a physicist, as you know, but . . .

—I don't know anything about you.

—Well, now you know I am not a physicist. In any case, I was thinking that the amount of radioactive material that could travel that distance must be infinitesimal.

—It is. But, however minute the amount may be, it can't just be a coincidence. The helicopter that crashed in Turkey was collecting air samples to detect signs of nuclear testing. That's what they would have been looking for, traces of argon-37. The pilot said they flew in some large equipment with them to Turkey. It would have been a MARDS—Movable Argon Detection System—or something like that. In any case, it's a big machine that can detect argon-37. An underground nuclear reaction will turn the surrounding calcium into just that. It's a pretty reliable way of detecting a nuclear site. You can't hide from it. You can't cheat. Calcium's everywhere, in sand, in rocks, in people, and some of the argon that a nuclear blast would create will eventually escape into the air, no matter how deep the explosion.

—You implied there are other isotopes of argon. Would it react to any of them or just this one?

—It would have to be just this one. There's a whole lot of argon-40 in the atmosphere, everywhere, other isotopes as well. But, I agree, it does seem odd that these artifacts would react to something so specific . . .

—Can you . . .

—I'm sorry. I didn't mean to interrupt. I meant to say unless, of course, they were designed that way. It would really be clever if they did that on purpose.

—**What do you mean? Who is "they"?**

—This might sound a little crazy, but hear me out. Suppose you encountered some civilization that's too far behind technologically for you to engage in any sort of dialogue with. Anyone capable of building these things would have scared the hell out of people six thousand years ago. They would have been seen as gods, demons, supernatural beings of one kind or another. Now, say you wanted to leave something for them to discover, but only once they had evolved to a certain point.

—**How would you measure their evolution?**

—You'd want to know when they reached a sufficient understanding of the universe for you to be able to communicate with them in a meaningful way. It would most likely have to be measured technologically. It seems reasonable to assume that most or all species similar to humans would go through more or less the same evolutionary steps. Make fire, invent the wheel, those types of things. Flight might be a good criterion, or spaceflight. If you can look up at the sky, it's safe to say you'll eventually try to find a way to get up there, and space-faring species might at least be open to the idea of not being alone in the universe. Unless you were there to observe, you would need a way to detect whatever evolutionary landmark you chose. If you hid these things on a moon, for example, you'd know they'd only be found once they're able to reach that far.

From where I stand, being able to harness nuclear energy would also be a pretty good criterion. Now—and this is the clever part—if you designed these things to react specifically to argon-37, they could only be discovered once that civilization managed to tap the power of the atom. This is all pure speculation, or course, but if that's what they did, I'm impressed.

In any case, I think we have to take another look at the panels. We're going to need a linguist after all.

—I thought you said there was no point?

—That was before I knew about the argon. If that site was built there for us to discover, there has to be something in it that we can figure out. If you were to build a structure, say a temple, for your own people, you'd write things in it that make sense to you. But if you were building that same temple for someone else, you'd want what you write to also mean something to whomever you built it for. There's just no point in writing a message if you know the person you write it for will never be able to understand it.

—Quite a few established linguists have already looked at the markings and come up with nothing. What makes you think the outcome would be any different this time around?

—I can't tell you why it would work now. I do have a pretty good idea why it didn't work the first time around. They were looking for something that wasn't there.

—And you now know what it is we are looking for?

—I haven't the faintest idea. But I think that's a good thing. I think those who looked at it before failed because they knew too many things, or so they thought.

—You will have to be a little less philosophical.

—I'm sorry. Generally speaking, people tend not to question what they've been told was true. Scientists are no different; they've just been told a lot more things. As a physicist, it would never occur to me to question the four fundamental forces, for example. I take them for granted, like every other thing I learned, and I try to build on that. We always look forward; never look back. But this thing . . . it's different. It challenges us. It spits in the face of physics, anthropology, religion. It rewrites history. It dares us to question everything we know about ourselves . . . about everything. I must sound pretty philosophical again.

—**A tad.**

—I'd like to try someone not as well trained, some hotshot student maybe, someone who doesn't need to throw the rule book out the window because he hasn't read it yet. We need to look at this from a whole new angle. I'll contact the linguistics department and see if they have someone to suggest.

—**It is an interesting concept. You want to find someone who is more or less unqualified because the people that were actually proficient have all failed.**

—I wouldn't quite put it that way, but yes, someone who's really smart and who's less encumbered with preconceived notions. It sounds a lot better when I say it.

—**It does. I suppose there is little to lose by trying, but you will forgive me if I do not exude enthusiasm. Did you receive the forearm from Turkey?**

—Yes, it arrived two days ago. We couldn't figure out if and how the hand was supposed to attach to it. Both parts have smooth, solid endings, nothing that would resemble a mechanism or a fastener. The end of the forearm is slightly concave, the wrist a bit convex but there's nothing to hold the pieces together.

—**It was my understanding that both pieces were now joined.**

—They are. My point is that I have absolutely no idea how it works. We just moved them close to one another to see how they would fit and they were drawn together like magnets. My assistant almost lost a hand. I can't talk intelligently about how the parts attach except to say it made a very loud, and very cool . . . *swoosh* sound . . . when they did.

—**Can you take them apart?**

—We haven't been able to. It's clear the amount of mechanical force required is more than what we can handle. I didn't want to risk damaging anything. I'd rather concentrate on finding the other pieces. I can't wait to see what the rest of the body looks like. We can try to take it apart once we finish building it.

—So you think there are more of these things buried somewhere?

—Oh yes. It's killing me not to have it all right now. I may be getting ahead of myself, but I can't see how there wouldn't be. I could understand these being some sort of monuments or art forms if we had found another hand, a head, even a foot, but a forearm doesn't seem like something you would build for its own sake. It's not my area of expertise, but I can't see a forearm playing a strong part in religious beliefs. And if I read the report correctly, there was no chamber surrounding it in Turkey either; no walls, no markings. It's much too large to fit in the chamber the hand was found in, so it must have been buried elsewhere on purpose.

—I agree, but they could have built just one arm, in which case, all we could hope for is another piece.

—Maybe. I still think there's an entire body out there, just waiting to be found.

—I hope time will prove you right. I really do.

—I can tell you that if I were able to build something so magnificent, I wouldn't stop at an arm.

—Based on what you now know, can you devise a process for detecting the other parts, if they exist?

—If the rest of that body is out there, I'm fairly certain I can come up with a way to find it. I just have to figure out how to make a lot of argon-37 and how to disperse it efficiently. It might take a while to find all the pieces even once we have a method in place.

—How long?

—Impossible to guess. Months. Years? If the body is divided along the major articulations like we'd expect, there should be at least fourteen pieces; three for each arm and leg, that makes twelve, a head and one or several pieces for the torso. I can only hope that piece in Turkey was the exception and that the rest of the body parts are closer to where we found the hand.

If I'm correct, and they want us to find these things, they would have buried the pieces on land, where we can get to them relatively easily. I hope so, because searching the ocean is a completely different story.

I'll have to request more funding from the NSA. I'm not sure how long this might take, but I'm absolutely certain I can't do any of it on our budget.

—Forget the NSA. Just tell me what you need.

—Forget the NSA? Remind me whom you're working for exactly? Wait. Don't answer that. I'll send you a list of equipment. We'll also need a delivery system, possibly an airplane or a helicopter that can fly long distances. We'll need a crew, I guess, and a team to recover what we find. This part might get complicated. As far as body parts go, what we found were the smallest ones. They'll only get bigger.

—We have teams that can handle the recovery. I will see about finding you some pilots.

—We'll also need a bigger room if this works.

—How big?

—Well, if the proportions are normal, or human, he, or she, would be over two hundred feet tall. We'll need a warehouse even if we lay her on the ground.

—You still believe it is a girl?

—More than ever.

FILE NO. 009

INTERVIEW WITH CW3 KARA RESNIK, UNITED STATES ARMY

Location: Fort Campbell Army Base, Kentucky

—You again. What do you want now?

—I only want to ask you a few simple questions.

—What if I don't want to answer?

—You are free to leave whenever you want, but it would be wise of you to stay.

—Why do I feel like this is a test?

—Because you are very perceptive. I am initiating a project to which you might be able to contribute, in one manner or another. You have, on the one hand, witnessed certain events and demonstrated certain skills that might give you a significant advantage over other potential candidates. On the other hand, your impulsive nature and your inability to work well with others are of concern to me, as they are to your superiors. With your permission, I would like to ask you a few simple questions and for you to answer them honestly. Is that something you feel you can do?

—Answer questions? Isn't that what I've been doing already?

—I was not questioning your ability to answer questions. You have already shown great skills at eluding any inquiry of a personal nature by answering with another question. I am asking whether you believe you are able to answer honestly.

—Does it matter if I'm not?

—It certainly matters if you entertain any hope of being selected for this project.

—You've already called me impulsive and unable to work well with others. It sounds as if you have a pretty good idea of what you think of me.

—Let me present this to you in another way. Let us assume that I already know you are not suited for whatever task I have in mind, and that I have purposely chosen to fly here and waste several hours of my time for no other reason than to make your life a bit more miserable. Under this scenario, it would seem preferable for you to get through these questions as fast as you can so that you may return to whatever it is you do, now that you can no longer fly helicopters. I might also not be a complete imbecile and have a genuine interest in your answers. Either way, you have ten seconds to answer each question. Are you ready?

— . . .

—What are your three worst qualities?

—My three . . . Last we met you called me—what was it?—obdurate, volatile, irascible. I guess that's three. I'm also vindictive, and I never forget anything. How many is that?

—What are three qualities you admire in others?

—Loyalty. Honesty. Courage.

—OK. You must answer the following statements with true or false. First one: You trust reason rather than feelings.

—You want me to answer that with true or false? It's a bogus question. I know you want me to answer true, but sometimes you need to listen to your gut.

—Then it sounds like your answer should be false.

—But if I say false, you'll think I'm an emotional time bomb.

—I might already be thinking that. I might also think you are completely heartless. You still need to answer with true or false.

—False.

—You often think about mankind and its place in the universe.

—I do.

—So your answer is true?

—Yes.

—You feel at ease in a crowd.

—False.

—You are usually the first to react to an unexpected event, like an accident.

—Hmmm . . . True. I guess.

—You like to assume responsibility for something.

—True.

—In a social event, you position yourself in the center of the room, rather than on the sides.

—That's an interesting one. I can't remember the last time I was at a social event.

—Let me repeat the question. In a social event, you position yourself in the center of the room, rather than on the sides.

—I don't think I do. No . . . False.

—You have difficulty expressing your feelings.

—That's another bogus question. It depends on the feeling. I have no problem expressing anger. I don't think many people do. I could say the same about joy, gratitude, frustration, amazement. Things like love, fear, shame, desire, helplessness, now that's another story.

—That is a very well considered answer to a completely different question. Now please answer this one with true or false.

—But I can't. I just told you there is more than one answer.

—This is unfortunate because this is a true or false question. Average it out. Do you have difficulty expressing your feelings?

—Yes . . . or true! My answer is true!

—There is no need to get angry.

—I'm not angry.

—If you say so. You have a problem with authority.

—You don't need a test to figure that one out.

—It is a question. It is part of the test.

—Oh. True . . . What? You're surprised? I know, now you'll ask me why someone with authority issues would choose a career in the military.

—This is an interesting conversation you are having with yourself. Can we move on?

—Yes, we can. I talk when I'm nervous.

—You believe in the existence of extraterrestrial intelligence.

—What?

—You heard me.

— . . . False. What could that possibly tell you about me?

—That you do not believe in extraterrestrial intelligence. Had your answer been true, I would now think the opposite.

—You're very helpful.

—Thank you. I will now give you the beginning of a story and you have to finish it in one or two sentences. Do you understand?

—I think I do.

—Tommy sits on the doorstep alone . . .

—Really? You want to understand the depths of me and you come up with "Tommy sits on the doorstep alone." That's just stupid . . . Why don't you just ask me what you want to know?

—We could be here for quite some time if you do not answer the questions. It is a very simple exercise; it should pose no problem for someone of your intelligence.

—Don't insult me.

—I am not. I saw your file, remember. Your qualification testing shows you have an IQ somewhere between 125 and 130. That would make you moderately gifted. Therefore, as I said, it should not be a problem for someone of your intelligence to complete a small story in one sentence or two, even under a time constraint. Shall we proceed? Tommy sits on the doorstep alone . . .

—Fine . . . His friends said they would come get him, but they didn't. Tommy's making up great stories in his head. When his friends finally come, he doesn't want to play with them anymore. Moderately gifted?

—Next story. On the way to the supermarket, Lisa found a lottery ticket on the ground . . .

—Do you come up with these yourself or did a team of psychologists create these little gems? I mean, would anyone really say they'd steal it? Then again, what if there's no one around? It's not like you can put an ad in the paper . . .

—I do not belie—

—Never mind! Sure enough, there was a name and address on the back. She returned the ticket to an old man who lived a few blocks down. When the man died, she found out he put her in his will and left her everything. Is that touching enough for you?

—Very well. I will now enunciate a word, and you will tell me the first word that comes to mind. What is the first thing you think of when you hear . . . War?

—Death.

—Luck?

—I don't know . . . Friend.

—Defeat?

—Rise.

—Country?

—Gratitude.

—Father?

— . . . Loss.

—Trust?

— . . .

—Ms. Resnik?

—Fund. Are we done?

—We are for now. I have a few more questions, but they are not part of the test.

—And yet you're still going to judge me based on my answers.

—I will, but in a much more subjective way. Can you tell me what a Night Stalker is?

—It's a member of the 160th SOAR, Special Ops Aviation Regiment. It's an elite force. They specialize in low-altitude night-flying operations.

—Are they good?

—They're the best of the best.

—And you are one of them.

—I am now!

—Why now?

—I lost my flight status. I got a teaching job at the Sabalauski Air Assault School after I hurt my eye, but you already know that.

—So you teach them how to fly but you cannot fly with them?

—I know you expect me to see some irony in there, but I never could. It's special ops. They don't take women other than in a support role.

—Who is "they"?

—The US military doesn't allow women in combat or special operations.

—How does that make you feel?

—How does what make me feel? That women can't join special ops? I knew that when I joined the Army. There are still a lot of rewarding jobs for women in the military. Do you wanna know if I'm upset I can't fly anymore? You bet I am. It feels like my legs were cut off.

—You like flying that much?

—Most kids want to become firemen, policemen, fighter pilots, astronauts. Most people change their mind when they get older. I always wanted . . . No, that's not true; I wanted to be a princess. But I knew I wanted to become a helicopter pilot the minute I saw one hover over our house. I must have been five or six. I haven't changed my mind ever since, never questioned my choice to join the armed forces. It's who I am. It's the only thing that really makes me feel alive.

—Could you fly if they let you?

—Could I? Yes. I could. I see fine.

—Let me ask you this. Why were you in Turkey?

—I'm really trying not to be a smart-ass here, but you're making it difficult. You'll have to be more specific.

—I mean why did they send you? This seems to be the type of mission the law is designed to keep women away from, and you just told me there is an entire regiment of people who specialize in just that sort of thing. Why did they send a twenty-four-year-old woman with an attitude for such an important mission and not SOAR?

—The commander knew me. I flew support missions for him in Afghanistan. And it's NATO, things are a little different. In any case, all the commander has to do is call it recon, or support, then I can go. There are some really good women pilots in the Army. Good commanders find ways to use them.

—One last question. What if I told you I could get your flight status reinstated? What would you be willing to do?

—Anything.

—Be careful how you choose to answer. You might regret it later.

—Then tell me what I have to do.

—Would you be willing to put your life at risk?

—That's a ridiculous question. Anyone who gets in a military helicopter knows they're putting their life at risk.

—Would you be willing to put the lives of innocent people at risk?

—If I trust there's a good reason behind it. It doesn't really matter what you ask me. Like I said, I'm willing to do anything if there's a purpose to it.

—You are a soldier in the United States Army. Presumably, you are not always told the reason for everything. Have you ever been sent on a mission without knowing its purpose?

—It happens. Not as often as you'd think, but it happens.

—Then how do you know it was worth putting your life in danger? You do not strike me as someone who would blindly trust anyone.

—I guess I didn't do too well on that test. You're right, I don't trust people easily, but I have faith in numbers.

—Interesting.

—I do. I think people are scared, and dumb, and selfish on their own, but put enough of them together and they'll be half-decent. The Army's a big clumsy machine, but I trust it to do the right thing more often than not.

—Can you keep an open mind? Are you willing to challenge what you know to be true?

—I suppose no one ever thinks that they're close-minded. You tell me.

—Thank you very much for your time, Ms. Resnik.

—Oh, again with the cryptic ending. Come on! Tell me more . . . No? Ask me more questions, then! Don't go . . . I'll tell you more stories about little Tommy sitting on the stairs!

FILE NO. 017

INTERVIEW WITH CW2 RYAN MITCHELL, UNITED STATES ARMY

Location: Joint Base Lewis-McChord, Washington State

—Good morning, Mr. Mitchell. Dr. Franklin tells me you are making progress.

—Oh yeah. Like she says, all you need is some faith and trust . . . and a little bit of pixie dust . . . We've been flying all over North America for just over four months now. It's sort of like crop dusting at night, only from a lot higher, and it's probably a lot more illegal. Operation Tinker Bell, that's what we call it. It was too easy, flying around leaving a trail of magic powder behind.

—Is the compound working?

—Definitely working. Hats off to Dr. Franklin, she sure can cook. ARCANA, she calls it. It means "secrets," or in this case Argon-Rich Compound for Aerial Nocturnal Application. I think she just liked the acronym. When we first started, pretty much everyone but Dr. Franklin thought this was a complete waste of time, but we found another arm piece in Vermont our first week out. We almost crashed again, though. Kara thought . . .

—Pardon me. Kara?

—Chief Warrant Officer Resnik. I'm sorry. We've been working with civilians for a while now. I guess it rubs off. She and Dr. Franklin thought we'd be fine flying at eight thousand feet, but when the arm piece we found activated, our engine stopped just like it did in Turkey. Fortunately, we were high enough for autorotation, and she was able to restart the engine before we hit the ground. She's really amazing to watch. Not the most tactful person you'll ever meet, but the girl can fly.

—I am happy to see you two are getting along. I was hoping you would. Do I detect a hint of infatuation in your voice?

—I wouldn't go that far. I'm well aware of the Army's fraternization policies, but you'd have to be made of stone not to find her attractive. She's built like a swimmer: long legs, very strong, and shoulders that would put most men to shame. I don't know how to say that without sounding like a jerk, but the men at the base say it makes their day just to watch her walk away. She has the darkest hair for someone that light-skinned. It just makes her eyes jump out at you. That pale green, it's very . . . disconcerting. Well, you've seen her. You know how hard it is not to stare at her eyes.

—I never noticed. You must realize you are not operating in a typical military environment. You would not be jeopardizing the chain of command.

—Actually, we would be. In the Army, the co-pilot is second-in-command. That means she's my superior. We have our own tiny little chain of command to jeopardize, and the Army is pretty serious about the Uniform Code. It doesn't matter anyway. I find her attractive, that's all. And believe me, she's not the least bit interested. She acts like she barely tolerates me.

—Coming from her, I would take that as high praise. Let us get back to the mission.

—Yes! We've divided the country into a grid. Each box on the grid is roughly the square mileage we can cover in one night, based on the time it takes to get there from the nearest Army base. We can cover a good portion of the map from here, and we go from base to base to clear the boxes farther east and south. We're just about halfway through the grid right now.

—**Have you been able to disperse the compound from a safe distance? I would rather the two of you not nearly die every time you discover a new body part.**

—We have, sir. As I mentioned, we almost crashed our first week out, so we went up to fifteen thousand feet on the next flights. We were unsure whether it was close enough for the pieces to activate before we got too far away to see them. It took about a month before we found another part, a lower leg, then a foot, along the Kansas-Missouri border.

—**A foot?**

—A big one. I was hoping it would have some giant toes, but it looks more like a fancy thick-soled boot than a foot. It's a beautiful piece though. Dr. Franklin said she had good taste in shoes.

It turns out flying higher is also a lot faster, the ARCANA dispersal pattern is much wider at high altitude so we need fewer passes to cover the same area.

—**So you found five pieces so far?**

—Six. We just found a thigh under the Tennessee highway. That thing is huge!

—**How large is it?**

—I'm not really good with measurements, maybe sixty feet. Big enough to make a hell of a mess, I'll tell you that. The highway was completely destroyed for about half a mile. The way Dr. Franklin explains it, these things are buried very deep underground, around nine hundred feet deep, and they rise to the surface really, really fast when they're turned on. I'm glad we're in a helicopter. I sure as hell wouldn't want to be around when these things come up. It's got to feel like the world's coming to an end.

—Thank you, Mr. Mitchell. I just realized that, while Dr. Franklin talks about you on a regular basis, this is the first time you and I have met. It is a pleasure to finally make your acquaintance.

—Thank you, sir.

—Tell me a little bit about yourself.

—There's very little to say. I'm a soldier in the United States Army.

—I know you can do better than that.

—What can I tell you? I'm from Detroit. My father was in the Army. What else . . . I went to Henry Ford High. I played ball.

—Baseball?

—Football, sir. Trojans. I was a cornerback. I enlisted after graduation.

—Was your father a helicopter pilot, as well?

—No, sir. He was a mechanic. I never had any taste for it so I applied to Warrant Officer Candidate School. I thought I could do something different.

—He must be very proud of you?

—Yes. His father was also in the military. It's sort of a family tradition. I wanna thank you for taking me on board, sir. I know you didn't really choose me, but I'm really glad to be here. I'm very grateful. This is more exciting than anything I ever imagined.

—I chose the both of you because of how well you complement each other. I would not have chosen Ms. Resnik had she not worked so well with you in Turkey. There is no need for you to feel any less deserving.

—It's OK. I understand. I'm the co-pilot. She's great. You were right to pick her.

—I will take your enthusiasm to mean you are adjusting well to your new working environment.

—Oh yes. Very well. Dr. Franklin takes very good care of us. We spent nearly a week with her before we flew anywhere. She brought us up to speed, showed us everything she'd been doing. She made us feel like we're really part of the team, not just some grunts doing the legwork. That hand is amazing. Do you really think it came from . . . you know . . . out there?

—Dr. Franklin certainly thinks so. I have neither the knowledge nor the inclination to disagree with her.

—I wouldn't dare either. She's very motherly. I can't imagine what she'd be like if she were mad. I'm sure it's not something I want to find out. She's very nice. And she's incredibly smart. She tries to dumb things down when she talks about what she does, but there's still a lot I don't really understand.

—That is why we chose her. How are things in the laboratory? Is everyone getting along?

—Yes, sir. Dr. Franklin is in a great mood. Kara—sorry, Chief Resnik—and her, they get along great. It's hard to tell at first, but they're a lot alike. They have completely different manners but they both have that drive, that sense of purpose. I think they even look alike, when you get a good look at them together, like sisters, or cousins. They have the same dark hair, the same intense stare. They seemed to make a connection right away.

—I was told Mr. Couture has arrived.

—The linguist? Yes, he showed up. Some cocky French-speaking kid from Montreal. Vincent, I think that's his name.

—Have you two had a chance to interact?

—Not really, we don't see much of him. They moved the panels to another room; that's where he spends most of his time. They say he's real smart. I thought he would have a French accent, but it's nothing like I imagined. He sounds . . . German, or something.

—**He is Québécois, not French.**

—I know where he's from. I just thought they spoke, you know, French. He sounds funny when he speaks any language, actually. Dr. Franklin has him speak to her in French. She says she never gets to practice. Even Kara gets a word in here and there. I think I'm the only one who can't understand anything he says.

—**It sounds like you do not really like him.**

—I wouldn't go that far. We're just very different people. He reminds me of the kids we used to pick on in high school. I don't like to think about that.

—**You are not proud of the way you treated people as a teenager? You do not strike me as someone who would take pleasure in bullying others.**

—Well, it's not like I beat up or tortured anyone, but I wanted to fit in as much as the other kids. Football team . . . you know how it is.

—**I do not.**

—The guys on the team used to make jokes about kids that were less athletic. They would pick on them in the hallways, any chance they got. I was smart enough to know it was wrong, but not brave enough to stop them. I didn't stand up for the weaker kids and maybe I should have.

—**You were a teenager yourself. It seems unfair to judge your actions through the eyes of an adult.**

—Maybe. Look, I don't lose any sleep over it. You just asked why I don't . . . I thought it might . . . It doesn't matter. I'm sure we'll get along fine once I get to know him. Can I ask you a question?

—Certainly.

—Why are we doing this?

—Do you believe that artifacts left on Earth by an ancient alien civilization are not worthy of our attention?

—No, I mean why are *we* doing this? I understand how amazing this is, and I can see why Rose is on board, but why is the military involved?

—First of all, the military is not. As far as the Army is concerned, you and Ms. Resnik are on a training assignment. But to answer your question, I feel a discovery of this magnitude might have repercussions that the scientific community is not best suited to handle. You saw what happened in Turkey. We needed crowd control, an extraction team, someone to handle the local authorities. I feel these are all things best accomplished by people with military training.

—Do you think what we're after has military applications?

—That is not my primary concern. I do believe we might learn something—a lot, actually—from this discovery. Whether what we learn is of military interest or not, only time will tell. I am absolutely certain, however, that this project has a better chance of success with you and Ms. Resnik on board.

—Thank you, sir. I just don't wanna find out I was part of someone's secret agenda.

—Do you think I would tell you if you were?

—Probably not.

—Then rest assured, Mr. Mitchell, we are all in this for the greater good.

FILE NO. 031

PERSONAL JOURNAL ENTRY—CW3 KARA RESNIK, UNITED STATES ARMY

We killed a child today. We killed a little girl!

We should have seen this coming. It was bound to happen at some point. The highway should have been a wake-up call, but we were so caught up in finding the next piece. It's easy to forget that when these things were buried, there was basically nothing around, just woods and plains. It was just pure luck that we found the first four pieces where we did. And now that little girl's dead! They're all dead!

We were so happy. We were making good progress, moving through our grid faster than we had planned.

It was such a beautiful day too. I got up earlier than usual and made it to the lab early in the morning. Since we fly at night, we never really get to spend time with Dr. Franklin or anyone else at the lab. But they were all there and we got to talk for a few hours, swapping anecdotes, learning about one another's work.

Mitchell and I left around 10:30. We drove over to the base to prepare our flight plan. We flew straight to Nellis Air Force Base, near Las Vegas. My eye didn't bother me as much as I thought it would. It doesn't hurt anymore, but it gets watery after a few hours. It's not so bad at night, but this was a long trip during daylight and it had me worried a bit.

We slept for a couple hours when we got to Nellis, then we took off again. We had to cover the northern part of Arizona. This was the farthest we'd gotten from the base. It was a long day, but we were excited to fly over the Grand Canyon, neither of us had ever seen it. We wouldn't really see anything at night, from this altitude, but it still felt good, like a layover in Paris. You never leave the airport, but even so, you're in Paris.

Our flight was uneventful, right up until the end. We were heading west near the south edge of the Grand Canyon when I noticed some lights flickering to my left. This was different from the other times we found a body part. There was a patch of white lights. It was there before but neither Mitchell nor I had been paying any attention to it. There was a turquoise spot right in the middle of it, and lights flickering all around. I've been in Iraq. This looked like someone had dropped a bomb in the middle of town. I looked at our map. It was Flagstaff.

I dove down and headed south toward the turquoise spot. As we drew closer, we got a bird's-eye view of the damage. The piece—from above, it looked like an upper arm—had obliterated a whole city block. Some houses on the edge had been torn in half. There were electric poles down; sparks were flying everywhere. A lot of the remaining houses were on fire.

I landed in a restaurant parking lot, about three blocks away. We started running toward the flames. Several people wearing next to nothing were running the other way. It was chaos. The fire department hadn't arrived yet, neither had our recovery team. A few people were fortunate enough to get out of their homes in time to see them reduced to nothing. They were running in the streets, trying to avoid fallen electric lines. I could see the telltale glow coming from a large crater where two large houses used to stand.

A woman in her nightgown ran out of nowhere and latched on to me, screaming, "Amy! Amy!" She kept screaming her name, pulling me by the arm toward the edge of the crater. "She was in her room! Amy was in her room!"

Her house appeared to be in fairly good shape from the front, but the back half had been ripped right off. It was like a dollhouse—you could see every room, every piece of furniture. Amy's room was on the edge, it was just . . . Mitchell pulled the mother away from me, doing his best to restrain her. "She's gone," he told her, holding her as tight as he could. "She's gone."

The hole was all muddy and filled with debris. There must have been a water line running somewhere. There were telephone poles sticking out like ragweed, chunks of bricks. We could see the front end of a car. All of it was mixed with mud and rocks. There was no way to even try to look for survivors.

There was this dog, a Bernese mountain dog, not a puppy, but you could tell he wasn't fully grown. It was just standing there, right on the edge, barking at a patch of debris. There were lots of dogs barking, but this one kept jumping and barking at the same spot. He was just so intent, staring at some random spot. There was nothing there, nothing but mud, some clothes, a microwave oven.

Mitchell and I left the crater and went through a couple of the houses that were on the edge. Nothing.

Only eight people died that night. That's what they told me. Most apparently ran out when the ground started shaking. Only eight . . . I pushed a button fifteen thousand feet away and I killed eight people, ordinary folks who never did anything to deserve this. They must have been so scared.

They tell me there was nothing we could have done to save any of them. I know that's not true. We could have not gone over there. We didn't have to do any of this. I wish it were as easy as saying I was just following orders. I chose to go. I'm responsible.

Everyone seems to have found a way to bury this, everyone but me. They've all shown great concern over me, lots of care and compassion. I don't deal well with that kind of attention. I know it's not pity, but I'm used to being the one taking care of people.

Mitchell comes to see me as often as I let him, which clearly isn't often enough for him. He really cares, everyone can tell. But I don't want to talk to him about this. He was there, just like I was. He's the one who actually pushed the button. He must feel as responsible as I do. And if we keep flying together, I don't want this to get in the way.

I've been spending a lot of time with Dr. Franklin since it happened. She wants me to call her Rose, as if I ever could. She's holding herself together really well, considering. She's the one that orchestrated all of this. The weight on her shoulders must be unbearable.

She comes every morning before her shift, sometimes she stays for a few hours. She plays the part of the big sister very well. She's the only one who gets me thinking about something else. She brings me a new book every couple days, bad ones; they're all horribly corny love stories. But she reads them too, and we laugh about them when we're done. We have the same kind of humor for that kind of stuff. I guess she's been as lucky as I have when it comes to relationships.

She's never asked me to talk about what happened. She knows I've talked about the incident with everyone else. It's all they wanna talk about. I don't need to go through the events a thousand times to remember. I was there. I'll remember how it went down for the rest of my life. I remember every detail; what the people were wearing; the picture frames on the walls of those houses that were torn in half. Dr. Franklin understands that. I'm grateful for that. I'm not sure I could go through this if it weren't for her.

I know she still believes that some good can come of this. I can tell. For a while, I thought she was just driven by scientific curiosity, but now I know, she believes it's worth it. She really thinks we can gain some knowledge that will help people. It's nice to see that kind of conviction remain after such a tragedy. I wasn't expecting it.

Speaking of surprises, Vincent showed up yesterday. I certainly didn't think he would, since we barely know each other. He only stayed for a minute, but he brought me a present, as he called it. A gift card, $25 at the Home Depot. I laughed my head off. That was the point, I guess. Then he just said goodbye and left. It was touching in some strange way. I don't know anything about him. He spends all his time alone in the other room, so we never have a chance to talk.

Dr. Franklin told me they've put together a leg, and it's not what we expected. The knee bends the wrong way, apparently. It has an extra joint, so we're still missing a piece above the thigh. She says it's like the hind legs on a horse. I can't wait to see it, but I'm not ready to go back yet.

It must show. Ryan said our nameless friend asked him how he'd feel about taking over. Ryan wasn't thrilled about the idea, but he said he'd do it if I told him to. He said they could find me some work on the ground if I wanted out, that everyone would understand.

How nice of them. Ryan's such a Boy Scout, he doesn't even know when he's being played. I get the feeling we're dealing with someone who doesn't easily take no for an answer. Push comes to shove, I think our "friend" would put a gun to my head before he ever let me quit.

What would I do anyway? Go about my business as if nothing ever happened? I couldn't even talk about it to anyone. This is gonna sound incredibly selfish, but I'd get bored to death unless someone started World War III or something. Who could go from this to carrying crates from base to base? And I need to know. I mean, how could anyone start something like this and not know how it turns out? I'd lose my mind.

I just realized our personal journals are saved on the lab servers. I'd be really surprised if "you know who" wasn't listening to them. Hey! Asshole! Two things I need to say to you. Number 1: Don't do that. Number 2: I'm guessing you chose me for a reason. You didn't have to pick a girl with a busted eye and an attitude. I never quit anything in my life. You didn't learn much from that stupid test of yours if you think I could ever leave this behind.

Like I said, I just need some time to sort things out, but we have to finish this. That little girl, all those people . . . We have to see this through.

FILE NO. 033

NEWS ARTICLE—CATHERINE MCCORMACK, REPORTER, *THE ARIZONA REPUBLIC*

TERROR IN FLAGSTAFF—8 DEAD IN BOMBING ACCIDENT

More than half a city block was destroyed last night in Flagstaff, in what authorities are calling a terrorist plot gone wrong.

Suspected domestic terrorist Owen Lehman died last night around 1:00 A.M., along with his 15-year-old son and 6 other people, in what appears to be a tragic bomb-making accident.

Lehman, who had been denied disability benefits back in 2012, had been sending increasingly hostile letters to the Federal government. "The language used in some of his recent correspondence was considered threatening. We took it seriously," said FBI Agent Robert Armstrong from the Phoenix field office. "Trace elements, as well as fragments recovered on-site, lead us to believe Mr. Lehman was attempting to build a large explosive device, which must have accidently detonated." The FBI had been monitoring Mr. Lehman for several months but lacked sufficient evidence for an arrest. "Obviously, we wish we knew then what we know now," said Armstrong, "but we believe the intended target was the Social Security office on Woodlands Village Blvd."

When asked about the absence of any fire damage, Armstrong added: "The explosion ruptured waterworks directly below Mr. Lehman's residence. That created some sort of landslide, which swallowed most of the debris and put out the fire. We got lucky. It could have been a lot worse."

Nearby resident Clarissa Parlow said Lehman was well liked by his neighbors. "He had a quiet way about him. He seemed shy, more than anything. I guess you just never know about people."

Further investigation is under way. Governor Udell plans to address the media later today when he visits the site.

FILE NO. 034

INTERVIEW WITH ROBERT WOODHULL, ASSISTANT TO THE PRESIDENT FOR NATIONAL SECURITY AFFAIRS

Location: White House, Washington, DC

—I don't know who you think you are, or whom you think you answer to, but this is the Office of the President, not some subcommittee you can just lie to for funding. How the hell did the NSA let that happen?

—It was out of their hands.

—Well, then, if it was out of their hands . . . Do I even want to know how you got them to agree to this?

—They did not agree or disagree to anything. It was just . . . out of their hands. I felt there was nothing to gain through their continued involvement. I do not know how or why they got involved in the first place. They are cryptology experts. They analyze phone calls. Giant artifacts left behind by alien civilizations seem a tad out of their league. If we need to talk about this project over the phone, then I will ask the NSA.

—It's nice to see you have such great respect for our national agencies. One question. Who are you to tell the NSA what they can and can't do? Forget that. Just who the hell are you?

—I have the utmost respect for the National Security Agency. I also hold my dentist and my accountant in very high esteem. I have not, however, asked either of them to lead our research team.

—You didn't answer my question.

—What were you told when you took this job?

—Nothing! I was told to cooperate with you as much as I could in the interest of national security. Well, I think this, right now, may be as much as I can.

—You might want to "sleep on it," as they say, in the interest of national security.

—You killed eight people, you son of a bitch! Eight US citizens—a child, for God's sake! A six-year-old girl, with curly red hair and bright blue eyes.

—Would you feel any better if her eyes had been a different color?

—Her face is on every television in every living room in the country.

—It was an unfortunate incident. I wish I could say it was not foreseeable, but that would not be entirely true. The probability of finding a piece in a densely populated area was deemed acceptably low. We had a contingency plan and it was executed without flaw. We did our best to control a bad situation.

—And a great job you did! A bunch of soldiers shoving a crying mother into a truck. That played so well on CNN.

—We have a cover story.

—I know. I've read it! A homemade bomb accidentally went off in the home of a suspected domestic terrorist. Gotta love that. You'll put the entire country on alert just so you can hide your precious little statue. What about that family you're blaming this on? I'm sure their relatives will be thrilled to know Uncle Owen was a terrorist. This isn't a game, you know.

—You and I both know I did not do anything that this country has not done a dozen times before. And while you might be too proud to admit it, your approval ratings will jump twenty points because of this. Oh, do not give me that look. You have many talents but acting is not one of them. The election is less than a year away. How many presidents have lost an election during a crisis? Will you really stand there and tell me you did not think about that? Not even for a moment?

You can admit it. You were not a causal factor in this tragedy and you bear little to no responsibility for the death of that little girl. I see no reason for you to feel shame because you stand to benefit from it.

And, for the record, it is not a statue. It appears to be some sort of vehicle.

— . . . There was nothing in the report to suggest . . .

—Your report may be a bit outdated. I assumed we would not find all the parts on US soil, so I put together a second team to fly drone planes at very high altitudes outside the United States.

—This is just surreal. When was that?

—About six months ago.

—Six months! But you had barely started the search six months ago!

—Why delay the inevitable? We started with the Arctic since it is mostly uninhabited. We found something under the ice on Ellesmere Island, something you will find interesting.

—Don't you think you should have talked to, let me see, me, before you did anything that stupid?

—My dear Robert. I thoroughly enjoy talking to you. You can rest assured I would have come to you without hesitation had I thought for a second it was something I needed to do.

—Go to hell . . . And what does Canada have to say about being invaded?

—They barely knew we were there. They are so worried about Danish ships challenging their territory, they probably welcome having us patrolling the area.

We found the torso. It is big, very big. On the surface it looks like every other piece, but we found a very small hatch on the back. This one is hollow. There is a large chamber inside, with what appears to be a control room.

—You mean it can move? Like a robot?

—That is our current assumption. We can confirm it once we find the rest of the pieces.

—OK. I wasn't expecting that one, but we already have plenty of things that can move, on land, in water, in the air, in space even. Does it have any offensive capabilities?

—We will know when we have all the pieces. As I said before, we really need to expand our search outside the United States.

—How many other countries do you have in mind?

—What do you mean?

—What do I . . . ? It's a simple question. How many countries?

—All of them, of course.

—Let me get this straight. You want this president to authorize violating the airspace of every single country on the planet so you can spread radioactive material over them, all in the hopes of finding parts of a giant alien robot. Is that all?

—No, it is not. He needs to be prepared to do a lot more than that. This is only the beginning. I cannot emphasize enough how important it is that he be clear on this.

Flying over other countries uninvited is easy. If we do this right, no one will ever know we were there. But if it works—and it will work, eventually—these body parts will surface. Some will surface in the middle of nowhere, but some will definitely surface where you do not want them to. They will come up hard, and they will come up fast, and they will destroy things. You thought Flagstaff was bad. Imagine what one of these things will do to downtown London or Paris. How about the Red Square in Moscow? A lot more than eight people will die, a whole lot more. They will be as innocent as the ones that just died. More little girls with curly red hair.

Most importantly, my people will not always be there in a matter of minutes to collect the pieces, which means other people will. They most likely will have no idea what they are looking at, but it will not take them long to figure out that it is worth their attention. Most likely, they will also not be happy about their little girls being crushed into the Earth.

You will need to get the pieces back from these people. You will ask nicely at first. Some of them will listen. Some of them will not.

What then? There will already be a whole lot of blood on your hands. Will you stop there? You really need to ask yourself: "What am I prepared to do?" If you and the president are not willing to go all the way, there are other players in this game who might not have the same reservations.

—Don't threaten me. Don't *ever* threaten me. You might have enough pull with this office to force me to listen to you, but if you ever threaten me again, you'll spend the rest of your miserable life in some third-rate country being water-boarded ten times a day. I know people too. Do I make myself clear?

—As always, my dear Robert, you are the epitome of clarity. Empty threats aside, my point still holds. This was never something we were going to be able to do without leaving this country. You have to remember—and you should have figured this out when you read my first report—these things were buried three thousand years ago. All those borders you are so worried about flying over, they are nothing but color lines on a map. None of these lines existed three thousand years ago.

—I understand how much more convenient it would have been to dig up these things a couple millennia ago. Somehow, it doesn't make the idea of violating the airspace of every ally or enemy we have any less insane. Unless, of course, you're willing to give all the world leaders that map and color-lines speech you just gave me. I'm sure they'd be happy to let us in, if only they knew about the color lines.

—You can mock me as you please. At the end of the day, you will realize that this has to be done. You may not like it—I certainly do not—but it must be done nonetheless.

—Does Dr. Franklin know about this?

—Not yet. I thought you would like to know first.

—About the torso being hollow, or about there being a second team?

—Both.

—You kill me, you know. You didn't tell her you had put together a second team? I'm sure she'll be thrilled to hear that one.

—That is not your concern.

—You're probably right. I want you to tell her—about the torso, that is. You'll have to tell her about the other team anyway. She'll be pissed off. I want you to tell her to figure out how this thing works and what it can do. I don't care if they have to work around the clock, just tell her to do it. Then I want to talk to her. I sure as hell don't trust you with any of this. Now *if*—do you hear me—*if* she tells me she can make it work, then you'll have the full support of this office. If she says she can't . . . Well, let's impress upon her how it would be in everyone's best interests that she can.

—You want me to threaten her.

—I want her and everyone involved—that means you too—to understand that the more chips we put on the table, the more difficult it becomes for us to fold.

—So you want me to threaten her.

—You make it sound like I'm ready to kill her.

—Are you?

—No! Why would I do that? I was merely suggesting we could replace her if she doesn't deliver.

—You do not think she has "delivered" already?

—She has. But if she can't take us the rest of the way, maybe someone else can. She should be aware of that. I'm not suggesting we replace her now, just that we let her know it's a possibility. That same reasoning also applies to you.

—It really does not, but I can see why you might think it does.

—What's that supposed to mean?

—If you had an employee you knew was leaving in six months, just how much responsibility would you be willing to give her?

—I don't see your point.

—You work for someone who may lose his job after four years, who has to quit after eight. I am merely pointing out there are many things of interest to this nation that require a more long-term commitment.

—I'll be sure to mention that to the president.

PART TWO

BREAK A LEG

FILE NO. 037

INTERVIEW WITH DR. ROSE FRANKLIN, PH.D.
Location: Underground Complex, Denver, CO

—Definitely a girl! I couldn't stop grinning when they brought the chest in. Her breasts aren't that large, given her size, but they're still bigger than my car. Perky . . . She must have been the envy of all the giant girl robots back in her day.

—I have not seen it yet.

—Well, you really want to see this. The breastplate and the middle of the abdomen are smooth. I think she's wearing some type of sleek armor, like the Amazons. Two large turquoise arteries are running down her sides behind large ribs. It's as if part of her anatomy is exposed. There is a large-scale V-shaped armor piece carved into her back, going all the way to her waist. It's magnificent, very humbling.

—I appreciate your attention to details. I am not blind to the aesthetics of the device. Some of its parts are indeed striking. You convey your appreciation for this particular piece in a very eloquent manner . . .

—It's *pieces,* plural. The chest and abdomen are separate pieces. They were just joined together when you found them.

—Thank you for correcting me. I was saying that I would prefer if you focused on the functionality of these pieces, plural.

—As I said, you need to see them. You can't ask about the Sistine Chapel and expect me not to mention the ceiling. The aesthetics aren't merely a side note, they're as important as anything else. You can't look at this thing and not know it was built to intimidate. Anyone who came face-to-face with this thing was meant to be awed and terrified at the same time. Form follows function.

—That the life is recognizable in its expression. That form ever follows function. That is the law.

—Who said that? Was it Frank Lloyd Wright?

—His mentor. I apologize for my previous comment. I should know better than to question your judgment.

—It's OK. I get a bit carried away. But the torso is magnificent, and very large.

—How large?

—Very large. It's . . . big. Roughly the size of a six-story building. We had to relocate.

—Yes, this is an impressive structure. I got lost in the tunnels after they showed me in. It took nearly twenty minutes before a security guard found me and brought me here.

—This place was completely empty before we moved in. Security's a little thin once you get past the front door.

—What can you tell me about this facility?

—They call it the Ark. We're right beneath Denver International Airport. It was built at the height of the Cold War as an alternate command center in the event of nuclear war. It also houses living spaces for nearly five thousand people, and it holds the world's largest underground storage facility.

—It sounds like a description of Cheyenne Mountain.

—Pretty much. Apparently, since Cheyenne Mountain was seen in just about every sci-fi movie you can think of, it would probably be high on a target list and might not withstand a direct hit from modern missiles. They built this facility in the late eighties to be used as a command site and long-term shelter when the Continuity of Government plan is invoked.

We've been given access to the storage area. It's over a hundred thousand square feet with a three-hundred-foot-high ceiling. If we manage to put her back together, she'll have room to walk around; now that we know she can walk.

—You can give me a tour later. I assume you found the opening.

—Yes, there's a hatch at the top of her back, right between her shoulder blades. You can barely notice it, but there is a handprint carved into the door that responds to body heat. When you press your hand onto the handprint, the door slides in. Of course, you know all this since your men already went in.

—I sense a bit of frustration in your tone.

—I don't know if you want to call it frustration, but I was told I was in charge of this project. Then you tell me you had teams searching the Arctic without my knowledge, using my formula. So, no, I'm not entirely happy, and I'm wondering what else you haven't told me.

—I wanted to let you finish the search on US soil. I suppose I could have told you before. I am telling you now. You are no longer in charge of the search effort. Everything else is your domain.

I want you to focus on making it work. It is much closer to your area of expertise and it is where you have excelled in the past. I hate to have to remind you, but you are not a military strategist. You almost lost your pilot when you hit your first road bump. Believe me, things are going to get very unpleasant once we take this search onto foreign territory.

—Look, I really don't care if I run the search or not. I just want you to be straight with me. I've never asked for anything since we started all of this. I'm asking now. Don't go behind my back.

—I will keep that in mind. Now tell me about the torso.

—Behind the hatch, there's a small tunnel, about four feet across that leads to another small door with a similar handprint—it's made of a material I can't identify. This one leads to a spherical chamber, about nine meters wide. That's about thirty feet.

—I am familiar with the metric system. Thank you.

—The chamber rotates inside the torso based on its incline. Basically, it's a big gyroscope. The concept is beautifully simple. The sphere is heavier at the bottom, and it floats in some sort of liquid. Gravity does the rest. If you tilt the body, the inner sphere stays level. The sphere appears to be translucent. You can see the dark metal through the milky substance it floats in. The interior is dimly lit though there is no apparent light source. There are no windows of any kind.

The floor of the chamber is flat, split into two crescent-shaped decks. The rear one is raised about three feet, with two steps on each side to get down to the front section. It seems designed to accommodate two people, two pilots. I call them animators. I like the puppet analogy better since it's not really a ship.

The upper deck is very minimalist. There is a beam that descends from the ceiling about halfway through. Attached to the end of it is a black helmet—like a scooter helmet, with a dark, opaque visor—and what looks like an armored straitjacket. It has metal braces that close over the forearms and upper arms and it's articulated at the shoulders and elbows. It also has a wide brace that wraps around the chest. There are glove-like devices at the end of each arm. Standing right in front of it is a small metallic round column, about three feet high.

—Have you determined its purpose?

—We have no idea what it does, but we really haven't tried anything yet.

The bottom deck is much more elaborate. There's a crescent-shaped console, about two meters wide, with maybe two dozen symbols carved onto it. Some of them are the same curvy ones we found on the panels in the hand chamber, others we haven't seen before. In front of the console, where you'd expect a chair, there is a round circle. I wouldn't call it a pool because it's only half an inch deep, but it's filled with some milky liquid. It's very smooth, very silky, like liquid Teflon. Rising from the floor, right in the middle of it, is a shaft, about three feet high. There is another black helmet attached to that shaft, and a matching set of leg braces with stirrups hanging about an inch from the liquid floor.

It would appear that one person operates the arms and trunk, while another controls the legs, plus whatever else one can do from the console. That's where it gets interesting.

—Before you go on, have you decided who will control the upper body and who will work the legs?

—I haven't decided yet. The leg station is the one that controls loco-motion and every other function on the console so there's an argument for Kara sitting there, standing there, whatever. On the other hand, I believe it may be physically harder to move the legs and Ryan is a very strong man. We'll probably try both and see what feels more natural.

—So what is it?

—What is what?

—You said: "This is where it gets interesting." Irony is not one of my favorite modes of communication, but I can still recognize it. I assume you were about to serve me with some bad news.

—The leg braces are not suited for human anatomy. They were clearly designed for someone with leg articulations like that of the robot it-self. I always assumed that the people who built this at least looked like us. If they weren't human, that is.

—Will that be a problem for the pilot?

—Perhaps I didn't make myself clear. The knees are backward! So yes, it's a problem, unless we can get a really smart ostrich to control the legs. We'll have to find a way to adapt the controls to fit our anatomy.

—What about the console? Are you making any progress deciphering the symbols?

—Not really. Vincent took a quick look at the console but now he's back to working on the panels. He feels there's a better chance of interpreting the symbols in context, seeing how they combine together, than by looking at them individually.

—He feels . . . Are you having second thoughts about choosing him?

—What makes you think I . . . ?

—You are distancing yourself from his opinion. That is unlike you. You tend to give credit to others when you succeed and you take responsibility for other people's failures. It suggests to me that you are having second thoughts.

—Sometimes. He's absolutely brilliant, don't get me wrong. He understands things that are well beyond his area of expertise. We had an interesting conversation about extrasolar planets the other night. It turns out he reads about astrophysics in his spare time, just for the fun of it. If anyone can figure out the symbols . . .

I just hope his ego doesn't get in the way. He respects me, and it's easy for me to like him. He can be a little abrasive if you don't live up to his standards. I have a feeling he's even more demanding of himself. I'm worried the longer this drags on . . . He's managed to get on Kara's good side, though, and that's not easy. It certainly makes all our lives a whole lot easier.

—I read his file. I believe he is more resilient than you give him credit for.

—You rea . . . He has a file?

—Your hairdresser has a file and you see him once a month. Vincent Couture is a foreign national on US soil, with direct access to top-secret-level information on a daily basis. He has several files, very large ones.

—You have a file on my hairdresser?

—Yes. He really needs to file his taxes. As for Mr. Couture, if you wish to replace him . . .

—You misunderstand. I'm sure if it can be done, Vincent can figure it out. I'm just not sure anyone can decipher these things. It might not be possible at all. That's what I'm really worried about. I'm afraid of what it will do to him. I don't think he's ever been faced with a problem he couldn't solve. He might just self-destruct if he feels like he's failing.

—I do not wish to appear insensitive, but without a basic understanding of the symbols, we cannot make this machine work. How Mr. Couture reacts to failure seems rather inconsequential when weighed against the biggest scientific discovery in history. If you suspect he will not succeed, you must replace him immediately. If your only concern is that his ego might be irreparably bruised, I promise we will use the considerable resources at our disposal to get Mr. Couture the best help money can buy. Thirty hours of therapy should not break our budget.

—He just needs more time.

—He has a week.

FILE NO. 039

EXPERIMENT LOG—CW3 KARA RESNIK, UNITED STATES ARMY

Location: Underground Complex, Denver, CO

This is Kara Resnik recording. Today is September 20. It is . . . 10:25 A.M. Dr. Rose Franklin is monitoring my vitals from the lab during the experiment. Hi, Dr. Franklin! We're about to test the controls inside the device. We've attached the complete left arm to the torso, and now we're gonna see if I can make it move. That's if I ever get up there. I'm making my way up the stairs now, with a barstool.

We should really set up the elevator for this. Even without the legs, this is pretty high. It's hard to move with all those sensors glued to my head and chest. I'm afraid I'll rip out the wires. It's bad enough I have to bring up furniture. When you speak to our mutual friend, ask him if they found anything resembling an alien stepladder in the Arctic. If anyone else ever listens to this, you should know that the hatch that leads inside the torso opens about four and a half feet from the floor. It's not that big of a jump, but you'd need to be about eight feet tall to close it from the inside, or to open it again. The moral of this story is: Don't go in there alone, or bring a barstool. Also, don't forget to pee.

I'm about thirty steps from the top. Why am I the one going up the stairs anyway? I know, I'm the arm pilot, the singular arm pilot. But since this thing doesn't have legs for now, maybe we could, you know, share a little. Ryan's twice my size, I'm sure he wouldn't mind carrying that stool up fifteen flights of stairs.

I'm not whining. I'm . . . climbing. I'm at the top. I'm just . . . gonna catch my breath for a minute . . .

I'm staring at the hatch. These aliens have really . . . ordinary hands. It's a little bigger than mine, but it looks like it could be anyone's handprint. Pressing my hand on it now. I can feel everything vibrate a little. It might be lining up the hatch inside the sphere with this one. It's opening.

I'm almost to the other hatch. Why is this walkway so small? OK it's open. It'll just take a second to . . . drop my stupid barstool on the floor . . . and . . . I can make my way in.

I'm in. The room is still well lit. The light is very . . . cozy, like a room with a fireplace. I just closed the inner hatch. I'm off the barstool, now approaching the top station. Rose, I know you think this looks like a straitjacket, but it's pretty badass if you ask me. Take it off that pole hanging from the ceiling and I think it would make Batman proud if you spray painted it black. I'm sliding my arms in . . .

I can't seem to get my fingers to fit into the gloves. Wiggle, wiggle . . . OK, the hands are in. Gloves are just a little stiff. Closing the arm braces. I'm trying to . . . clip the front closed with my big metal fingers. I think that's how it goes. I'm closing the large metal brace around my chest.

Let me see if I can move with that thing on. Mobility is good, as resistance is minimal on the arms and hands. It's a bit harder to move my chest. I can bend forward to touch my toes, but I can't crouch. I can barely flex my knees before I run out of leash. I can't move away either. It'll be hard to pick anything up from the ground. Strike that. I'm an idiot. My legs don't count. Ryan can crouch from the other station, and I can grab stuff from wherever the ground will be . . . for me. That'll be weird. I know everyone's excited, but it might take a while before we get the gist of this two-pilot thing.

Of course, that'll be the least of our problems, unless there's a video screen or something in that helmet, because, well, we can't see outside. I can't see anything but metal. And the visor on the helmet looks completely opaque, so if there's no screen, then I won't see anything at all. Use the Force, Luke! Maybe that's it. Maybe this is a really big Jedi training thing, to see if you can move a ten-thousand-ton dummy around with your eyes closed.

I don't think there's anything else I can try before I put on the helmet. You know, this really looks like a helicopter helmet. I'm putting it over my head now. I wonder if . . .

AAAAAAAARRRRRRRHHHHHHH . . .

FILE NO. 041

PERSONAL JOURNAL ENTRY—
DR. ROSE FRANKLIN, PH.D.

I'm angry. I'm angry with everyone. I'm angry with myself. I should know better than to experiment with things I don't understand and assume everything's going to be fine. That was stupid of me. It's not as if the leg controls left us with any doubt. This device wasn't built for humans. Who knows what this thing can do to us? How could I ask Kara to try something I know nothing about, on her head, and not have a medical team with her?

She's still at the hospital. She said the pain was so sharp, she lost consciousness almost immediately. We found her hanging by her arms at her station, like Christ to the cross. The helmet had turned itself off. It took nearly a half hour for the paramedics to reach her and get her out. She could have died a thousand times over.

When she came about she was completely blind. We almost lost her twice on the same day. Kara being Kara, she ripped out her IV the minute she woke up and tried to feel her way out of the room. She tripped over something and knocked herself unconscious on a metal cabinet. They had to close a cut on her forehead, eight stitches or so.

There were superficial burns on her face. The doctors treated them and wrapped a bandage around her head to cover her eyes. She was supposed to keep it on for a few days. Of course, she removed it after only a few hours. She said it was itching . . . The doctors scolded her halfheartedly. They've seen her a few times already—routine exams, some cuts and bruises—so they were probably surprised she kept it on that long. I was.

When I stopped by the hospital to see how she was doing, the whole room was agitated. Doctors were arguing amongst themselves, kept calling in other doctors to examine her. I asked what was going on about a dozen times, but I couldn't get anyone to listen to what I was saying. Kara threw a lamp at the wall. That got their attention.

The doctors told her that her eye was fine. She didn't seem ecstatic enough, so they went on to explain that her retina had somehow been repaired. I didn't believe it myself, but they showed us the before and after pictures. It didn't take a medical degree to see it. That helmet had fixed her. It probably detected an eye injury and proceeded to repair it. I can only hope that's why it was so painful.

It's hard to express how relieved I am. Kara's fine. Better than fine, really. This is closer to a miracle. So why am I angry? Well, I was so happy. I rushed back to the lab and I tried on the helmet myself. Stupid, right? It didn't do anything, so I asked Ryan up and had him try it on. I had every lab assistant come in and give it a go. When that didn't work, we tried the helmet at the other station, all of us. Why risk one person's life when you can go for half a dozen? Oh, and the helmet's broken. As far as I can tell, the other one was already broken when we found it. Neither of them work anymore.

What was I thinking? It repaired her eye? For all we know, these aliens might have one big eye. Maybe they have eighty of them. They might have the eyes of a fly, they might have no eyes at all. It could have ripped her skull in half, disfigured her, turned her into something she's not. A million things could have happened to her, most of which would probably have killed her.

It's my job to keep her safe, to make sure nothing happens to her. I sent her up there and she trusted me. She trusted my judgment, she trusted that I wouldn't send her in if I thought she could get harmed. I'm supposed to be a scientist. I don't know what I am anymore.

Kara's scheduled for an MRI tomorrow. We should know if there's any brain damage. If I had half a brain myself, I would have waited for the results before letting anyone back in the sphere. It's too late for that, but I'll have the doctors run a lot more tests before I let Kara back in there. We should wait a few weeks anyway, she might exhibit more symptoms as time goes by.

I hope she's OK, with all my heart. Not just for the sake of the project, I don't think I could live with myself if I let anything happen to her. I've grown a lot closer to her. I've grown closer to all of them, but I really like Kara.

I'm not the only one who likes her. Ryan hasn't said a word, and we all let him think we haven't noticed, but of course she knows. I know. Vincent knows. I'm sure the robot knows by now. I wish Ryan only the best—who wouldn't?—but I hope his crush disappears on its own. I certainly hope they don't end up together. I love Kara, but she'd end up hurting him, a lot.

That being said, the two of them are doing great. It took a while, but he's learned to leave her enough space. I have to give Ryan credit for that. They complement each other quite nicely. They work well together. They'll have to if they're going to stare at each other all day.

So, I have an incomplete robot with broken controls, one infatuated pilot and one injured. I'm not sure where that leaves us. The helmets are a major setback. I don't know when, or if, we'll be able to fix them. Even if we manage to get them working again, there's no guarantee we can wear these things without ending up in the hospital. They weren't meant for us, after all.

Which brings me to the leg controls. Ryan's really got a bad deal on this one. His helmet doesn't work and his legs bend the wrong way. I wish I could find a way to modify the leg controls to fit our anatomy, but there's too great a chance of permanently damaging the controls if we start tinkering with them. I can't reproduce the metal that was used if we break something on that station. I'll try just about anything before I let anyone approach it with a blowtorch.

Ryan has it in his head that he can work the legs facing the other way, with his back to the console. He'll have to walk backward all the time. I think it's insane but I have nothing better to offer so I'm inclined to let him try. Walking is a lot more complicated than people think. We do it unconsciously, but it's a lot more difficult if you have to think it through. Make a comment to someone about the way they walk and see how awkward they become. It's complex, and hard to decompose.

They won't be able to keep the robot balanced if Ryan doesn't get the movements perfectly right. It's a tall and narrow structure, and the center of gravity is going to be really high. It's scary enough as it is, and I can't imagine how bad a fall would be once we get the legs on. It would probably flatten a city block or two.

I brought in some engineers to create a computer simulation. It will connect to the leg controls and to the other station and convert the pilot's movement into a computer model of the robot. We'll be able to see the results on computer screens. It takes weight, speed, and several other factors into account. It should at least give us an idea of whether or not what we're trying to do is possible.

So, if we get the helmets working without killing ourselves, if Ryan can control kilotons of metal while walking backward, we'll be left with the console. Ryan will be facing away from it, so someone else will need to handle that.

Right now it doesn't work, of course. Vincent seems no closer to interpreting the symbols that are on it than he was when he first came in, and we have absolutely no idea what it does. This might be unprofessional of me, but I say we can cross that bridge when we get to it. We don't know how complex it will be to operate. We might need a physicist, or a soldier, or maybe someone who's really good at video games.

I know we're supposed to make these journal entries to help us cope with stress. Hell, I'm the one who suggested it. But I have to say, right now, it's not helping. Do I think we'll eventually solve all these problems and make this thing work? I . . . I think getting to the moon probably felt like an impossible thing to do at first. Who am I kidding? Right now, I don't think we have a chance on Earth.

I might feel differently in the morning. Either way, I'll get up and go back to work. There are simply too many breakthroughs waiting for us if we can understand how this machine works. We already know it can perform medical wonders. Who knows what else it can do?

That also scares me. Am I ready to accept all that may come out of this if it works? It might give us a cure for everything. It might also have the power to kill millions. Do I want that on my conscience? I wish I knew where this journey will take us, but I don't. All I know is that this is bigger than me, my self-doubt, or any crisis of conscience. I now truly realize how profoundly insignificant I am compared to all this. Why does that make me feel so much better?

FILE NO. 042

EXPERIMENT LOG—CW3 KARA RESNIK, UNITED STATES ARMY

Location: Underground Complex, Denver, CO

This is Kara Resnik. Today is September 22. It's three in the morning, so no one is monitoring me. I'm probably gonna get in trouble for this, but what else is new? Dr. Franklin came to see me at the hospital today—well, yesterday now. It's obvious she feels responsible for what happened to me. I tried to make her understand this wasn't on her. I mean, it's not like I wouldn't have tried that thing on my own if she'd waited another day. She seemed devastated. Apparently, the whole project is on hold until they see if I suffer from any aftereffects. We'll see about that.

She also told me I broke the helmet. I mean, really? I didn't do anything! I just put it on my head, because . . . it's a helmet? That's what you're supposed to do. I don't buy that it's broken either. I had an MRI today, I don't have the results yet, but I'm pretty sure that alien device didn't scramble my brain, so I don't see how my brain could have broken it. OK, it's not the best reasoning ever, but it re-paired my eye, for God's sake! Doctors couldn't do that, and that thing did! I'm sorry, but I don't think a machine that can do eye surgery after being buried underground for three thousand years is gonna break on account of my little head.

I'm not as smart as everyone else, but I think the pain was so intense because it repaired my eye. That, or it figured out that my brain isn't what it's supposed to be, and it adapted somehow. Either way, if it's smart enough to fix me, I'm pretty sure it'll find a way not to kill me. I have a gut feeling it may have—what's the word—imprinted, when it adapted to my brain, like a baby duck. If I'm right, it thinks I'm its mommy now. I think that's why it won't turn on for anyone else anymore.

I know that wouldn't explain why the other helmet doesn't work, but like Dr. Franklin always says: one thing at a time. You can't solve every problem at once. You see, Dr. Franklin: I was listening. Now I'm trying to solve one problem. I know what you're gonna say: I haven't even been discharged from the hospital yet. You and the doctors told me to stay put and get some rest. Well, I can't rest if everything's stopped because of me; and I don't want to worry about that helmet knocking me out every time I put it on. This is me finding some peace of mind, so don't get too mad when you find out what I've done. Unless I die in the next ten minutes. Then you can get mad all you want.

Also, don't get mad at the hospital staff either. They probably thought I was going to the cafeteria, considering I told them I was going to the cafeteria.

I'm at the top of the stairs now. I think next time, if there's a next time, I'll bring two barstools with me, just for the satisfaction of throwing one down as hard as I can. I hate these things now. From now on, I'll stand when I go to a bar.

You know what I'm doing, so I'm sparing you the play-by-play. Crouching, crouching. Opening the inner hatch . . .

I'm inside the sphere, going to brace myself in. I'd be lying if I said I wasn't a little nervous. This seemed like a much better idea an hour ago. Then again, I get sweaty palms when I wanna ask a guy out, so, par for the course.

I have the helmet in my hands. I'll put it on now, before I chicken out. Be nice, little fellow, Mommy's here . . .

AAAAAAAHHHHHRRRRR!

Son of a . . . Helmet's off! *Come on!* What is it *with* this thing?! It burned like hell. I couldn't even keep my eyes open. Mommy's pissed! Obviously, it wasn't as bad as the last time if I'm still talking, but that thing really hates . . .

I . . .

I'll be damned. I can't feel much with these gloves on, but I think the cut on my forehead is gone. I can tell you the stitches are gone for sure.

OK, I must be crazy, because I'm putting it on again. I don't see what else it could fix, except maybe some self-esteem issues. I wanna see what it does when it's not healing things.

. . .

Whoa. This is just amazing! . . . Ha-ha! I don't even know where to start. As soon as I put it on, the visor went from dark to clear and suddenly I could see everywhere. I mean, I can see *everywhere,* not just inside the chamber. I can see through the metal outside the torso, I can see the lab.

I can still see the sphere, the liquid around it, but all of it is translucent. In fact, if I focus on something outside, I can see it clear as day. If I look at something inside, then what's outside gets dimmer. It gives a bronze hue to everything, like an old photograph.

Let me look around for a while. This is awesome. I know I sound like a complete moron, but I can't find the words. What . . . *is* . . . this?

There's a hologram, a miniature of the robot—about one foot tall—projecting out of the small column in front of me. It's really cute. Dr. Franklin, I wish you could see how cool that thing is. I mean, I know what it'll look like when we have all the pieces. It's . . . out of this world. No pun intended. Other than the legs being weird, she looks like a normal badass-warrior human being. The head looks human, and there's only one. Nice. The hologram is moving its head when I move mine. When I move my arms, it does exactly the same thing. It mimics every movement of my upper body. I suppose it will also move its legs as well once we get the other station working.

I'm flailing my arms around like a madwoman. The actual robot arm isn't moving an inch. That's probably a good thing because I'd have destroyed everything in the lab, but the hologram has no problem moving at all.

Dr. Franklin, I just realized you'll probably never experience any of this firsthand, if the helmet won't work for anyone but me. It breaks my heart that you can't see what I'm seeing after all you did. But it works! You were right, Dr. Franklin! And you see there's no reason to wait. Everything's fine. Oh, and you're stuck with me, for good.

Don't worry about the arm not moving. It will probably work when we connect all the pieces, like those old Christmas lights from when I was a kid. If a single tiny light was missing, none of them would work.

I wish I could try the other station. I know, baby ducks. There's only one of me and I can't be at both stations at the same time. Still, it'd be nice to know if it works . . .

FILE NO. 047

INTERVIEW WITH VINCENT COUTURE, GRADUATE STUDENT
Location: Underground Complex, Denver, CO

—Dr. Franklin said you had a breakthrough.

—I did. It's not language!

—Already you lost me.

—I couldn't figure out the meaning of the symbols. The more I thought about it, the more I realized I wasn't supposed to.

—Now you have really lost me. Please say something, anything, that will make sense to me.

—The people that looked at this before me, they couldn't come up with an interpretation because they lacked a . . . a frame of reference. They didn't know the grammar of that language. They didn't know the vocabulary. They didn't even know what this was about. They needed something to compare it to. Do you know what the Rosetta Stone is?

—I do.

—Well, so you know it's a piece of rock, like the name says, with three sections of text carved into it, one on top of the other. The top one is written in ancient Egyptian hieroglyphs, which no one understood when the stone was discovered. The middle carvings are Demotic, another Egyptian script, and the bottom one is Ancient Greek. That one we knew. What's so great about the Rosetta Stone is that all three texts are about the same thing. Do you know what it's about?

—That, I do not know.

—It's a *décret*. A decree?

—Yes.

—Basically, it establishes the new king as a god. Because Ancient Greek was a known language at the time, it was used as a starting point and they were able to recognize key elements in the hieroglyphs by looking at repetitions. They were able to figure out how Egyptian hieroglyphs worked because they had the Greek version of the text as a reference.

—But whoever wrote on the panels did not leave us a Rosetta Stone.

—Maybe they did. Logically, without a frame of reference, we shouldn't be able to do anything with this. They would know that. But if Dr. Franklin is right, this was left for us on purpose. So I started thinking, what if *this* is the Rosetta Stone? What if this isn't a message written in a different language but a key to interpreting something else? It would have to be about something we already have in common, something universal. Then it hit me. It's not words, it's math!

We may not be as advanced, or evolved, as the people who wrote this. We might not be able to understand things that would seem trivial to them. But the one thing that we absolutely, positively, must have in common is some form of math. We both need to count things. I think they kept this thing simple enough so we could understand it, but they made sure we could get as many important concepts as we could out of it.

There are seven curvy symbols on the panels, and each has a dot in the middle. All of them also appear on the console. If you count the number of curvy lines in each one, you get the numbers one through seven. It's so obvious once you think about it, it just makes me mad not to have seen it before.

—So the markings on the walls are a series of numbers?

—More like a series of equations. There are several of them, enough for us to interpret the other symbols, the ones that are made of straight lines.

Look at this one, for example. Here we have the number 2 . . . Oh! I skipped over the part where you have to read from right to left. I'm sorry . . . So, from the right, the number 2, some unknown symbol, 2 again, some other unknown symbol, then the number 4. Now fill in the blanks: 2 something 2, something 4.

—2 + 2 = 4?

—Exactly. So now you know the symbol for addition and the one for equality. That last one could mean something a little different, like the result of an operation. I don't know precisely but we're in the ballpark.

—Wait. It could also be 2 x 2 = 4. How can you be certain it is not multiplication?

—That's why there are so many sequences. We can use other formulas with the same symbols to verify our hypotheses. Here we have the same symbols used with other numbers. If this were a multiplication, it would read like 3 x 2 = 5, but it works if it's an addition.

—What of that little line on the left? You ignored it. Is it not a symbol like the others?

—It's definitely a symbol. I was getting to that. That vertical line appears at the end of every formula, except for two that end in a small square. The vertical line seems fairly pointless until you look at the two formulas with the square. If my interpretation is correct—and I'm pretty sure it is—these two would read $2 + 1 = 1$, and $4 \times 3 = 10$.

—But that is wrong . . .

—I think that's the point. The vertical line tells us that the equation that precedes is true, and the square tells us that it's false. These two symbols might be the most important ones. Obviously, we now have symbols for true and false, but these are such powerful concepts, they might also be used outside of mathematics. If you look at my notes, you'll see that both symbols also appear next to each other on the console. True and false don't seem that useful for piloting a ship, but they probably use the same symbols for something similar, like yes and no, go and stop . . . Ryan thinks it's likely akin to proceed, cancel . . . something like that.

—Mr. Mitchell? I did not know you discussed this with anyone but Dr. Franklin.

—Well, we basically live in a bunker, the four of us. I have my own little area where they installed the panels but—how do I put this?—I get bored . . . So I nose around a little. We went out for a drink a few times. Actually, they went out for a drink a few times and they felt bad about leaving me here so they asked me to tag along. Rose and I have gotten to know each other a lot more, since I report to her, but I like hanging out with Ryan and Kara. Ryan's a nice guy. He's a little too Captain America at times, but he grows on you.

I like Kara. She doesn't open up much, with us, anyway. I don't think she has someone to talk to on the outside either. I don't know how she does it. She seems to be coping well, though. It could just be a facade, but if it is, she's good at it. Either way, we seem to get along OK. We have the same kind of humor. Dark . . . we say *pince-sans-rire*.

—Deadpan.

—Yes. Probably a little *too* deadpan. Ryan thinks we're just mean.

—So . . . please correct me if I am mistaken. You are saying the panels are a key to understanding whoever built this, through mathematics. You have discovered symbols for addition, multiplication, equality, truth and falsehood, as well as the numbers one through seven.

—We have a lot more than that actually. The formulas also include symbols for subtraction and division. Most importantly, we can interpret any number, if I got this right. As one would expect, some of the formulas have results that are higher than 7. Their mathematical system seems to be base-8. They only have seven symbols for numbers, plus the dot. Do you know how a base-8 system works?

—Enlighten me?

—It's very easy to understand, just very hard to use—for us, that is. We have a base-10 system—ten symbols for numbers, if you count the zero. Basically, when we count, we go up to nine—1, 2, 3, 4, 5, 6, 7, 8, 9—and then we run out of symbols. So we add a digit, and we get 10, which means one set of 10, plus nothing. Then we go through our nine symbols again: 11, 12, 13, etc. And we run out at 19, so we add one to the second position and we get 20, which is two sets of ten, and so on.

Their system works the same way, but with fewer symbols. They count through seven, then add a digit, and they end up with 1 plus the dot, which you can think of as zero, or as a placeholder if you prefer to see it that way. That means one set of 8, plus nothing. Then they go on with their seven digits: one-one, one-two, one-three, etc. Remember, one-two doesn't mean twelve, it means eight plus two. It gets much more confusing for us when we add more digits. Something like 2222 means two, plus two times eight, plus two times 64, plus two times 512, so 1170 in total.

Now, just to make this more fun, remember how the formulas read from right to left? Well, so do the numbers.

Dr. Franklin tells me the console doesn't work yet, so we can't know what it's used for. Whatever it is, since all the digits are on it, you can bet Ryan will have to punch in numbers, and he'll have to do it *in base-8*. I wouldn't say it can't be done, but it's extremely hard to learn, you have to do pretty complex math in your head just to read the numbers. At least, writing direction shouldn't matter when you punch in numbers on a keyboard. Still, 12345 their way is 5349 our way. 12345 our way is 30071 their way.

Oh . . . no. I see the look on your face but I'm not that smart, I wrote it down before you came in. I can't imagine having to do this on the fly.

—That is not what I heard. They say you are brilliant, once-in-a-generation brilliant.

—That's not true, unfortunately.

—Modesty does not become you, Mr. Couture.

—I've been accused of many things, but modesty, not so much. I'm smart. I'm really smart. Drop me in a room with a hundred people, chances are I'm smarter than ninety-nine of them. But there's always going to be that someone. I met a lot of people at the University of Chicago who could outthink me. I met some I couldn't even understand, and not because of my English. It wasn't because I lacked technical knowledge in their field or anything like that either, they were just . . . It's like playing chess. Some people can only see what's in front of them, others can see several moves ahead. I'm a couple moves short of the great ones.

—Do you believe you are the smartest person here?

—Maybe, maybe not. Rose can definitely think on her feet. Alyssa might have a few IQ points on both of us.

—Who is Alyssa?

—The geneticist. Rose brought her in to figure out why Kara's the only one who can use the helmet. She's not a people person, but she's a math genius. She might have figured out the panels long before me if she'd been around. I'm not sure what you want me to tell you. Do I think I'm smarter than you? Is that what you're asking?

—**Are you?**

—Without a doubt. It doesn't mean I think you're an idiot, but I'd be lying if I said no.

—**Fair enough. In my experience, people with superior intellect have a tendency to react poorly to failure. Did you ever think you might not succeed?**

—I suppose what you're asking is whether or not I ever doubted myself. No, I did not. But, there was always a good chance we were never going to figure this out. I knew that. Rose knew that. Those who didn't need to ready themselves for some serious disappointment.

—**What do you mean?**

—Well, long shot doesn't even begin to describe this. I'm amazed we actually got this far. *If* we manage to get the leg controls working, and *if* the pilots can make her move without crashing, and *if* we can figure out how to use the console, we might be able to use her. That is, of course, *if* we find all the other pieces—it's a big planet. There's also a distinct possibility that she just won't work even if we do get all the pieces. She might just be broken, you know. Then, well, all the king's horses and all the king's men . . .

—. . .

—Humpty Dumpty? I think that's how it goes. I'm just saying, these things are buried in the dirt. The reason for that might be slightly less romantic than what we're all hoping for . . .

FILE NO. 092

INTERVIEW WITH CW2 RYAN MITCHELL, UNITED STATES ARMY

Location: Joint Base Lewis-McChord, Washington State

—Nothing happened.

—That is not what I heard.

—What did you . . . ? I don't understand. How could you . . . ?

—Each of us has a specific function in this project, Mr. Mitchell. Dr. Franklin is in charge of all scientific aspects of this mission. You are a pilot. I know things.

—I don't know what you want me to say.

—I asked a very simple question. What happened?

—We had *one* kiss . . .

—Mr. Mitchell. It would make things easier for both of us, especially for you, if we could forgo the part of this conversation where you take me for a complete idiot . . .

—OK, it was more than a kiss but it's not like we defected to Russia or anything. I don't think the Army has anything to worry about.

—You keep forgetting. I am not the Army, nor am I concerned with
their code of conduct. I have no interest in seeing either of you
court-martialed. I will, however, grow tired of asking. Just tell me
what happened.

—Well, we've been at this for five months now, full-time, and alone.
After a while, we either end up killing each other or we grow closer,
there's really no in between. We spend what? Twelve hours a day
together in the sphere? Six or seven days a week. It seems pointless to
go into details, but let's just say it didn't take long before I started
thinking about her for the other twelve hours.

But Kara's Kara. So every time I tried to get closer to her, she'd
back away and give me the cold shoulder for three days. I tried to give
her some space, as much as I could while being in the same room. It's
really hard spending that kind of time with someone without the conversation eventually slipping into personal territory.

After a while, I got tired of being called by my rank and last name
every time I mentioned anything not work-related. You'd be surprised how many things will strike a chord with her. I still don't
know what happened to her, but apparently anything having to do
with family, children, or relationships will make her mad. I mean, I
really tried, but anyone who gets edgy when cats come up as a conversation topic has some serious emotional issues.

A few weeks passed. I just kept my mouth shut and focused on
getting the big girl walking. We tried a few things, but each time our
computer model ended up flat on her face. It happened so often at
first, we had to remind ourselves she would wreck a dozen houses if
that happened for real. Turns out, even if I get the leg movements
right, Kara still has to move the arms and torso in sync for her to keep
her balance. Turning is even more complicated.

I started calling every movement out loud—left knee up, leg forward, left foot down—so she could shift the weight at the right time.
After about a month of that, she started anticipating my movements,
reading my body, the way I would move my shoulders before lifting
a leg, things like that. I got pretty good at reading her too. I spend my

entire day looking at her, since I'm facing away from the console. You do this from sunrise to sunset every day, it starts to feel natural, like you actually need the other person for something as simple as walking. She noticed I even stopped moving my arms when I walk on my own. She says it gives me a Terminator kind of look . . . The liquid guy, not Arnold.

—Does that mean you can make her walk?

—No, not quite. Even with Kara helping with the balance, I'm still short one leg joint. I can't seem to get the upper legs to move quite right. She has really short thighs between her hips and her actual knees. I don't have that; my legs connect to the braces just below. I have to thrust my whole body upward at every step to get a natural movement out of her and it's really hard to keep that going for more than a few steps.

But we're making progress. Perhaps that's what got Kara to open up a little. Perhaps it's because we started pulling even longer shifts. But one night she asked me out for a drink. It wasn't the first time, but she always made sure Dr. Franklin or Vincent tagged along. We usually go to the Aviator's lounge at B-Gate. Our exit inside the terminal is past security so it's convenient and Dr. Franklin can smoke. She doesn't, really, but she likes to light one up when she drinks. She mostly stares at it. Anyway, it closes at ten thirty so we drove to a real place that's open late. It was a bit of a dive, but anything where normal people go feels pretty special these days.

I don't know if I was nervous, or just really tired, but I got drunk. Plowed. One bourbon, one bourbon, one beer. I don't *think* they had Scotch anyway. I was on my second round when I started talking. She basically just listened to me spill my guts to her all night long. I was still mad at her, so I did it the mean way. You know: "I can't stop thinking about you but you're the coldest person I've ever met"—that kind of thing. She just sat there and listened. When I became a bit too incoherent, she dragged me to her car and drove me home without saying a word.

I wanted to hide under a rock the next day. More than anything, I was waiting to see what kind of hell she'd put me through for this. She didn't. We just went through our routine. She was quite cordial actually. Nothing the next day either, then the next. After a week had gone by, I assumed she had decided it was best to pretend it didn't happen. I was still reasonably embarrassed and inclined to agree.

A week later, she stopped me on the way out and asked if I still wanted to take her out to a real dinner. I tried to look like I thought about it before saying yes. I was going to pick her up on Sunday. I was at home getting ready when she called to cancel: "It's not a good idea, we work together, blah blah blah."

I should have been mad but I thought it was mostly funny since she was the one who invited me. We went through this dance one more time until I finally had it. I just stopped by her house on our night off and told her to hurry up. She didn't argue. I must have looked more confident than I was.

She offered me coffee but I told her I'd wait in the car. I should have said yes to that coffee, because she made me wait out there for a good half hour. I was flipping through radio stations when I saw her walk out. Wow! is all I can say. I'm not sure I would have recognized her if it wasn't her house. She wore a short skintight red dress, heels, the works. It made her legs look . . .

—Longer?

—Yes. I was looking for something more . . . Anyway, she had done something to her hair. I couldn't tell what it was . . . something though. She even had makeup on. The whole thing was totally unlike her, but she just looked amazing. She obviously felt a bit out of character. She wasn't nearly as bold as usual. She looked amazing and . . . vulnerable.

—Did you like that?

—That she felt vulnerable? I don't know. Maybe.

—There is no shame in admitting it.

—I don't get satisfaction out of making people feel smaller if that's what you're saying. I liked that I was having some sort of effect on her, you know. I wouldn't want her to be like that all the time. She's brash. That's who she is. Still, it was special.

I don't know how to explain it to you. All I think about is spending time with her. Do you understand what I'm saying? I spend twelve hours a day alone in a small room with her, and I still want . . . I don't know . . . More. It's like wanting a cigarette so bad, then you smoke a whole pack and you're still craving.

—Did you start smoking?

—No. It's just a figure of speech. I couldn't think of a better one. I wanna feel like I'm reaching her somehow, like she's letting me in. That night I did, for a while. It felt good.

—I understand. How did your evening go?

—I took her to a Brazilian steakhouse. It was a little out of my price range, but it was worth the money just to walk in there with her holding my arm. We had a really nice meal. I don't know if you like steak, but if you do, you should try that place sometime.

—I do, and I might. Please continue.

—This time I made sure I stayed sober. She didn't. The lady likes red wine. About halfway through the second bottle, she started talking. How her mother never approved of the men she was with. How her mother was right every time. I'm not sure but she made a comment in passing that led me to believe she was married once.

—She was not. I can tell you that much.

—Maybe I misunderstood. Whatever happened, I could tell there was a lot of pain involved.

I drove her to her house after dinner. I was about to get out of the car to get the door for her when she grabbed my arm. She undid her seat belt and jumped on my lap. Next thing I knew my seat was down and my shirt was coming off.

—That sounds like more than a kiss to me.

—Maybe. But the kiss is the only part where I felt she was really with me. I don't think I mattered after that. It was cold, angry sex, you know. It felt like she was getting back at someone. This is gonna sound stupid, but I was jealous of whoever she was thinking of. He obviously meant more to her than I did at the time. Anyway, she was done pretty fast. Then she got out of the car without saying a word. That was it. That was a week ago, and we haven't talked about it since.

—Do you *want* to talk about it?

—I'd like to know where we stand. If that was just the wine, I suppose I'll handle it. But I think she could use someone who'd take care of her. I don't think I'm the best man on Earth or anything like that, but I'd be good to her.

—I do not wish to be presumptuous, but if I may offer a bit of advice: Ms. Resnik is in need of many things. In my humble opinion, "someone who'd take care of her" is not one of them.

—I know. I know. Believe me I know. It's a cat-and-mouse thing, or is it the chicken or the egg? She backs off because I come on too strong. I come on stronger because I feel her slipping away.

—"Cat and mouse" implies a love of the chase. "The chicken or the egg" refers to a causality dilemma. You were attempting to refer to the situation as the latter.

—That's what I meant.

—I know. Unfortunately, it is an inaccurate interpretation of the facts. The situation you describe does indeed reinforce itself through a feedback loop. However, the expression suggests that the initial cause cannot be determined. In this case, it can.

—You mean me, right?

—I do. Just let her come to you on her own terms.

FILE NO. 093

MISSION REPORT—OPERATION CLEAN SWEEP

First Sergeant Dylan Rodriguez, U.S. Army, Transportation Specialist

Mission was a success. No friendly casualties.

We used an abandoned Russian air base near Semey in Kazakhstan as our home base. We'd been flying UAVs over eastern Siberia for three days when one of the drones picked up something in Tuva. It was right in the middle of nowhere, just east of a town called Sizim. It's a pretty inhospitable region, rocky hills surrounding green valleys along the Kaa-Khem River. There's really nothing there, so the good news was we probably had some time before anyone showed up. The bad news was transport would be more difficult.

We took two Kazakhs with us on the chopper. We wanted to drop them near Kyzyl. They said they weren't sure we could get our hands on a big enough truck there, but they knew a place in Abakan. It would mean waiting for an extra five hours but it seemed a safer bet. We flew in at night and dropped them into Khakassia before we headed toward Sizim. We were approaching the crater. There was some light flickering around it. It took a few seconds before we realized we were being shot at.

The helicopter dropped us about a mile away and we doubled back on foot. We waited for sunrise to get a better sense of what was going on. Turns out the artifact had turned a marijuana field inside out. There were peasants running around the field, some of them with AK-47s. They seemed to be more concerned about their crop being lost than with whatever it was that destroyed it.

Transportation was about six hours away and Sergeant Ortiz decided to make contact with the Tuvans. We didn't have the Kazakhs with us but Ortiz speaks a bit of Russian. I think they recognized our guns, or maybe it was the sergeant's accent, but after a couple minutes, they put down their AKs. We could make out one word in what they were saying: Americanyetz! Americanyetz! I don't know what they think of Americans in Tuva, but they sure seemed happy we weren't Russians.

One of the Tuvans went back to the village to get some help. He came back with a dozen more men. With the eleven men in our squad, that meant about forty able bodies. They helped us dig out the artifact and wrap some ropes around it. It took about an hour. Then we sat down with them and waited for the truck. That's when the Russian army showed up, sort of. It was a small truck with two men in it. If I had to guess, I'd say they were in on the marijuana trade and were coming to get a cut or something. Anyway, we hid behind the artifact as fast as we could. The Russians got out of the truck and started yelling. One of the Tuvans approached them smiling, then drew a pistol and shot both of them in the head point-blank.

The Kazakhs showed up with the truck twenty minutes later. It took about ninety minutes to load the artifact, then another ninety to bury the Russians and get rid of their truck. The Kazakhs told us there were a few checkpoints on the way to Khakassia, so we decided to head south on M54 and get air transport out of Mongolia. We met our contact at the border and flew to Afghanistan on a C-17.

—End Report—

FILE NO. 094

INTERVIEW WITH ROBERT WOODHULL, ASSISTANT TO THE PRESIDENT FOR NATIONAL SECURITY AFFAIRS

Location: White House, Washington, DC

—This is not exactly like fixing an old car, Robert. They will get it done, in time.

—I hope you're right. You wouldn't want to go down in history as the idiot who started World War III for a giant paperweight.

—You certainly have a flair for the dramatic.

—Not really. You're doing a great job at it so far. You've managed to single-handedly start the Cold War again.

—And how exactly did I achieve that on my own?

—Your drone planes just unearthed a very large hand in a place called Tuva.

—I know.

—That they found a hand or that there is such a place as Tuva?

—Tuva is a small republic in southern Siberia. I also knew about the hand. I did not know you had been made aware of it.

—Well, you're using US troops for your little pet project. Don't be surprised if they report to us when there's an international incident. And good for you about Tuva. I had to look it up . . .

—Forgive me if I do not share in your pessimism but the mission was a success. We retrieved the hand without any loss of life on our part, and logic dictates the Tuvans will not tell the Russians anything. I fail to see what the problem is.

—That's the thing. They don't need to tell. The Russians know.

—What do they know?

—Everything. They know everything down to the smallest detail. The Russian ambassador gave me the play-by-play this morning. Sounded just like First Sergeant Rodriguez, with a different accent. One of their planes was nearby when the hand emerged. It crashed a few miles north. They had a satellite over the site about an hour before your men arrived. He even showed me the video. The part where two Russian officers get shot is much more dramatic on television.

—I assume they are not pleased.

—That's the euphemism of the century. I don't even know where to begin. Mongolia's pissed because we put them on the spot. Russia followed your truck all the way to their front steps. Moscow demands an official apology, which they obviously won't get since we're adamantly denying we had anything to do with any of this. They also have this thing on satellite photos, so they know what it looks like. It would be easier to come up with a cover story for a nondescript body part, like a forearm, or a calf, like you did in Turkey. But the hand, well, it looks like a big hand, even from a thousand miles up.

You know that by now they've tortured every Tuvan they could get their hands on, so I'd say they know even more than they did before. There's a reason we hire local mercenaries for black ops; it's called plausible deniability. You sent a bunch of friggin' Puerto Ricans with M-16s on a mission into Siberia. They didn't exactly blend in, you know.

—We cannot assemble new teams in every part of the world in a matter of hours. Furthermore, involving mercenaries would pose a significant security risk. We buy mercenaries. Mercenaries are easily bought. That is what mercenaries do.

—Well, for now, Russia thinks we discovered an ancient temple or something, which is fine, but how the hell do we explain why US troops are now in the business of pillaging archaeological sites?

—You do not.

—What?

—Explain. You do not admit anything, and you do not explain anything. But you give them something.

—What do you have in mind?

—Anything. Something they want more than a big hand. That should not prove too difficult. Dismantle a missile base somewhere. They would probably love for you to take those Patriots out of Poland. They will rub your face in it for a while, but they are absolutely not going to escalate the situation into something that can get—excuse the pun—out of hand, not if you give them a way out.

—Somehow I don't think the president will be too keen on weakening our position in Eastern Europe just so you can keep playing your little game.

—You know as well as I do that most of these bases are just window dressing, straw men designed to make smaller countries feel a bit mightier. Give the Russians anything they can spin politically. They will have their victory and everyone will go home happy.

—Let's just hope, for both our sakes, that the next part turns up in France, Australia, anywhere they don't speak Russian.

I also had an interesting conversation with the president this morning. He wants to know what you plan to do with that robot of yours if you get it to work. The idea was always to extract advanced technology from it. So far, your people can't even repair it, let alone reverse-engineer anything we can use. If your people can't do that, what are we supposed to do with a twenty-story robot? We can't use it without other nations asking questions, and there's no point in hiding it in that basement forever.

—I say take her out. March her down Constitution Avenue. Let everyone wonder what she can do. If you want a bigger deterrent, find a meaningless war in the middle of nowhere and annihilate one side. From what Dr. Franklin tells me, conventional weapons could not even put a scratch on her. I believe she could have driven the Iraqis out of Kuwait by herself. Are you going to tell me you would pass this up? You know this is worth a little squabble with Moscow.

—Maybe. I'm still not convinced that robot is all that you say it is. While you're here, can you tell me what you're doing about getting the controls to work for someone other than the Resnik girl?

—We are . . .

—Yes?

—Why do you ask?

—It's just a question.

—It is not. What are you not telling me?

—Fine. I received an e-mail from someone on your team. Alyssa . . . something.

—Ms. Papantoniou. She is a geneticist.

—Well, Ms. Paponiou.

—Papan . . .

—Whatever. She thinks we can't rely on that pilot of yours for something this important. She says she's too unpredictable.

—Is that all she says?

—No. She says that studying her should be a priority but that Dr. Franklin won't give her the resources she needs. She also says you won't do a thing about it.

—And what do you think?

—I think you have what looks like a mutiny on your hands, and I don't find that the least bit reassuring.

—I find it mostly annoying. But if it can make you feel better, I will let you decide what needs prioritizing. We do not have a complete robot. What we have cannot move. If and when we find the missing pieces, then it may or may not move. One of the control helmets does not work for anyone at this point. That nonfunctioning helmet is at a station designed for a creature with a different anatomy that we also cannot operate. What we do have is one functioning helmet, one station we can actually use, and one pilot able to use both the helmet and the station. So, Robert, where do we focus our efforts? Choose wisely.

—Hey, it's your show. All I'm saying is you should have a better handle on your people. But even if we don't need to deal with it now, that . . . Alyssa person's got a point. What are we going to do when the Resnik girl is too old? God forbid she gets hit by a truck a week from now. What if she wakes up one morning and decides she doesn't want to do this anymore? Say she decides it goes against her values. Say she gets pregnant and doesn't want to risk her life anymore. What would we do then?

—Believe me, she will not. None of them will. They would not give this up for all the gold in the world, let alone for principles. We will have a few more years to analyze it. We will find a way to make it work for someone else. There is always a chance that her children could work the controls.

—You want to *breed* pilots? You'll forgive me if I don't bring your suggestion to the president.

—I do not think it will come to that, but why not? Breed them. Clone them. Ms. Papantoniou would certainly not object. Who knows what we will be able to do twenty years from now. In any case, this president will be long gone when that decision needs to be made. I think this robot will still be advanced weaponry long after you and I are buried.

—I don't share your optimism. This whole thing scares the hell out of me. I can't help but think it will all blow up in our faces.

—Do you like superheroes?

—Oh, I'm not in the mood for a metaphor right now.

—Humor me. Who is your favorite superhero?

—I don't know. Superman. No, the Hulk.

—OK, now imagine for a minute that—what is he called when he is not the Hulk?

—How should I know? I'm not twelve! Wait one second . . . Lisa, what's the name of the guy who turns into the Hulk when he's angry? . . . She doesn't know . . . How about Superman? . . . Superman is Clark Kent . . . Thank you, Lisa.

—Imagine that Clark Kent walks into your office one day and offers his services to fight for America. You are given the opportunity to recruit a near-indestructible soldier with superhuman strength who can fly faster than a supersonic jet fighter. Would you say no because Mr. . . .

—Kent.

—Because Mr. Kent might someday fall ill?

—That's it? That's your point? I can tell you this: I'd certainly think about it if I had to start by invading a dozen countries to pick up body parts from Mr. Kent all over the map.

FILE NO. 118

INTERVIEW WITH CW3 KARA RESNIK, UNITED STATES ARMY

Location: Underground Complex, Denver, CO

—Yes, I slept with him! Are you happy now?

—I did not mean him.

—Well, which one *do* you mean? The one in jail, or the one in the hospital? I slept with both of them, so take your pick. I sleep with everybody. That's just the kind of girl I am.

—There is no need to be on the defensive. I am not accusing you of anything. I just want to know what happened.

—You're not accusing me? Now that's a relief! You can just go ahead and say it. It's not a matter of opinion. I know this is all my fault. Believe me, I know.

—You can start by telling me what happened with Mr. Mitchell.

—I don't know what to tell you. We spent so much time together. He's kind. I'm not used to men being kind. I've made the wrong choices every single time when it comes to men. Ryan, he's . . . a good guy. Leave it to me to pick Mr. Right and still get it wrong.

I mean, I knew better. I knew this wasn't for me. He just . . . wore me down. I caved in, and I was hoping I'd wake up the next day and all the pain would be gone, all that self-doubt. But, of course, I felt exactly the same. You don't erase a lifetime of mistakes by sleeping with some man in a car, no matter how kind he is. I tried. I swear.

—You saw him again after you made love in the car?

—We didn't make love in the car. I jumped him. I had too much to drink. That was me being . . .

—Self-destructive?

—I was gonna say "me being me," but that works too. He knew, that's the worst part. I was hoping he didn't, but he knew. I felt horrible. So yeah, we went out again a couple times. I figured, he'd seen me at my worst and he stuck around. The least I could do was to give it a real shot. I mean, that's what people do. Isn't it? They find a decent, good-looking man who doesn't judge them and treats them like a princess. They realize how lucky they are and they never let go. Isn't that how it's supposed to work?

—I wish I could offer a piece of wisdom. Sadly, romance is not an art form I have ever mastered. As unsuccessful as your attempts at relationships may have been, you are still the expert in this room. Is there something about Mr. Mitchell that you find off-putting?

—No! Nothing! There's nothing. If I could describe the perfect man, all the qualities I'm looking for in someone, it wouldn't be too far off from Mitchell. He's a bit clingy at times, but overall he's great company. I love the way he looks at me. I like seeing myself through his eyes. I don't know. Maybe it's me I can't stand. Maybe I don't like the effect I have on him, how he loses himself when I'm around.

—Would you prefer he paid less attention to you?

—I . . . We spend every minute of every day alone in a space the size of my bedroom. There's no one else he could pay attention to. I can't put it into words. I . . . I wish I didn't feel like everything was about me. Then again, I'd probably find him too distant. Maybe I'm just nuts.

—Did you sleep with him again?

—Does it really matter? I tried to make it work. Deep down, I knew it wouldn't take but I tried. I never stopped really. I was still trying. Then the unthinkable happened.

—What do you mean?

—The end of the world. Stars falling from the sky.

Mitchell and I spend most of our time alone in the sphere, but once in a while, someone will come up for a few minutes. The techs will come up to check the equipment. Dr. Franklin likes to climb in once a day just to say hello. We're always pretty happy to see other faces. Vincent is our most frequent visitor. He comes into the sphere a couple times a day to look at the console. We usually take a break to chat.

—What do you talk about?

—Anything and everything. Work, sports, the weather. That time he walked us through the number symbols while he was there. Did he show you how the numbers work? It's insane. I just can't wrap my head around it. Anyway, it was late. We were all really tired and we started joking around, showing Vincent how the controls worked. Ryan was doing the moonwalk with the robot. I was doing disco moves on my station. We were all watching it on the computer screens. We were having a really good time. The helmet was just sitting there. We were laughing so hard, we didn't even notice when he reached for it.

—Who did? Mr. Couture?

—Yes. He put it on. Then he fell to his knees and screamed. It was all happening in slow motion. We just stood there. Ryan looked at me, and we both knew what had just happened. We knew everything had changed. After what seemed like an eternity, we got out of our braces and we helped him up and out of the sphere. Dr. Franklin kept asking: What happened? What happened? Neither of us could get the words out.

—**What happened?**

—Ryan was out. That's what happened. Everything he had, all he had worked for, gone. Just like that. I've seen men die in combat, but I'd never seen anyone lose everything in one instant and have to live with it. I wish I could have held him in my arms at that very moment, told him everything was going to be all right, but we had to take care of Vincent.

—**Why do you think the helmet turned on for Vincent and not for anyone else?**

—Hell if I know. DNA. Brain configuration. Fate. The universe having a very sick sense of humor.

He spent a couple days in bed. He actually listened and kept his bandages on the whole time. When he came back, the station turned on for him, as we all expected. The console lit up as well. Dr. Franklin couldn't hide how thrilled she was, despite her best efforts. Who could blame her? She'd been hoping for this for so long.

Once the helmet activated, I could see the leg movements on my hologram. There was another small hologram on the console, just like mine. Of course, Vincent's legs didn't fit the controls any more than Ryan's did, so the hologram didn't help much. He had to face away from it, just like Ryan. And just like Ryan, he couldn't get the leg movements right. But Vincent wasn't nearly in as good a shape as Ryan. I wish I could say we were back to square one.

Vincent had to learn everything from scratch. Seeing the legs move on my hologram helped a little, but we still had to call out every movement. It was . . .

—**Discouraging.**

—You got that right. It took Ryan and me close to six months to get the hang of it, and we had to do it all over again with someone who ran out of breath after five minutes.

Ryan was very . . . gentlemanly about the whole thing. He took Vincent under his wing and taught him every move a thousand times over. Vincent also went into this with the best of attitudes, considering . . . He knew he was taking Ryan's place, and he was reminded of it every day having him as a coach. He knew he was slowing us down as well. He hit the gym real hard, lifting weights every night after we left; but you can't make up for years of military training in a few weeks.

Ryan had them build a replica of the leg controls. For three months, he worked side by side with Vincent, having him shadow every movement he made. Slowly, but surely, Vincent began to get it right, for only a step or two at first, then for minutes at a time. After a while, Ryan was mostly encouraging him, pointing out a few mistakes here and there. I could tell he was beginning to feel useless. I became much tougher on Vincent, doing my best to make him look as bad as I could so Ryan would have something to work on.

But that was only the half of it. Vincent and I couldn't help but get along. We always made each other laugh and this was no different. Working in the sphere, it does something to people. Ryan looks like an underwear model, but Vincent and I, we have chemistry. Soon, Ryan began to feel like a fifth wheel. It was horrible to watch. He was losing the most exciting job of his life, and losing me at the same time. He had front-row seats to watch me grow closer to Vincent. What's worse is he was asked to play a part in it.

Vincent's not a good man by any standard definition. He's not evil or anything, but he's self-absorbed. He has an ego the size of New England and he's not particularly nice to people. He actually says he doesn't like people. He's a genius, but he's a bad person. I know, because I was attracted to him, and it was obvious it ran both ways. After a while, you had to cut through the sexual tension in the room. Maybe it was because we both knew it was the worst thing we could do; maybe having Ryan in the room made it all the more forbidden.

All I can tell you is that it was palpable. I did my best to ignore it. I even asked Ryan out a few more times. He wouldn't sleep with me. He couldn't stand the idea it might have been out of pity.

—Was it?

—Ryan began leaving the sphere early. Dr. Franklin eventually found him some work in the lab to keep his mind at ease. I don't think he could stand being in the same room with me anymore. I feel terrible for saying it, but I was beginning to resent him for giving up. It's awful, I know, since I didn't think we had a future together, but part of me wanted him to fight, for his job, for me, for anything.

One night, Vincent and I were working late. Ryan had left early and we had just heard Dr. Franklin close the door on her way out. We listened to the silence for a few moments, waiting for the inevitable. Vincent got out of his station and climbed up to mine. He smiled and slowly moved in front of me. I was still braced in, my arms stretched out in the control suit. He undid my belt, took off my pants and wrapped my legs around him. He didn't say anything, not a single word; he just stared at me the whole time. It was . . . Never mind.

We locked the lab behind us and walked out through the exit in the maintenance building. I followed Vincent outside; two blinding lights appeared out of nowhere. I was still covering my eyes when Vincent shoved me back inside as hard as he could. I hit the ground pretty hard and knocked my head on the stairwell ramp. There was a loud bang that shook the whole building. When I got out to see what had happened, Ryan was still in his truck, both hands on the wheel. The front end had embedded itself about a foot into the cement wall. Vincent was lying facedown on the hood of the truck, his legs crushed into the wall.

PART THREE

HEADHUNTING

FILE NO. 120

INTERVIEW WITH VINCENT COUTURE, SENIOR INTELLIGENCE ADVISOR (DCIPS)

Location: Hospital for Special Surgery (HSS), New York, NY

—I remember going to the zoo with my father. I must have been five or six years old. It was a good hour from Montreal and my dad didn't like to drive. He also didn't like crowds. But I had been begging my parents since the middle of winter and my mom finally convinced my dad to take me. I was so excited. It's all I could talk about. Will there be lions? Will there be zebras? "I don't know, son, you'll just have to wait and see."

We finally left on a sunny Sunday morning. My father gave me a present for the ride. It was one of those wooden puzzles; just a cube made of small indented pieces of wood that only fit in a particular way. I remember thinking it was really pretty. My father, of course, insisted I take it apart and put it back together on our way to the zoo. "You have an hour," he said. "That should be plenty of time." Well, it wasn't. I was still working on it when I saw the giant Zoo sign. Of course, I immediately put the puzzle back into the box it came in and I started naming every animal I could see on the signs. Look Dad, a zebra! He said: "Great! Finish your puzzle, then we'll go." I said I didn't want to but he reminded me that, in our family, when we start something, we see it through to the end.

I worked on that thing for another two hours while he read a book. I could almost make the whole cube, but in the end, I would inevitably end up with one or two pieces that didn't fit. I knew I must have put a couple of pieces in the wrong place, but there were just too many and I couldn't remember what I did the next time around. I kept doing the same thing over and over again. By noon, frustration had turned to despair. I started crying. My father just kept on reading. I couldn't think anymore. I was shaking, frantically jamming pieces together. By two o'clock, I was just hysterical. My father put his book away. He started the car and drove straight home.

We didn't talk for the rest of the day. After my mother tucked me in, he came into my room and told me I had learned a valuable lesson that day, much more valuable than seeing some caged animals.

—**What was the lesson you learned?**

—I suppose he meant that emotions get in the way of judgment, that I might have succeeded had I not been so eager to do something else.

—**You must have been an exceptionally smart child. This would seem difficult to grasp for a five-year-old.**

—Oh, I'm saying this now. I had absolutely no idea what he meant at the time. I just wanted to see the zebras. My father was a philosopher. Literally, I mean. He was a philosophy professor. We didn't always get along once I got older but I worshipped him when I was a kid.

—**What did your mother do?**

—She was a teacher too, until she met my father. She gave up her career when I was born. She was a really smart woman, but her heart was bigger than anything else. She wanted me to play sports, to spend some time with other kids my age, but my dad thought it was a waste of time. He said I was born with a brain that worked better than most, that it would be a shame not to use my gift. He didn't think I could do that throwing a ball with a bunch of half-wits.

My mother insisted, but I told her I didn't want to. I loved my dad. I did everything I could to make him proud. It must have driven my mother crazy. She left us, eventually. We were both crushed. I don't know why it came as such a surprise. It wasn't hard to see that one coming. Any woman in her right mind would have dropped that selfish egotistic man in a heartbeat. She probably just found some half-decent guy who paid a modicum of attention to her every now and then. I know she didn't leave because of me, but I think she might have stayed had I not ignored her as much as my father did. I was so bent on pleasing him. At times, she must have felt like she didn't even exist. She wasn't a cynical woman, not for a second. This would probably just make her really sad, but you can bet the irony wouldn't be lost on my dad.

—The irony?

—Oh yes. I worked all my life at being the smartest I could be. My dad always told me I could make a real difference someday. Most people don't really have a purpose, a sense of purpose anyway, beyond their immediate surroundings. They're important to their family but it doesn't go much beyond that. Everyone is replaceable at work, friendships come and go.

I had the chance to be a part of something much larger than me, but it's not because of how much I learned, or how smart I am. The one thing that made me special, what made me truly useful, turned out to be my legs. And now I'm about to lose them both.

—What makes you think you will lose your legs?

—The doctor left a few minutes before you walked in. He said there's no choice but to amputate. Both legs.

—I do not wish to appear insensitive, but you seem to be handling the news fairly well.

—I spend most of my time sitting down thinking, really. That's what I'm good at: sitting and thinking. I figure, so long as I can do that . . . I never paid much attention to my body. Didn't eat that well, didn't exercise much, didn't play sports. I do think I'll miss walking. Walking was good.

—Is that all you are feeling?

—What do you want me to say? Life is unfair. I didn't deserve this. In the grand scheme of things, I don't think what I'm feeling is all that important. If you can't get the controls to work for someone else, then it's all over for everybody. Putting that helmet on was a really stupid idea.

—Guilt is a normal feeling. Some form of resentment would also seem appropriate.

—I'm heartbroken about losing all of this, if that's what you wanna hear. I mean, who wouldn't be? I don't know why, but I keep thinking of that astronaut who got grounded seventy-two hours before liftoff because he was exposed to the . . . How do you say *rougeole*?

—The measles. You are referring to Thomas Kenneth Mattingly, II.

—That's him. I can never remember his name. I'm sure he was pissed. I'm sorry if I'm not devastated enough for you. To be honest, I was pretty sure it was all over when I saw that truck coming. Everything just went . . . dark. How's Kara, by the way? She must be pretty shook up.

—She is doing fine. She feels responsible, but she will be OK. She would have come but . . .

—No, she wouldn't have.

—Perhaps, but she is genuinely grateful. You might have saved her life. She said to tell you to hurry up and get back home.

—Ryan?

—There is not much I can tell you. He has been reluctant to speak, at all. He is being held at Fort Carson. Have no fear, Mr. Couture. He will pay for what he did to you.

—What good would that do? I'm many things, vindictive isn't one of them. I can't imagine how he must feel.

—Love makes people do some crazy things.

—Nah. Love makes you get really drunk and punch through a wall. That man had everything he cared about taken away from him, everything. I did that. I didn't do it on purpose, but I'm the one who turned his world upside down. Not so Captain America after all, I guess. I didn't think he had it in him . . . I'm sorry, I'm not laughing because of that.

—You find it humorous that Mr. Mitchell is losing his mind?

—No. That it's you sitting by my bed. Not my family, not my friends—not that I have many—not Kara or Rose, you. Mr. Warm and Fuzzy. It's like waking up from a coma and having the cashier at the grocery store at your bedside. No offence.

—None taken.

—I guess that's what they meant when they said to be nice to people. No tears for the narcissistic Québécois.

—I doubt that people would be lining up by the hundreds but, in the interest of fairness, no one knows where you are.

—You know, I get that you don't want to tell people your name, but wouldn't it be easier to make one up? Something cool, Charlie, M., anything. Then again, maybe you're better off without one. "What's in a name?" he said.

—So Romeo would, were he not Romeo called, retain that dear perfection which he owes without that title . . .

—An educated man? Somehow, you didn't strike me as the literary type.

—English literature. Magna cum laude.

—Oh! Please, do tell!

—I think not. But if it makes you feel special, the president does not know this much about me. Did you know we are only missing three pieces? We found both of the small thigh pieces in China, about ten miles from each other. We should have the other parts soon. We have covered about 80 percent of the globe.

—Good for you. I just hope they're on land.

—What do you mean?

—Well, 70 percent of the planet is covered by water. When you're done surveying every continent, you'll have gone through about 30 percent of the Earth's surface.

—Dr. Franklin believes that . . .

—I know what Rose said. She thinks they desperately want us to find these things. But did you notice we keep finding them in the middle of nowhere? We got almost half of them in the United States. Do you know what was in the U.S. three thousand years ago? Not much. The Arctic isn't the most convenient place to look for things either.

—If I did not know you better, I would be tempted to call you a pessimist, Mr. Couture. Let us worry about that. You concentrate on getting back on two feet.

—Funny. An hour from now, I won't have any feet to get back on. I just need to figure out how to work a wheelchair. It can't be that hard. I've seen some really stupid people in wheelchairs. And I'll worry about whatever I want. I think I have plenty of time to do that. I always wanted to learn Cantonese. I just never found the time.

—I want you to listen to me very carefully. No one will take your legs. You may not believe in fate, but there is a reason the robot chose you. It is what you were meant to do. It will take some time, but you will get back into that sphere and make that robot walk. You will make us all proud. And you need to get back to Chief Resnik.

—Where do you get this stuff? They'll still take my legs, but that was a nice speech. And you know as well as I do Kara and I are over.

—I do not think she is the type of person who would abandon you because of a handicap.

—I know that. She's loyal as a dog . . . that doesn't sound so nice when you say it out loud. Anyway, that's my point. She'd be with me for all the wrong reasons. She'd be unhappy, but she'd stick around out of some twisted, misplaced sense of duty.

—What makes you think she would be unhappy?

—They're cutting my legs. I won't be able to walk. I won't be able to stand, to get food out of the top shelf. I'll need help taking a bath. I'll probably soil myself. I'm already cynical, I don't think this will suddenly turn me into a ray of sunshine. I wouldn't wanna live with me. I wouldn't wish that on anyone, especially Kara. She should be with someone she can be proud of. Last thing she needs is changing diapers.

—Did you know that Ken Mattingly never contracted the measles? He did fly to the moon on Apollo XVI, and later took part in two space-shuttle missions. No one will take your legs, Mr. Couture. I give you my word.

FILE NO. 121

INTERVIEW WITH DR. PAVEL HAAS, CHIEF OF SURGERY

Location: Hospital for Special Surgery (HSS), New York, NY

—How is Mr. Couture doing?

—His femur, tibia, and fibula are broken in several places on both legs. He has no patella to speak of, on either leg. His knees have just been obliterated. There's nothing but small fragments piercing through his flesh like shrapnel. To put it mildly, his legs are gone.

—He is under the impression that you will cut them away.

—He's right. They're prepping the OR as we speak. We'll take him upstairs as soon as we're done here. We'll cut his legs about midway to the knee. There should be enough left to attach prosthetics if we're lucky. It will take some time, but most patients in his situation eventually learn to walk again. I know it sounds terrible right now, but you have to believe me when I tell you, this is what's best for him.

—That is more or less what he told me. I am sorry to tell you that an amputation is out of the question.

—I don't want to be rude, but this really isn't up to you.

—How I wish that were true. Unfortunately, there are a great many things that fall under my responsibility and this happens to be one of them.

I can see your mouth opening slightly, which would suggest that you are waiting for the first opportunity to interrupt me, so I will save you the time and give you the only justification you are going to get.

That man is in a unique position to do something remarkably important for this country, if not for mankind. More to the point, he is the only one who can, and he needs his legs to do it. I apologize if this is more succinct than what you were hoping for, but it will have to do under the circumstances.

—You can't . . .

—Please do not interrupt. I understand you are in a position of au-thority and the nature of your work probably makes you unaccus-tomed to being contradicted. But if what I have been told is true, we do not have a lot of time before sepsis sets in, so I hope you will forgive me for being blunt.

If you insist on pursuing this course of action, these two men will escort you out of the building and drive you away. I do not want you to think I am threatening you. You will not be killed, and no one will inflict physical pain upon you. You will, however, wake up in a strange room and never see the outside of it for the remainder of your life.

I just want you to have all the facts so you can make an in-formed decision. Unfortunately, you will need to make that deci-sion in the next thirty seconds.

—I don't know how I'm supposed to answer that.

—You do not have to answer. You just have to do exactly as I say. I was told you are the best at what you do. That is why we flew him here. That is why we chose you. It will take me about ten minutes to get someone almost as good to replace you, but I really hate having to settle for second best.

—You don't understand. I can't salvage any of the bones—not me, not anyone else. It's not a matter of will, and threatening me won't change anything. I can't "wish" his bones back together. And I can't just make him new legs out of thin air.

—Sure you can. You wrote several papers on titanium implants and you have the highest success rate in titanium total hip replacements. You may or may not lack some of the mechanical engineering skills to create implants of this size, but we can remedy the situation with one phone call. I believe you already have all the equipment you need, but if you require anything else, I will have it flown here within the hour.

You will enjoy unlimited funding, and you may use any and all of the resources of the United States Army, the NIH, the NSF, NASA, as well as those of agencies you have never heard of. If you require anything, simply call this number and mention your name. Someone will make sure that you get all that you need. It is vital that you realize the colossal amount of resources at your disposal. I would not want this experiment to fail because you assumed certain technologies did not exist, or that certain materials were unobtainable. Right now, at this very moment, you are the most powerful person in the medical field on the planet.

—We'd have to replace every single bone in his legs. Basically, we'd be inserting whole mechanical legs inside his tissue. It's never been done, there's a reason for that. The human body is hostile to foreign objects. I'm not even sure we could salvage enough muscle for them to be functional, but his body would absolutely reject such a large implant. I can guarantee it. We'll just end up killing him.

—That is precisely what I was talking about. You need to understand how much you do not know, and you need to understand it very quickly. In about twenty minutes, you will receive a call from someone at the US Army Medical Research and Materiel Command. They will provide you with a new immunosuppressive agent they have been working on. That should help him accept his new legs. They will also send a muscle-building agent that . . .

—I can't inject a patient with something I know nothing about.

—It is a myostatin inhibitor, much more efficient than anything else you may have read about. I am confident it will come with some sort of label. They tell me it works wonders on mice. Do not waste precious time pretending. We both know you are as curious as I am to see it work. You will get to use experimental drugs the FDA will not even hear about for another decade.

—You obviously don't care about my opinion, but I want to make sure you understand. He could live a very productive life with prosthetics if we amputate now.

—He will live an astoundingly productive life after you build him new legs.

—I need to think about this.

—You do not. You made up your mind about twenty seconds ago. You see, Dr. Haas, our jobs are not that different. We analyze the situation, we gather as much data as we can before we take action, and we try to anticipate every possible outcome. I did my job as thoroughly as I hope you will do yours. You gained a tremendous amount of the knowledge we are now asking you to use during two extensive studies funded with corporate money, one on tapered titanium cementless total hip replacement, and the other on tissue response in failed titanium implants. In 2006, two of the patients participating in your hip replacement study rejected their implants, one of them died of complications. Interestingly, there is absolutely no trace of these two patients in any of your grant proposals, or in any of your publications. Somehow, however, their data show up in a tissue-response study they never took part in. You switched the patients from one study to the next, as if nothing ever happened. No harm, no foul, except for a dead patient.

—That woman had a heart condition she didn't tell me about. I would never have chosen her for this study had she not lied in her application.

—I have no doubt. Putting her in your report would not have saved her. You just made the preliminary results look this much better to the people paying for it.

More to the point, when you immigrated to this country, you also neglected to declare that you were arrested for driving under the influence. I realize it is only a misdemeanor in the United States, but it is a criminal offence where you come from.

You are egotistic enough to believe that the rules do not really apply to you, that these little white lies served a greater good, and that you were actually helping others. It is not uncommon with people of your background.

—My background?

—Raised in precarious conditions by a poor family with traditional values. First one in the family to get a college education. First to rise out of poverty. It sounds cliché, I know, but we have become very proficient at this sort of profiling. One thing is certain: you are a survivor, Dr. Haas. You are definitely not one to throw away your life, your family, and your career for something as petty as principles.

When you leave this room, you will make sure that enough of the remaining living tissue in Mr. Couture's legs is preserved while you construct his new bones.

—If we do this, and by some miracle it works, I can guarantee he'll wish he had died on the operating table. He'll beg for us to end his life. You simply can't imagine the amount of pain he'll have to suffer. Every minute of every day will be the worst of his life. Will you be the one to tell him that?

—I would rather not. That is a horrible thing to tell anyone, especially before life-threatening reconstructive surgery. Will he suffer any less if we tell him that he will?

—No. He'll go through hell no matter what; if he doesn't die first.

—Then I see no reason to tell. I want him in as good a mental state as humanly possible. I want you to tell him everything will be fine.

—I want the record to show that this procedure is being done against medical advice and that I am participating under duress.

—I am recording this conversation so anything we have said so far is on the recording. You may call this a record, if you wish. If you were referring to the hospital records, then no. This is your idea and yours alone. You are performing this surgery because you firmly believe this is the best solution for your patient and you have every confidence in its success. There will be no reference to this conversation, in any form, whatsoever. Let me be abundantly clear on this. Any mention of my presence, of my very existence, to anyone, will have dire consequences for both you and your loved ones.

—What kind of consequences?

—I have not yet had time to ponder an appropriate response, but I can guarantee that you will never see your children again, even if the operation is successful.

—What if it isn't?

—Then you will almost certainly lose your medical license.

—No. I won't say anything. But what if the patient doesn't survive? What are you threatening me with?

—Why would I threaten you if you do exactly as I ask? I am not evil, Dr. Haas. That said, you will most likely lose your medical license, along with your house, your car, and everything you own. I would expect some jail time. You are about to perform absurdly complex, insanely risky, and completely unnecessary experimental surgery on a stable patient without his knowledge or consent. What do you think will happen if he dies?

Before you go, I also want you to take a look at these designs. You will need to integrate them into your leg structure.

—What are they?

—Knees.

—I'm not a mechanical engineer, but it looks like they . . .

—Yes, Dr. Haas. They do.

FILE NO. 126

INTERVIEW WITH ALYSSA PAPANTONIOU, PH.D., GENETICIST

Location: Denver Public Library, Civic Center
Park, Denver, CO

—It is an interesting accent you have, Ms. Papantoniou. Is that from the Balkans?

—Yes, most of Greece is in the Balkans.

—You must be from a region I have not visited. It is very unique.

—Thank you. I'm curious to know why we're meeting at the p . . . public library. I'm sorry. I get nervous when I t . . . talk to people.

—There is no need to apologize. I did not want us to be disturbed. It is a pleasure to make your acquaintance.

—The pleasure is mine. What did you want to di . . . discuss?

—It has come to my attention that you disapprove of the direction this project is taking. I would be remiss if I did not take such complaint seriously, especially coming from someone of your intelligence.

—Thank you very much. I didn't mean to go over your h . . . head.

—So it was an accident?

—I . . .

—It does not matter. Now, tell me, what is it that you find so objectionable in the way that Dr. Franklin is leading her team?

—I have all the respect in the world for Dr. Franklin. She is a very good physicist.

—But?

—But she does make mistakes. She's not as . . . she's not as brilliant as you think she is. I often find it necessary to d . . . double-check her calculations.

—I am certain she appreciates.

—More than anything, Dr. Franklin is too . . . fragile. She lets her feelings for the members of her team cloud her judgment. She treats Kara and Vincent as if they were her ch . . . children. Kara is a stubborn, unyielding person, and I feel it is . . . irresponsible to rely entirely on her good will for this project to move f . . . forward. I have requested, on several occasions, that she submit to a series of tests to determine why the helmet will only activate for her, and Dr. Franklin has systematically refused.

—Is that statement really accurate? I was told that Ms. Resnik submitted a saliva sample and that you performed an analysis of that sample. In fact, I remember seeing a report in which you conclude that there is nothing out of the ordinary about her genetics.

—I did perform some genetic and biochemical tests and found no chromosomal anomalies, nor any obvious mutation. But there are a lot more tests, mitochondrial analysis. I haven't even done a full genome sequencing. I could study her brain structure, her eyes might also be the answer.

—Dr. Franklin also performed a retina scan if I am not mistaken.

—I meant that I could study a sample of her eye, not a picture of it.

—Could these other procedures wait until we have recovered all the pieces from the robot, and solved our more immediate problems?

—You don't understand. It's not just Kara. We can't . . . we can't move forward without Vincent now. What if he doesn't survive? What if he can't w . . . walk again? Understanding why the helmet worked for Kara might be the key to replacing Vincent as well.

With all due respect, there is too much at stake here to worry about personal feelings, or some mild dis . . . comfort while I insert a needle into someone's eye. I thought you of all people . . .

—You thought I of all people?

—I thought you were . . . pragmatic, that you understood what needed to be done. Maybe you've also become emotionally attached.

—Are you questioning my judgment?

—Let me ask you this. If we needed dogs, and not humans, to control this machine, would we not already have a dozen pu . . . puppies to spare?

—Puppies . . . I find the question is a lot more interesting than any answer I could provide. But I thank you for shedding new light on the situation. I have found your comments both insightful and interesting and, I promise you, I will take everything you said under advisement.

—Thank you. That's all I ask.

—Good day, Ms. Papantoniou.

FILE NO. 129

INTERVIEW WITH ROBERT WOODHULL, ASSISTANT TO THE PRESIDENT FOR NATIONAL SECURITY AFFAIRS

Location: White House, Washington, DC

—**What can I do for you, Robert?**

—SecDef has moved us to DEFCON 3.

—**The Russians?**

—Amongst others. The Chinese spotted us leaving their territory. They've lodged a formal complaint with the UN.

—**Since when do you care about the UN?**

—I couldn't care less about the UN, but the Russians were all ears. They put two and two together very quickly. They still don't know what we're after, but they know it's not just some ancient artifact, if we're willing to enter every country uninvited to get it. The Turkish government also made your little visit known to the Russians, which didn't do anything to help.

They are now blaming us, officially that is, for the death of their soldiers in Siberia. They are calling our little incursion a deliberate act of provocation. The Russian ambassador left for Moscow about an hour ago. They're cleaning out the embassy as we speak. You can almost hear the shredders all the way down here. It's only a matter of time before China follows suit.

—Have they increased their military readiness?

—You could call it that. In the past three hours, we've seen more naval activity out of Russia than we have since the Cuban Missile Crisis. The entire Northern Fleet is on alert, so is most of the Pacific Fleet from what we can tell. There are over one hundred ships operating in the North Atlantic alone.

—Submarines?

—The *Severodvinsk* set to sea this morning along with two Borei-class subs. The White Sea Base looks like it was abandoned. There are five Delta-IVs roaming around, just as many Delta-IIIs, even their big old Typhoon. Basically, everything with a nuke that is seaworthy is now out there. We haven't seen any unusual action on the Chinese side, but I wouldn't be surprised if they sent out part of their fleet as well.

—They are bluffing. You know that.

—So are we. Bluffing doesn't mean what it used to. No one wants an all-out war, and everyone knows it. Both sides know the other doesn't want a fight, so we push each other against the wall, a tiny bit further every time. It's all about saving face but, basically, we're playing chicken, and both sides think that they can do whatever they want because the other guy will never use its nuclear arsenal. It probably won't be today, but someday . . . someday one of us is gonna be terribly wrong.

We've deployed our attack subs, of course. If China steps in, we'll send even more ships to go against their ships. Our aircraft carriers are already on full alert. If we send them out anywhere in the general direction of Asia, they're gonna launch everything they have and send it our way. You can see where this is going.

Nothing good has ever come of a naval standoff. I know it looks big on the map, but an ocean can get crowded real fast, and I sure as hell don't like putting my fate in the hands of a dozen half-blind sub captains trying not to bump into anything.

—Do we really need to always respond in kind? Could we not simply do nothing and let the Russians posture for a few days? I never understood the merits of proportional response.

—I'm not sure there are any. It's just what we call human nature for people with too much firepower in their hands. Ever been in a bar fight?

—I assume this is a rhetorical question.

—Well, that's how it starts. You bump into someone, make them spill their drink. They yell at you and push you away. You pretend that you apologized while you poke at their chest. Everybody "proportionally responds" until someone gets their teeth knocked out. No one really wants to fight, but no one wants to be the one to back off either. It's a hundred times worse with military men, and a hundred times more so with politicians.

So we're gonna do our thing, they're gonna do their thing, and if we're really lucky we won't send twenty million people to their deaths in the process.

—We were all aware of the risks when we agreed on this course of action.

—That's a bit . . . That's a pretty distorted way of looking at the situation, don't you think?

—How so?

—We didn't exactly agree on anything. You presented us with a *fait accoupli*. You told us what you were doing after the fact and you threatened . . .

—*Accompli.*

—What?

—The expression is: a *fait accompli*. It means done deed. *Accoupli* is not even a word. I never understood why people use words they do not understand.

I made my intentions abundantly clear when I asked for your assistance. You chose to help. You did not have to supply troops. You could have said no. You also had the means to stop me at any time. You could, at any point, have had me and every member of my team arrested, imprisoned, or even killed. Had you said nothing, it would have been the perfect example of a tacit agreement, but you went farther and you set out certain conditions, under which I would have "the full support of this administration." I can understand your desire to distance yourself from this decision, given the current state of affairs, but you did make a choice. That choice will not cease to be yours because a lot of people might die as a result.

—What about you? You're fine with that? The end justifies the means, is that it?

—You make it sound as if I were irrational. Yes. I do think this particular end justifies considerable means. I draw the line somewhere, like everyone else. I just draw it based on reason and not emotions.

—So you'd let a few hundred people die? Would you stop for a thousand? How many lives are you willing to sacrifice for this? A million?

—Certainly not. But a thousand seems like a reasonable figure.

—You're an asshole, you know that? Isn't that just a bit arbitrary?

—Of course it is. Most things are. Eight people died while we raced the Soviets to the moon. Another fourteen lost their lives in the Challenger and Columbia accidents, and yet the space program is still around. Space exploration is important enough to justify the death of twenty-two people. Had 22,000 people died, things might have been different.

We lost about three hundred soldiers liberating Kuwait. Most would think that was reasonable. Over four thousand Americans died in Iraq. Some might say it was too high a price to get rid of Saddam Hussein, some might not. Obviously, the Administration thought that it was worth it at the time.

Over twenty million soldiers died during World War II. Twenty million, in the military alone. There had to be a lot of people who believed that their particular end justified some unfathomable means.

I honestly believe that what we are doing is much more important than going to the moon, or getting our hands on a few barrels of oil. In my opinion, it more readily compares with inventing the wheel, or making fire. I realize that others might disagree. I wish I could tell you exactly how many lives this is worth losing, but I cannot. At some point we might decide that we could live with 1,151 dead, but not 1,152. It is, by definition, arbitrary.

What I can tell you is this: in an underground warehouse in Denver, there is definite proof that we are not alone in the universe, undeniable evidence that there are civilizations literally thousands of years ahead of us technologically, and we are drawing closer to being able to use some of that knowledge. This can be a leap of monumental proportions for all mankind, and not just from a technological standpoint. This will change the way we think of the world, the way we see ourselves. This will reshape this planet, and we have an opportunity to help steer that change. How many lives is that worth to you?

—Let's just hope no one else has to die, shall we? We could use some good news, and soon. Speaking of which, did you get that little mutiny of yours under control?

—As a matter of fact, I did.

—Good. The president is growing tired of all this. He's also heard about your little stunt at the hospital.

—Exactly what nefarious deed of mine are you referring to this time?

—You forced a doctor to put some crazy metal knees into the linguist. Did you think no one was going to find out?

—Well, he needed knees.

—That's not how the president sees it. Up to this point, he's been willing to overlook certain risks to the population and he's given you a fair amount of leeway when it comes to international law, but you've just crossed a line that wasn't meant to be crossed. You performed very risky—experimental is an understatement—body-altering surgery on an American citizen without his consent.

—I apologize. I did not know that this was frowned upon.

—This isn't funny.

—It is somewhat funny. First of all, I did not perform anything, the doctor did. Second, Mr. Couture is not an American citizen. He is from Montreal. It is a large city, about the size of Boston, in that very large country just north of here. You may have heard of it. They play hockey.

—That was just an expression.

—"American citizen" is not an expression. Are you seriously telling me the president is unhappy because I did not let some doctor saw off our best chance of success? I can shoot Mr. Couture if need be, but he finds surgery morally reprehensible? It makes him uncomfortable? Ill at ease? Tell the president we gave him really good knees. Better yet, tell him to give Mr. Couture a medal. That will make him feel better.

If Mr. Couture survives, our chances of success will be significantly greater than they were before the surgery. May I also remind you that the alternative was to have a leg pilot without legs? There was a unique window of opportunity and I took it. I would do it again without hesitation.

—The next time you want to turn someone into the six million dollar man, you should get his permission first. As far as the president is concerned, what you did is tantamount to torturing the guy.

—I respectfully but vehemently disagree. You can tell the president whatever you want. He is your responsibility.

— . . .

—Robert?

—You know, that medal's not a bad idea.

—I was being sarcastic. You cannot give . . . Never mind. Yes. Give him a medal.

FILE NO. 141

INTERVIEW WITH DR. ROSE FRANKLIN, PH.D.
Location: Underground Complex, Denver, CO

—Where's Kara? She didn't show up today.

—**On assignment. I wish I could tell you more, but she will be back in a few days. I heard you went away as well.**

—You don't miss much, do you? Yes, I went to visit Ryan.

—**I did not know he was allowed visitors.**

—He's not. But government psychiatrists are allowed, apparently.

—**They did not check your credentials?**

—The NSA never asked for my ID back. It says Doctor on it . . .

—**I must say I am moderately surprised. This seems a bit out of character for you.**

—I don't know if I should be offended or flattered.

—**You should feel neither. I was merely pointing out that your recent behavior is uncharacteristic of your personal disposition. You** are extremely brave, but also very rational and methodical. This seems somewhat rash, impulsive. These are words that more easily come to mind when speaking of Ms. Resnik.

—She suggested it . . . She said you'd bail me out if I got into trouble.

—I would not count on it.

—Well, I couldn't just leave him alone out there. He had to know that people still cared about him. He seemed genuinely surprised to see me. He feels such shame over what he did; I don't think he expected anyone to show any concern over him.

He says the worst part is that he remembers everything about that night. The hours before are either fuzzy or completely missing from his memory, but somehow the alcohol didn't erase a single detail about the crash. He can still see Vincent's face when the truck hit. I told him I would visit him again if he let me.

—Mr. Couture is also very forgiving, considering. That seems to be a common trait in the scientific community. I assume Chief Resnik did not join you.

—No, she didn't, but it's different for her. She feels . . . responsible. And I wouldn't go so far as saying I forgive him. I think what he did is appalling. I also know everything he's been through. Surely, you can understand that.

—I understand that these are unusual circumstances and that heightened emotions are to be expected. I understand that a strong feeling of attraction can easily develop in stressful situations and that the associated loss can also be proportionally amplified. I also understand that under the same circumstances, you, Ms. Resnik, and Mr. Couture have not attempted to murder anyone. Mr. Mitchell tried to kill one of his coworkers, showed reckless disregard for the life of an Army soldier, and jeopardized what could be the most significant endeavor in modern history. I believe I understand perfectly.

—Maybe you're right. I just think that's not all he is. What he did, however horrifying, doesn't have to negate every other day of his life. He has a family, a mother that brought him into the world, fed him, bathed him. She dressed him for school. She drove him to soccer practice. You can't expect her to see this in black-and-white. She can't. Neither can I. I refuse to think of him in such simple terms.

You thought he was good enough before. Well, before hasn't changed. Everything he did, up until that day, is still true. Ryan knows he didn't just hurt Vincent, that he left a whole lot of lives in shambles. He has to live with that. I think that's punishment enough.

—Let us agree to disagree. I did not come here to discuss Mr. Mitchell, nor your emotional response to his current predicament. There were reports of an incident in the laboratory.

—You could call it that. Work on the console has completely stopped without Vincent. Kara was getting restless having no one to train with. The lab feels really empty now that Alyssa's gone.

—Where is Ms. Papantoniou?

—I thought you knew. Her work visa was revoked. Some technicality. She was sent back to Greece on Monday.

—I am sorry to hear that. I heard she was a brilliant scientist.

—She was. She had a hard time connecting with anyone, though; I don't think she had any friends here. I'll admit she was hard to deal with. She had really strong feelings about the way things should be done, but a lot of the progress we've made recently was based on her ideas.

—I did not know that.

—Yes. Since we found the second piece, all our attention has been focused on the robot itself. With Vincent unable to train, Alyssa suggested we take the opportunity to go back to the metal. We already know the parts activate in contact with radioactive material, but she wanted to know if it had anything to do with what they're made of. Anyway, now that it's just the two of us in the lab, I decided to have Kara help me run some experiments Alyssa had designed.

—I am somewhat perplexed. Did you not perform a metallurgical analysis of the material early on?

—I did, several times. Every piece is a solid block of metal, 89 percent iridium, 9.5 percent iron, 1.5 percent other heavy metals. I could go on about the physical properties of that alloy until morning. Only nothing I would say would mean anything because we know for a fact that it can't be true. This alloy should weigh ten times more. Metal doesn't shine light in fancy little patterns, and it sure doesn't move when you put pieces of it together. What science we do have tells us we're looking at a solid chunk of metal, but this has all the physical properties of a complex mechanism.

So I'm trying to devise experiments to find out more than what metallurgy says I can find out. I know it sounds a little iffy, and it should. I'm making this up as I go along.

I first exposed one of the panels to plutonium-238 and measured its light output. It turns out the parts don't just activate with radioactive material, they feed off it—any kind of nuclear energy, it would seem. Exposure to even a small amount of radiation increased the light output of the panel by about half a percent.

—Is that how these things power themselves?

—That would be my guess, but that's not the interesting part. We had originally managed to cut a small speck off one of the panels for analysis. I had it encased in transparent resin afterward. It was just sitting on my desk as a paperweight. When we noticed an increase in luminosity in the panels, I had the idea to measure how much energy the material could absorb. I put the fragment in a closed environment in direct contact with the plutonium. It turns out the metal does absorb radiation, but it saturates fairly quickly and needs to release the superfluous energy.

Upon discharge, it emits a very strong electromagnetic pulse. It knocked out the two computers that were in the room. It's possible the parts emit the same kind of pulse when they activate. It could be what brought down Kara's helicopter in Turkey, though an EMP wouldn't explain why her engine failed. Now that I know what to expect, I'll monitor anything I can think of. I'd also like to see if it feeds off other types of energy.

—If it had not been made a cliché by another fellow, I would call this fascinating.

—I'm glad you like that. But that's not even the good part. What's *really* interesting is that it also generates a strong energy field, strong enough to destroy surrounding objects.

—What do you mean by "destroy"? Like an explosion?

—No. Nothing explodes. The stuff around it is just . . . gone, vaporized, without vapor. I was running the experiment in a glass-enclosed environment. It made a perfect spherical hole in the glass—surgically precise, like a laser. There is no ash, no debris, no trace that the missing matter ever existed.

—How much energy could the entire robot absorb?

—A whole lot. If that little speck of metal can discharge enough energy to make a one-foot hole, I can't begin to imagine how much energy kilotons of this material can swallow. Obviously, I can't place any instruments anywhere near it, but once I figure out a way to measure the energy output from the small shard, I can extrapolate a figure for the entire thing.

—Could the robot withstand a hit from a missile or a bomb?

—It's complicated. Conventional weapons will generate heat, but most of the damage usually comes from kinetic energy. I have absolutely no idea how it handles kinetic energy. I can run some experiments. It might be as simple as putting a sledge to the panels and measuring the light output. I'll think of something.

I can tell you we applied some insane amounts of pressure trying to cut a piece off one of the panels. I really don't see how a shock wave could seriously damage her. It might knock her on her back if it's powerful enough. I just don't know enough about weapons.

—Do you believe it could withstand a nuclear explosion?

—I don't know. Maybe? I think a more important question is how much the sphere is shielded from what happens outside. It might be almost impossible to destroy the robot itself, but it doesn't mean all that much if everyone inside is dead.

In any case, if it did survive a nuclear blast, the energy the robot would release would probably be nearly as destructive as the blast itself, unless it can be focused somehow. The fragment I used only weighs a few grams, it's smaller than the nail of your little finger, and it made a hole about one foot in diameter. I'm just now realizing how powerful this thing might be. I must admit, she's beginning to scare me.

—What do you think she was built for?

—Up until now, I tried to ignore the fact that this might very well be a weapon, an enormously powerful weapon. But when I think about it, there's simply no reason to build something this massive for anything else. There's nothing practical about it. She'll weigh about seven thousand metric tons if we manage to put her together. She'll destroy anything she steps on. What worries me is that you could have walked through an army of ten thousand men with something a tenth of this size. There was nothing remotely powerful enough six thousand years ago to justify a weapon of this magnitude, nothing of this Earth anyway.

—You believe she is that powerful?

—We'll just have to locate the head to find out.

—We will have all the answers very soon. Unfortunately, we will need to go under the sea to get them.

—I thought about that possibility. I'm hoping it's not, because I can't get the ARCANA compound to disperse well under water. It'll take months to develop a new delivery system, and a whole lot longer to go through all the oceans. Whatever I come up with, I can already tell you that dispersal will be a lot slower under water. With a slower vehicle, like a submarine, it could take decades before we find anything. It might be wishful thinking, but I'm really hoping that whoever buried these things was afraid of water.

—**You misunderstood. What I meant is that I know exactly where the head is. It is beneath the sea. The Bering Sea.**

FILE NO. 143

INTERVIEW WITH CAPT. DEMETRIUS ROOKE, UNITED STATES NAVY

Location: Naval Submarine Base Bangor, Kitsap Peninsula, WA

—Please state your name and rank.

—Captain Demetrius Rooke, United States Navy.

—What is your current assignment?

—I'm in command of the USS *Jimmy Carter,* designated SSN-23.

—If I understand the designation correctly, that is a nuclear attack submarine.

—Yes, sir. Seawolf class.

—How long have you been in command?

—Five years in October, sir.

—I am not part of the military. You do not have to call me "sir."

—What would you prefer I call you?

—On second thought, sir will be just fine. Please describe, in your own words, the events that occurred on the morning of August 17.

—Very well. We left Bangor Base alongside the USS *Maine*. She's an Ohio class ballistic missile sub. We were on our way to SEAFAC in Ketchikan, Alaska, for a week of detection exercises when we got a call from SECNAV.

—You received a call from the Office of the Secretary of the Navy.

—No. I mean from the Secretary of the Navy himself.

—Does the Secretary of the Navy often call submarine captains directly?

—No, he does not. That was unusual in and of itself. His orders were *definitely* out of the ordinary. We were to intercept two Russian subs in the Bering Sea and secure whatever we found on the site. We were to avoid hostilities, if at all possible, but use of force was authorized if necessary.

I don't know if you've ever spoken to SECNAV, but he's a very *loud* man. He speaks slowly with a very deep voice. It's really impossible to misunderstand anything he says, but I asked him to repeat anyway. I don't think a sub captain has heard those words since World War II.

First, we had to head back to Bangor, to take an Army Chief Warrant on board as an advisor. Good-looking girl. We headed west from there. The trip is about sixty hours at maximum speed.

She said we were on our way to recover a new kind of power reactor, some new fission technology we couldn't let the Russians get their hands on. Apparently, it was on its way to a secret facility in Alaska when there was an incident and they had to drop it into the sea. Her helo was escorting the ship, and she was familiar with the device. That's why we had to bring her aboard.

She asked to be brought to the control room right away. One of my lieutenants told her we'd send for her when we reached our destination, but she insisted. Some words were exchanged. My XO had to intervene. I didn't think too much of it at first. I thought claustrophobia was getting to her. It's not unusual when people get on a sub for the first time. Tight spaces, small doors, low ceilings—some people have a hard time adjusting. It can make them irritable. I let her blow a little steam and left it at that.

—Did you bring her to the control room?

—Not right away, no. I sent for her about twelve hours from our target. She seemed calm and in control. We went around the Alaskan Peninsula and headed north from Dutch Harbor. After about ten miles, we made sonar contact with three objects. There was an Akula class sub lying on her side at the bottom of a small cliff. She appeared to be disabled. The *Saint Petersburg* was just sitting there, staring at us, about two thousand feet west of the Akula.

—The *Saint Petersburg*?

—Lada class. She's the lead ship. Really quiet. She was designed for this sort of thing. Blowing up subs, defending a base, things like that. They must have sent her when the Akula stopped responding. Whatever she was guarding, the "reactor," she seemed adamant about not letting us anywhere near it.

—You do not think it was a power reactor?

—It's not my place to say. It was a large object, about thirty-five feet in diameter, sitting in between her and the disabled Akula. Sonar said it was metallic. When we tried to get closer, the *Saint Pete* maneuvered herself between us and the target.

We stopped. The USS *Maine* tried to go around the Russian sub. We were hoping that having two ships to deal with might make her run. She didn't. She kept her nose straight at us and flooded her torpedo tubes.

—What did you do then?

—Nothing. Our other boat stopped. We waited. Submarines are slow, clumsy things. A lot of what we do is just sit and wait. We're good at that.

—You had orders to fire if necessary.

—I didn't think it was necessary. And I wasn't ready to get blown to bits quite yet. We could have taken her down, but not before she fired everything she had at us.

—How long did you wait?

—About a day. Like I said, we're good at waiting. The next morning we received an ELF warning that a Russian corvette was under way. It would get there in less than ninety minutes. We had to act quickly. A corvette is well equipped for antisubmarine warfare and she would no doubt bring the target aboard or tow it away.

I gave the order to flood and open our torpedo tubes, and we used the Gertrude to tell the USS *Maine* to do the same. The Russians responded in kind. That's when things started to get crazy. Our Army guest "suggested" we surface and warn the Russians that we'd destroy the object before we let anyone have it.

—Did you?

—No. I had no intention of doing that. There was a corvette coming. She then asked me—ordered me, would be a better choice of words—to actually do it. "Just fire on it!" she said. "Everything you've got!"

My orders were to recover that object, fire at the Russians if need be, not to destroy the very thing we came for. Naturally, I said no. She assured me it wouldn't be destroyed, but the blast would force the Russian boat to back off, and we'd gain enough time for the cavalry to arrive. I couldn't even be sure we had boats under way. She called me a fool for arguing with her.

—How did you respond?

—"You're out of order," I believe was my reply. I told her I would have her removed if she did not desist immediately. Then, and I remember this perfectly because it was the last thing I expected, she raised her voice to make sure everyone in command heard her and said: "I'm assuming command of this ship under the authority given to me by the president of the United States."

—Gutsy.

—You could call it that. I called for security on the double and I asked the Chief of the Boat to place her under arrest. The XO grabbed her by the arm, and then things are a little fuzzy. It was happening so fast. She got the XO in an armlock and slammed his head on a console. Two armed security officers arrived on deck. She round kicked one of them and broke the other one's nose with her palm before kneeing him and throwing him down. She must have grabbed a sidearm from one of the men because the next thing I knew, she had her arm around my throat and a gun to my temple. She backed us up against the wall to get a full view of the room.

Four more armed men came through the door. There was a lot of back-and-forth yelling. I could sense my men were losing their calm so I asked everyone to lower their weapons. I had to repeat it a few times, but they eventually complied. I asked her what the next move was. She gave me two choices: I could either fire on the object as she wanted or surface to confirm her orders. I certainly questioned her motives, but there was no doubt in my mind about her resolve. She would blow my head off, I was sure of it. Yet she remained fairly calm under the circumstances and I chose to believe she hadn't completely lost her mind.

I told her there was no way I would surface with a corvette only minutes away, but I would fire our torpedoes at the object if the USS *Maine* kept hers aimed at the *Saint Petersburg*. Only, I would *not* do it with a gun to my head. She had to let me go.

—She believed you?

—I gave her my word as a Navy officer. I took the gun away from her. The XO punched her unconscious, broke her nose in the process, I think. The men dragged her to the brig.

—Did you fire?

—I gave her my word. We shot two torpedoes at the object. Both were direct hits.

—**What happened?**

—Nothing happened. Well, not nothing, but not what you'd expect. When the torpedoes exploded, we braced ourselves for the shock wave that would shortly follow. We were fairly close to the target. The engine went silent, all the lights went out. All we could hear was the metal of the hull shrieking under the pressure. We started to slowly tilt upward and sideways, we all had to grab ahold of something. We hovered like that for about six hours, then we heard something attaching to the hull. They took us out in a rescue sub, a dozen men at a time.

Turns out they had sent a whole lot of boats after us: several frigates, two destroyers, and a cruiser. They must have been minutes away when it all happened. We could see the *Saint Petersburg* through the window in the rescue sub—her shadow, actually. There was a lot of bluish light behind her. She was missing part of her tail. A really clean cut, not like an explosion. You'd need a laser or a blowtorch to make a cut that clean. The rescue sub went out to help the Russians. They were lucky. The rear chamber was sealed when their tail was cut off; only two people had died.

I asked the cruiser crew: "What of the Akula?" They just stared at me blankly. It took several of us to convince them that there *was* an Akula class submarine at the bottom when we arrived. One thing's for sure, it wasn't there anymore. Poof! Like magic. There was no wreckage, no floating debris, no sign it was ever there.

—**What happened to the Army Chief Warrant?**

—Never saw her again. They told me she would be court-martialed. She must have been right. About her orders, I mean.

—**I thought you said she would be . . .**

—They also made it very clear to me that none of this ever happened. I don't think they'll put anyone on trial for something that didn't happen.

—Are you always this cynical? You seem to doubt a lot of what
you are told.

—It's all cockamamie, if you ask me. Military intelligence. They come
up with these really far-fetched stories, and just because we don't ask
questions, they think we're actually buying it. They forget that they're
talking to people who are trained not to ask questions. If it were up
to me, I'd rather they just didn't tell me anything. It's less insulting
than to be lied to.

—Do you believe I am lying to you?

—That would be hard. You haven't told me a single thing. But let's
give it a shot. Can you tell me what it was I fired at? It wasn't destroyed, just like she said. I saw it hooked to a crane when they
brought it aboard, but they had it covered in some black sheeting. I
fired two torpedoes at that thing . . .

—Let us say for a minute I could provide you with—how shall I put
it—an alternate story. I can assure you that you would find it so
preposterous that you would leave this room absolutely convinced
that you fired your torpedoes at a prototype reactor that was lost
at sea. So I will save both of us the time and leave it at that. I can
tell you this: what you did mattered.

—Thank you. I guess that's all I really wanted to hear. By the way,
that Chief Warrant, I'd like to shake hands with her some time. She's
got grit.

—I will let her know you said hi.

FILE NO. 161

INTERVIEW WITH CW3 KARA RESNIK, UNITED STATES ARMY

Location: Underground Complex, Denver, CO

—I can't stand it anymore. I feel like I'm watching him die, every day, all the time. If he's not unconscious, he's in agony. No one can stand that much pain all the time. I'm surprised he lasted this long.

—**He can walk, can he not?**

—No! He can't! You can't call that walking. You and I are walking. He can barely take a couple steps before his whole body starts shaking. Then he collapses and—to spare us—pretends it doesn't hurt as much as it does. I've had to pick him up from the ground three times today. No one wants to hurt him any more than he already is, so no one says anything.

—**And what would they say if they dared?**

—He just doesn't have enough muscle mass left.

—**Is he taking his drugs?**

—Religiously. But his body's adapting to the muscle-building agent. The doctor says his tolerance will continue to increase.

—We will find him new medication.

—You can't keep pumping him full of experimental drugs. His body's been through enough already.

—Would you rather we let him suffer?

—He doesn't have to suffer. Take these things out of him and let him rest. He can learn to walk with prosthetics when he's ready.

—You do realize that this project would essentially be over if he lost his legs. You would be willing to throw away all the work that he did, that you did, to spare him some pain for a few weeks?

—It's not a few weeks. And if the alternative is to watch him die, then yes, I give up. We're killing him! And it wouldn't have to be over. We can find a way to make the helmet work for someone else. We can rig the controls so he can maneuver with his arms. There are a hundred things we can do that don't involve torturing him. This? What we're doing to him? It's just wrong.

—From what Dr. Franklin tells me, we are decades—if not centuries— away from fully understanding the technology behind the helmet. I would also point out that you and Mr. Mitchell—a man in tremendously better shape than Mr. Couture—have worked countless hours in the sphere and were able to make her walk only for a few steps. You cannot seriously suggest that Mr. Couture could control robotic legs with his hands *and* operate the console with any kind of efficiency. That would be putting his life, and yours, at risk. Mr. Couture is a grown man. Why not let him make his own decisions?

—No. Of course, he'll take new drugs if you give him a choice. He'd do anything to get the project back on track.

—Some would call that dedication. I would hardly call it a problem.

—It's not just his body that's messed up. He's changed.

—Is he depressed?

—No, quite the opposite. He says this ordeal's made him see things differently. He keeps telling us how much he appreciates every little thing. You should see him with me. He's kind, he's . . . attentive. It scares the hell out of me.

—It is not uncommon for people to find positive aspects in a negative situation.

—I get that. I've heard it before: "Life's taught me a great lesson." "I now realize what the important things in life are." I even think it's true sometimes. But this doesn't feel right. That's not who he is. I think he's on the verge of a mental breakdown and he's finding ways of holding on to his sanity for as long as he can.

—It is kind of you to worry about your friend but I honestly believe he is making astounding progress, physically and mentally. Speaking of physical progress, how is your nose healing up? Are you still having trouble breathing?

—It's kind of me to worry about my friend? . . . You ought to listen to yourself sometimes. My nose is fine. I still have to breathe through my mouth when I sleep but it's getting better. They said I'll need plastic surgery if I want to get rid of the scar. I'm not sure I want to. It's a shame the helmet doesn't come down that far, I could have saved a nose job.

—That was a bold move you made. They could have shot you. They should have shot you. Do you realize how dangerous that was?

—I know. It's not like I planned any of it. They were either going to get us all killed or let the Russians take the head. I've never been really afraid of dying, but it would feel damn stupid to get so close to the last piece and let it slip away. I tell myself it was a calculated risk, but the truth is I acted on instinct. They just made me mad.

—An impulsive reaction is to be expected in your case. I am curious as to how you knew the head would not be destroyed?

—You can call it an educated guess. You know I've helped Dr. Franklin run some experiments. I assumed that if a tiny speck of metal could absorb a lot of energy, something that massive could withstand a couple torpedo hits. I know. You're gonna tell me it wasn't up to me to take that chance, that I could have ruined everything.

—I am not going to tell you anything of the sort. I chose you because of who you are. I sent you there for the same reason. Quite frankly, I would have fired myself. I am curious, however, as to how you knew it would disable the submarines. If my understanding is correct, an electromagnetic pulse does not travel underwater, and if it did, a submarine would likely be shielded from it.

—I thought about that, but an EMP shouldn't have done anything to my helicopter either. It's hardened against that. And yet it stopped my engine cold, twice. Whatever this thing shoots out, it's nasty. If it didn't work, the shock wave from the explosion might have at least pushed the Russians away.

—They are still searching for the other Russian submarine.

—I feel sorry for those people. I didn't think it would destroy their ship.

—*Obliterate* might be a better term. All that is left is a crescent-shaped hollow on the cliffside, and some very confused seamen.

—Won't they report what happened when they get back?

—What could they report? The other submarine was there, and then it was not. Their ships were there, and they know we did not leave with a submarine. What matters is that we recovered the head. Have you attached it yet?

—No. We haven't even unwrapped it. Dr. Franklin wants us to try everything we can on the console before we attach the head. If we can see the result on the hologram first, we can avoid accidents when she's functional.

—I thought curiosity would have the better of you.

—Well, it would have had the better of me. I would've put that thing on the minute we got back. At least we'd know if it works, right? Then out of nowhere, Vincent was back to his old self for a few seconds. He said: "One of those buttons could be a self-destruct." It was nice to catch a glimpse of him again. His eyes, they haven't been the same since the accident, but he looked at me like he used to for a moment. Of course, I didn't have anything smart to say after that. We all agreed to work on the console while Vincent gets better.

We didn't find a self-destruct, but we did find the command to disassemble her. There is a small button on the top left of the console, if you press it long enough, she lays down on her stomach, arms along her sides, and all the parts disconnect from one another, at least they do on the hologram. There's a hatch on top of the sphere for us to get out, since the sphere will stay level, but I don't know how we'll be able to reach it.

—Have you discovered any weaponry?

—Not yet, but it could be weeks before we try every sequence on the console, and some of the controls seem to have no effect on the hologram. These could be your weapons.

—My weapons?

—You know what I mean . . . All we can see right now is what makes her move. If there's a button that makes her eyes shoot little turquoise lightning bolts, we won't know until we can do it for real. We'll have to figure out these things once she's assembled if Vincent recovers enough strength.

—You mean *when* he recovers his strength.

—Sure, that's what I meant. Promise me you won't push him.

—You make it sound as if I could control him in some way. I cannot force him to do anything he does not want to.

—You sorta can, that's the thing. He listens to you. Don't ask me why. I can't, for the life of me, figure out why he'd trust you of all people, but he does. Don't abuse that trust.

—You and I both know that Mr. Couture puts more faith in your opinion and that of Dr. Franklin than he will ever put in anything I have to say. To suggest otherwise is simply preposterous.

—No, he trusts us . . . he trusts me for just about everything, but he knows how much I care about him, and Dr. Franklin too. He knows we'll always have his interests at heart. I guess, in some weird way, he trusts your . . . *objectivity* more.

—Do you believe I have lost my objectivity?

—Lost it? No. I don't think you really had any to begin with. I don't see how anyone can come into this and remain objective. Dr. Franklin is a scientist. If anyone can remain detached it should be her, but she's not a robot, she's curious, she's proud. She can't help but be blinded to certain things because of what motivates her. The same thing is true for me, and it's blatantly true for you. You have your own agenda and you're willing to go the distance for it. I'm not saying you're in this for your own personal gain—I think, in many ways, your motivation might actually be less selfish than everyone else's—but that doesn't make you any less biased. The only difference between me and you, when it comes to Vincent, is that you really don't care what happens to him if he can't do this. That's not objectivity.

—I can accept, and even understand, that you might question my motives. I find it more difficult not to respond when my integrity is questioned. Have I ever lied to you?

—A thousand times, I'm sure. Just don't lie to him, that's all I'm asking.

—I suppose I should be offended. Has it ever occurred to you to ask Mr. Couture if he believes I have misled him in any way? He is

an incredibly intelligent young man, more so than either you or I could ever aspire to be.

—Come on. Be honest for one second. If he said: "No, I don't wanna do this anymore," you wouldn't try to force him to continue, manipulate him, blackmail him, threaten him in some way?

—Who is being manipulative now? There are two possible answers to this question: one that you would not believe, and one that would make me a cruel and evil figure. So I can either appear cruel and dishonest, or honest but still cruel and evil. You have formulated a question for which the best possible answer is to admit than I am a dangerous manipulative blackmailer. You will forgive me if I do not give you the pleasure of answering it.

Fortunately for me, your question is entirely speculative, as Mr. Couture has expressed on several occasions, and to the both of us, his strong desire to help with this project in any way that he can. If, at some point in the future, his disposition changes and he wishes to remove himself from this enterprise, then you will have the only answer that really matters and we will know if I am everything you portray me to be. In the meantime, I hope you will not presume to know more about the needs and wants of Mr. Couture than he does, and that you will honor and respect the wishes of the man you claim to love.

FILE NO. 182

PERSONAL JOURNAL ENTRY—DR. ROSE FRANKLIN, PH.D.

Location: Underground Complex, Denver, CO

"We knew the world would not be the same. A few people laughed, a few people cried, most people were silent. I remembered the line from the Hindu scripture, the *Bhagavad-Gita*. Vishnu is trying to persuade the Prince that he should do his duty and, to impress him, takes on his multi-armed form and says, 'Now I am become Death, the destroyer of worlds.' I suppose we all thought that, one way or another."

Those are not my words. In fact, I had to look up the exact quote. Like everyone else, I only knew "I am become Death, the destroyer of worlds." We tend to romanticize good quotes, and I always imagined Oppenheimer uttering those words while staring at the mushroom cloud of a nuclear explosion. In reality, he spoke those words during an interview for an NBC documentary in 1965. He had had twenty years to think about it.

I've been giving a lot of thought to Oppenheimer and the Manhattan Project these past few days. I haven't been building a bomb, but it's becoming increasingly difficult to ignore a very simple truth.

I am building a weapon, and a formidable one at that. But that's not the truth I'm hiding from. There's no hiding from that. I spend most of my time understanding just how devastating it can be. I realize it may have been an instrument of peace, but not the kind of peace achieved through righteousness and understanding. This is meant to be a killing machine, one of such might and power that no one would stand against it.

It works. I'm afraid of it. I'm reminded of it every night in my dreams. All of us are. I keep showing up earlier and earlier in the morning, either because I can't sleep or because I don't want to go back to whatever dream I was having. Inevitably, someone's already there, or they show up a few minutes later. No one wants to talk about it, but we can all tell we're going through the same thing.

My dream is usually the same: she's standing over me, then she bends on one knee and brings her face a few feet above my head. She's staring at me with bright, blinding turquoise eyes; she looks like she's about to speak. That's when I wake up in a sweat.

After yesterday, I know I won't have the same dream ever again. We finally looked at the head.

Everyone was dying to see it. It had just been sitting there wrapped in a black tarp. I'd catch Kara trying to take a peek about once a day. I could have just unwrapped it, but it was too much fun torturing her. She would pace around it for twenty minutes, hoping the tarp would magically fall off. And then she'd walk off angrily.

Yesterday morning, I brought Vincent in his wheelchair and I told Kara it was time. We unstrapped the head and removed the cloth. She is stunning, but not at all what I expected.

She has thin lips and a very small nose. All her features are small, delicate. She almost looks like a child, innocent but controlled. *Chaste* is the word that comes to mind.

I can't decide if it's her hair or a very elaborate helmet, but her head is covered in wavy spines with intricate carvings. Turquoise light seeps between them. Some extend forward onto her cheeks and brow, others are sleeked backward toward her back armor. From her forehead, several spines join to form an axe-shaped appendage at the back of her head.

When we unwrapped her, I was expecting to cross the same intense gaze I see in my dreams, quailing at the idea to be honest, but it wasn't there. No blinding light, no gaze, no eyes.

She doesn't have eyes, only small recesses where they ought to be. It's very unsettling. You can't help but wonder just how aware of your presence she really is. I know she's not aware of anything, because I'm the one who put her together. But there's something about her . . . a presence. I think there's more there than a glorified toaster. Besides, I can't really be blamed for anthropomorphizing something that's anthropomorphic. Anyway, I doubt she'll leave me alone at night, but she'll have to find another way to scare me.

We had to use two cranes to raise the head. As soon as we attached it, the whole room started to shake. Her entire body stiffened for a second, then everything went back to normal. I asked Kara to grab a walkie-talkie, get up the elevator, and into the sphere.

She went in and braced herself at her station. I asked her to raise her right arm slowly. It was fantastic to watch. She moves! After all this, we finally got her working. We made her move her arms, rotate her head. She even bent down to pick up a storage crate. She's really gracious, delicate in her movements. I didn't expect such fluency. Of course, she crushed the crate with her fingers, but we can work on that. Kara's not that delicate herself.

We found weapons today. I haven't told our nameless friend yet. He'll find out soon enough. I just don't want to give him the pleasure of pretending he hasn't been waiting for this all along. We came upon them by accident. I was expecting we'd find weaponry at some point, but not so soon, and I always thought it would be lasers, a death ray, something futuristic. Maybe I just watch too many movies. I was wrong, it turns out our girl is old school. She has a sword and a shield.

Apparently, she was built for close combat. I don't know what she was supposed to fight, but it must have been big. The sword is a focused-energy weapon. Like a lightsaber, only wider, double-edged, more like a medieval sword. *Star Wars* meets *Lord of the Rings*. It's not turquoise like everything else. It's a very, very bright white. It's almost impossible to stare at.

What's really—I seem to use the word *cool* a lot these days—is that we can dial its length on the console. Vincent figured out that it works on a sixty-four-step scale—1 being the shortest, 64 the longest. At the lowest settings, it's almost like a dagger. At its longest, it's . . . We made a large hole on the floor when we tried it at 64. We stopped playing with it after that.

Fortunately, the shield is somewhat safer to experiment with. It's also based on controlled energy and we can adjust the size in the very same way. At the lowest setting, it barely covers her wrist. At the highest, it can cover her entire body. It's also not nearly as bright as the sword. It's almost transparent, in fact. You can tell something's there because it distorts light a little bit, like the exhaust of a car on a really hot day.

We discovered it can also be used as a weapon. It took another hole—in the wall, this time—to figure that one out, but the edge of the shield is very sharp . . . if you can say that about light.

The light in both the sword and shield appears to be self-contained. There's no sign of an electromagnetic field around either of them. Needless to say, I have no idea how they're able to manipulate photons as if it were regular matter. Yet, they seem to do with light as they please, like a sculptor would mold clay.

We haven't found any long-range weapons so far, but I'm certain we will. She's full of surprises. There needs to be a way for her to focus the energy release away from her. If she does, I'm sure that weapon will have a pretty long reach. She really needs to be able to control it or she'd be more of a danger to her own army than to the enemy's. All one would need to do is throw enough power at her and she'd obliterate everyone around. I wouldn't want to be anywhere near her when she gets into a fight.

On the other hand, if she can focus all that energy in one direction, she'd be a nightmare to deal with. Everything one would hit her with, she would throw right back. The more powerful the enemy, the mightier she would be. That, I have told already. But I hope we don't find out for a long, long time.

It's important for "the powers that be" to know that we have yet to uncover her more destructive powers. I fear they'll take her away from us the minute they believe there's no more weaponry to be found. We must use the time we have to discover as much as we can about how she works and what she can do besides leveling a city or vaporizing an army. I haven't told Vincent anything, but I think he understands.

All we need now is to make her walk.

We'll have to wait before we take her for a spin. Vincent's not ready. He can barely walk himself.

I hate to say it. We've already lost several months because of his injury, and I know Kara's more than eager to resume training, but it's a miracle Vincent's lasted this far. To push him any farther would jeopardize everything.

I would never tell him, because it would only make things worse, but I can't stomach what they've done to him. I understand the appeal, there's even a reasonably sound logic behind it, but we must draw the line somewhere if we're to remain human.

He hasn't tried reversing his knees yet. He wants to, but I don't. If I understand correctly, it's going to rip apart whatever muscle he has left on the back of his legs. They're just too short. It'll take months for him to build muscles that fit his new anatomy.

I realize that won't happen if he doesn't try his knees, but he's already in pain twenty-four hours a day. I'm not going to put him through even more. And it's not in anyone's interest to push Vincent to do something he's not ready for. It'll break him physically, and mentally. It will bring resentment, mistrust, and will put every member of my team at unnecessary risk.

I know he'll have to try them at some point. I don't think it'll be easier, or any less painful, if he does it a month from now. In fact, it'll probably be more painful because he'll have gained some muscle mass. But I'm hoping he'll have gained some strength as well, physically *and* mentally.

All that said, I can't wait to see her walk.

So, what's that simple truth I've been hiding from? It's not that I'm building a weapon. It's not even that it'll kill people. That's just a matter of time. What I've been trying so hard to deny is that I'm loving every minute of it. As much as I'd like to be principled enough to walk away from this, I'm having the time of my life. I'm a scientist, and this is what I breathe for. If I can learn to live with that, I might be able to sleep again.

I tried to find out what Oppenheimer's thoughts were while it was all happening. He had this to say in 1945:

"But when you come right down to it the reason that we did this job is because it was an organic necessity. If you are a scientist you cannot stop such a thing. If you are a scientist you believe that it is good to find out how the world works; that it is good to find out what the realities are; that it is good to turn over to mankind at large the greatest possible power to control the world and to deal with it according to its lights and its values."

FILE NO. 188

PRELIMINARY REPORT—DISAPPEARANCE OF FLIGHT ICELANDAIR 670

FAA Office of Accident Investigation and Prevention

Flight Icelandair 670 (FI670), scheduled for a nonstop flight from Denver International Airport (DEN) to Keflavik, Reykjavik (KEF), disappeared from Air Traffic Control instruments at approximately 10:31 on the morning of August 10. The Boeing 757-200 called ready for taxi from Gate A-43 of Denver International Airport at 10:16. Following instructions from Denver Ground, the plane taxied to Runway 17L through taxiways M and ED, holding short of the runway before contacting the tower. Flight 670 was cleared for takeoff immediately after assuming position on the runway. The entire communication between the tower and FI670 is reproduced below. Prior communication with ATC shows nothing out of the ordinary.

> **FI670:** Tower, this is ICEAIR 670 holding on Echo Delta for Runway 17 Left.
>
> **ATC:** Good morning ICEAIR 670. She's all yours, into position on Runway 17 Left.

FI670: Roger that.

In position, 670.

ATC: ICEAIR 670, you are clear to takeoff, Runway 17 Left, contact departure 1-2-6-1 in the air.

670, you're clear to go . . .

ICEAIR 670, I lost you on my screen. Can you read back?

FI670: Where the hell is that light coming from?

ATC: Can you repeat that 670?

ICEAIR 670, this is the tower, please respond.

670, please respond . . .

Investigators were on-site around 12:15 P.M. and FAA personnel were denied access to the site. However, the abundant news footage of the incident showed that only the southernmost section (estimate: two hundred feet) of Runway 17L/35R remained intact. A large crater, approximately fifteen hundred feet across, three hundred feet deep, covered the remaining part of the runway and the surrounding taxiways. The examined footage shows no sign of wreckage, no debris of any kind.

The complete absence of evidence, coupled with the extraordinary nature of the circumstances, strongly suggests that neither mechanical failure nor pilot error are responsible for the disappearance of flight 670 and that the aircraft could not be responsible for the destruction of Runway 17L/35R. The circumstances of the incident, while currently unexplained, clearly fall beyond the expertise of the FAA and no further investigation is warranted at this point.

INTERVIEW WITH VINCENT COUTURE, SENIOR INTELLIGENCE ADVISOR (DCIPS)

Location: Fort Carson Army Base,
near Colorado Springs, CO

—I don't wanna start at the beginning. Can we just stop? I . . . I don't wanna talk . . . I just need a few minutes to think. Where's Rose? I didn't see her. Where's Kara? I wanna see Kara.

—**Take a deep breath. You need to relax. I only want to help you remember.**

—Remember what? Where's . . .

—**No. Do not try to get up.**

—Where are my boots?

—**Let us start with something simple. Tell me the first thing you did this morning.**

—Someone took my boots. What's this? Is it a hospital gown? I can't find any of my clothes.

—**Please, get back into bed. At least sit down on the bed.**

—My clothes . . .

—**I will help you find your clothes. Now, sit down and look at me. I want you to focus on me. What is the first thing you did when you woke up this morning?**

—This morning . . . I . . . I did . . . I took a shower, and I went to the lab. I got to the lab early.

—**Very good. What did you do once you got there?**

—When I got where?

—**To the lab. You got up early, and you went to the lab.**

—Yes.

—**What did you do at the lab?**

—I practiced walking . . . I walked a few times around the lab, then I . . . I tried it with my knees reversed.

—**Good. I did not know that you had tried them yet.**

—A few times.

—**How does it feel?**

—How does what feel? I . . .

—**Your knees. How does it feel when you reverse them?**

—It hurts like you wouldn't believe. I tried them last week for the first time. Rose kept telling me to wait, not to rush things. I assumed you had talked to her . . . I'm not sure if you know how they work, but you have to stick your finger under the kneecap and push real hard. That hurts, just by itself, but the knees are spring-loaded, and they just yank your legs backward real hard. It's overwhelming. I fell face-first, the first few times. It just . . . It hurts like hell. It's like having a truck run over your legs.

—**Go on.**

—I . . .

—This morning, you went to the lab early.

—Yes, I did. I got there before anyone else.

—And you tried your knees . . .

—I wanted to see if I could go around the room. I made it about two-thirds of the way, then I fell down and I couldn't get up. It's really hard to get up with the legs in reverse.

—What did you do then?

—After I fell? Nothing, I just lay on my back and waited for someone to come. Rose came in about a half hour later. She brought my wheelchair over and helped me up. She had cinnamon buns. Coffee and cinnamon buns. There's this little tiny shop about two kilometers from the airport. They make the best pastries.

—What happened after Dr. Franklin helped you get up?

—We sat down and talked politics while waiting for Kara. She showed up around nine. She whined for a good fifteen minutes because we ate all the buns. Rose promised to go get some more, and we made our way up into the sphere.

We tried the shield again, then the sword. I asked Kara if she was up for a quick walk around the room. We radioed Rose. She didn't think it was a good idea. She told us to practice handling the shield at different sizes. We did for a while, but I could tell Kara also had that walk in the back of her head. I flipped my knees again. I took a minute to get through the sting, then I braced myself in the controls. "Are you sure you're up for it?" she said. Since I didn't answer, she got out of her station and helped me get into mine.

It's cold in here. Where are we? Is this a military base?

—It does not matter right now. Just keep going.

—I wanna see Kara. She was with me. Is she here?

—I will answer all your questions in a minute. I just want you to tell me what happened next. You braced yourself in. You were about to try walking for the first time.

—We did. I had taken off my headset, but I could hear Rose getting worried: "What's going on up there? What are you guys doing? Talk to me!"

I lifted my left leg. It took us aback for a second. The whole room began to tilt slightly when the sphere adjusted to the movement. I moved my right leg, then the left again. Rose was trying to stay calm: "OK, you did it, now stop and get out of there." I told Kara we'd go to the end of the room and back. I could feel my legs going numb, but I was too excited to stop. I took a few more steps, then my knees started to give. I'd never had to support more than my own weight with my knees backward, and I had to swing my hips upward and back at every step to keep the balance . . .

I don't wanna talk anymore. Can you take me to see Kara?

—I understand. It will only take a minute. You can ask any question you want afterward. It is important that you tell me everything that you remember.

—Kara and I tried walking for the first time. We just wanted to get to the end of the room.

—Yes. Your legs were weakening . . .

—Oh. I told you . . . I . . . My left knee folded about three steps from the end of the room. Kara was quick enough to raise her hand to the side to stop us from falling headfirst into the wall. I fell forward, both hands on the console. It was the strangest feeling. When my hands pressed against two buttons, I realized we hadn't tried that before, two buttons at the same time.

I was getting excited and trying to calculate how many combinations were possible, when I realized I had a hard time concentrating because of the noise. I hadn't noticed it a second before, but it was getting louder.

—What noise are you referring to?

—Hissing. The pitch was getting higher and higher. It was like a camera flash charging, only much, much louder. Then the hissing stopped.

It was complete silence. Everything turned white outside the sphere. It got so bright we had to cover our eyes. After a second or two, I felt the room darken slowly through my fingers. I looked around. It was as if we'd been transported to another place.

There was no roof anymore. I realized it was the sky above us. We were in the middle of a perfectly round crater, maybe half a kilometer across. Kara looked up; I saw the head tilt backward above my head. The ledge was at least five hundred feet higher than we were. There was a large plane, right on the edge. It was missing the tail end.

My legs felt perfectly fine as I spun the robot around to take a look behind us. There was a large building that stopped where the crater began. Most of the lights were out, but we could see the neon sign from our bar. It was Terminal B, most of Terminal B. Minutes went by before Kara told me to look up. There were three or four helicopters circling above us. I don't think they were military.

—No, they were not. Those were television helicopters. Our little secret is now on every television station in the world. What did you do after you saw them?

—We got out of our controls and sat on the floor in the middle of the room. Kara wrapped her arms around me and helped me lie down. We held each other for . . . I don't know, it seemed like hours, without saying a word. I must have fallen asleep. How did we get down?

—A Delta team took you down with a tower crane.

—It seemed like a long time . . . I'm so sorry. I'm so terribly sorry. We just . . . I thought you wanted us to move faster. I thought Rose did too, but she would never say it. I don't . . . We lost everything, didn't we? All our notes, everything . . . I don't know what to say. I'll find a way to make this right. We can fix this.

—I do not believe this, as you call it, can be fixed. We can only try to move forward from here.

—The helicopters. Is that gonna be a problem?

—Will it be the end of our project? I do not know. I know things will become . . . complicated.

—Now can I ask where we are?

—This is the base hospital at Fort Carson. You were flown here after they took you and Ms. Resnik out of the device.

—I don't remember flying. I don't remember anything after we lay down on the floor.

—They gave you a sedative. You were in shock. You became agitated when they tried to take you out of the sphere. They had to restrain you.

—Where's Kara? I wanna see her. Is she OK?

—She is fine. She is in a room a few doors down, sleeping. She stayed by your side for a few hours, but she fell asleep in her chair. I found her a bed.

—A few hours? How long have I been here?

—About sixteen hours. It is almost dawn.

—Wow. Where's Rose? Is she here too? She was . . . She . . .

—She was in the lab.

—In the lab? The lab is . . . No! She wasn't there. She went to get more cinnamon buns. She said she would.

—She never left.

—No! No! She said she would get more cinnamon buns! She went to get some. She said she would get more for Kara. You see, Rose and I, we ate all the pastries. Kara was mad at us. Rose said she would go and get some more. She wasn't in the lab.

—Mr. Couture . . .

—Rose, she . . . She cared about the little things. She cared about us. She made sure we knew we were appreciated. Every day. Little things, you know. Coffee, cake. She found some Kinder eggs somehow. She knew they reminded me of home. She would drop one at my station every now and then.

She could have left them in my locker, anywhere really, but she took time to take the elevator up to the sphere before I'd walk in, just because she thought it would make a better surprise. So, you see, she would have made sure Kara didn't stay angry. She would have gone to get more pastry.

—Mr. Couture . . .

—She said . . .

—VINCENT! . . . She's gone.

PART FOUR

BODY BLOW

FILE NO. 211

INTERVIEW WITH ROBERT WOODHULL, ASSISTANT TO THE PRESIDENT FOR NATIONAL SECURITY AFFAIRS

Location: White House, Washington, DC

—I feel as though I have been summoned by the principal.

—The reports are in. I thought you'd like to know how much damage you've caused.

—It was an accident, admittedly a foreseeable one, but an accident nonetheless.

—Let's talk infrastructure first. You have obliterated two buildings on Vandriver Street, just about half of Runway 17L-35R, as well as the east end of Concourse B. Fortunately, there were no planes leaving out of the east-end gates. They estimate the damage will be around 300 million.

—I am not very good with numbers. I assume this is a lot.

—How about this number, smart-ass: 311. That's the number of people you killed.

—How could there be so many? You said there were no departures in the portion of Terminal B that was destroyed.

—There were only a few employees in the terminal: concession-stand workers, janitors, some ground crew on the tarmac just outside. Forty-two people in total, all of them Americans.

There was, however, an Icelandair Boeing 757 on the runway when it happened. I think it goes without saying that all on board have perished, since the plane itself doesn't exist anymore . . . The flight was almost full, 193 passengers dead, 6 crew members. Most were Icelanders. Icelandic? Anyway. Eighteen were Americans.

There was also a Dash 8 taxiing to Terminal B, fifty-one dead. And you took out the tail end of a United Airbus 320, that's another nineteen. They were lucky, only the last three rows of passengers were vaporized, along with one crew member.

Three hundred eleven people in total, three hundred twelve with your scientist. One hundred nineteen Americans, about two hundred Ice . . . people from Iceland, two dozen Canadians, and a few people from nine more countries whose governments are publicly blaming us—rightfully so, I might add—and demanding an explanation. Some of them will get over it, but you can definitely add Iceland to the list of countries that want bad things to happen to us.

—Do we really need Iceland on our side?

—Well, we need *someone* on our side.

—Perhaps.

—That's it? One snide remark about Iceland? No expression of remorse, no apology, not one word about the people you killed?

—Could I erase 312 deaths with a few heartfelt words? . . . Then, no, I do not see the point.

—It might make you at least appear like a human being. In any case, you're probably the only person on the planet who doesn't want to talk about it.

There's pretty much nothing else on television anywhere in the world. Strangely, most channels are going the human-interest route.

—Why is that so strange?

—Giant robot magically dematerializes everything for half a mile. I just thought . . .

—People will not understand that part. Crying mothers are accessible. I find it rather typical.

—Maybe you're right. Heartbreaking stories though, you should hear some of them.

Husband surprised his wife and three kids with tickets to Paris for their anniversary. There is a fourteen-year-old girl in Memphis who will die in the next few hours because the heart she needed was on the Dash 8 that vanished. Lots of twin stories, both twins on the plane, one twin on the plane. There was a young couple, coming home from Thailand, with the daughter they'd been waiting for . . .

—You can stop. What are they saying about the robot?

—Anything and everything. Speculations range from a giant Mayan statue to . . . well, to pretty much what it really is, but everyone is completely baffled by whatever made that hole. The best explanation they came up with so far is some amazingly fast cover-up on our part. The press is suggesting we somehow got rid of all the debris from a large explosion, in less than ten minutes.

Regardless, we're gonna have to come up with something. I'll meet with the president this afternoon and figure out the best course of action.

—That will not be necessary. The president already knows what he will do.

—What are you talking about?

—He and I met this morning and we are in agreement.

—How dare you talk to the president without speaking to me first! I tell you what he wants, not the other way around.

—You can take it up with him if you want. He was not, in any way, obligated to talk to me.

—I will. As soon as this meeting's over.

—That will not be possible, I am sorry to say. He is in New York, meeting with the Security Council. He will make a public announcement this afternoon.

—What's the cover story?

—There is no cover story. He is going to tell them exactly what they saw.

—You mean he's gonna tell the world that aliens left giant robot parts on Earth thousands of years ago, and that we've been secretly assembling them in an underground base, all in the hopes of keeping it to ourselves?

—He will probably want to reformulate the last part, but if you turn on CNN at 3:00 P.M., that is more or less what you will hear.

—He's completely lost his mind.

—He seemed coherent enough when I met him this morning.

—He's gonna sound like a goddamn lunatic!

—Seventy-two hours ago, a giant robotic figure, about twenty stories tall, was seen by just about every living soul on this planet after it created a half-mile-wide perfectly spherical crater, obliterating part of Denver International Airport. What would you suggest? Routine military exercise? Weather balloons? I should also point out that the leaders of several countries already know that we did not build it ourselves since we had to steal the pieces from them.

—He's going to end his political career.

—He is trying to prevent World War III.

—Do you really think the other governments are just gonna say: "Oh! It's an alien thing! Never mind, then. Carry on!"?

—They will have questions, I have no doubt. They will want reassurances. But they will also have to come to terms with the idea that we are not alone in the universe. The president is hoping that realization is enough to bring everyone to some sort of agreement.

—OK, so we tell the Russians, the Chinese, the French government. Why go the extra mile and tell the whole world? Don't you think the population might react, let's say, unfavorably to aliens and a giant government conspiracy to boot?

—I do not believe the election is foremost in his mind at this juncture.

—I wasn't suggesting he might lose votes. I was thinking of something more along the lines of mass hysteria.

—That will not happen. People have been sufficiently desensitized.

—What?

—Desensitized. Made less sensitive. People have seen too many alien movies to be completely shocked by their existence. You expose someone to something long enough and they become . . . desensitized.

—We're talking about the real McCoy here, not some guy in a rubber suit on television.

—It does not matter. You train your soldiers to kill using video games. They blow enough people up on their computer and it becomes easier for them to kill with a real weapon. Why do you think your government funds so many war and terrorism movies? Hollywood does your dirty work for you. Had 9/11 happened twenty years earlier, the country would have been in chaos, but people have seen enough bad things on their television screen to prepare them for just about anything. We do not really need to talk about government conspiracies.

—So what's he gonna do?

—My understanding is that he will offer a compromise.

—Are you willing to share that thing? If they can't have it, I don't think they'll let us keep it either.

—That is what I meant by a compromise.

—So we'll share it with them.

—Not exactly.

—Then what? We'll just get rid of it?

—Precisely.

—Seems a little stupid to violate every international treaty we signed, get a bunch of people killed, only to destroy the very thing we were trying to get. You'd be willing to do that?

—I would not.

—Didn't think so.

—In any event, I am not entirely certain that we could. Destroy it, I mean.

—So what then?

—My suggestion to the president was to drop it in the Puerto Rico Trench.

—Where is that?

—Near Puerto Rico . . .

—Very funny.

—It is the deepest part of the Atlantic, about five miles deep.

—Could we get it back?

—Not at the present. That is the idea.

—You mean we couldn't reach it if we wanted to?

—We probably could. There are deep-sea vehicles capable of reaching these depths. James Cameron went 6.8 miles deep in a one-man submarine.

—The filmmaker?

—Yes, but "one," "man," and "submarine" were the important words. These are very small crafts, incapable of bringing back up anything that massive, even in pieces. We could reach it, but we could not bring it back. It is a solution drastic enough to meet the demands of our current predicament, but it is not a permanent solution. Someday, soon, new technology will exist, and we can revisit the situation.

— . . .

—You are atypically silent, my dear Robert.

—You know what? I don't believe you. You had me for a moment, but you're not the type to give up on something so big so easily. No pun intended.

—Dr. Franklin is dead. Over three hundred people died in Denver, and we are on the brink of a global conflict. *Easily* is not the first word that comes to mind.

—See, I think you're an arrogant, self-absorbed son of a bitch, but you're also a cold, calculated son of a bitch. You're the kind of guy who has backup plans for his backup plans. I don't believe for a second that you'd walk into something that big without a plan B.

—That is enough compliments for one day. I do have a plan B. Drop the parts in the Puerto Rico Trench and fetch them back in a few years when we are able to.

—I forgot to mention, I don't think patience is one of your best qualities, but whatever you say. Obviously, you wouldn't tell me if you had a plan. What will you do with your team, what's left of it anyway?

—They will go back to their lives. Chief Resnik is already flying missions out of Lewis-McChord.

—Wasn't she grounded? Her file says she has a bad eye.

—You should take another look.

—You falsified her personnel file?

—I did no such thing. Everything that was in her file is still there. Someone may, however, have gone slightly overboard with the black marker while redacting it.

—How very nice of you. I didn't peg you as a romantic.

—I did not say that I did anything. I said "someone" may have. However, I find it more productive to keep my promises. We may need her in the future, and I would not want her holding a grudge.

—What about the French kid? I mean French Canadian . . . You know what I mean.

—Mr. Couture, unfortunately, is on his own.

—Not so romantic after all, I guess. After everything he did for you, you're gonna send him back home?

—It was his choice. I offered him counseling. I called in a few favors and found him employment at DARPA. He declined both. He is not in the best state of mind.

—You think? Where is he now?

—Probably over the Great Lakes. His flight left at ten o'clock this morning.

FILE NO. 229

INTERVIEW WITH CW4 KARA RESNIK, UNITED STATES ARMY

Location: Joint Base Lewis-McChord, Washington State

—How long has it been, Ms. Resnik?

—Since we last met, or since Dr. Franklin died?

—Would not the answer be the same?

—Pretty much. And I'm sure you know the answer better than I do.

—I meant to ask how long it had been since we last met. And I genuinely do not know. I would say six or seven months.

—Nine.

—I see you were promoted. I am happy for you.

—I'm not . . . I barely get to fly since I made CW4. I spend most of my time planning missions. It's funny, I never paid much attention to any of it before. I just went to mission briefings and I flew my bird. I never really thought about how long it took someone to work out all the tiny details of my five-hour flight. Well, now I know.

I swear my head will explode if I have to spend another minute staring at a map. They're all desert maps, too. I spend hours staring at gigantic beige pieces of paper, squinting to figure out if one little square is ten feet higher than the one next to it.

—I take it you did not ask for that promotion.

—God, no! They called me in one day and broke the news. They said I have good leadership skills. How does that make me fit to look at maps and weather reports?

—People often confuse leadership with managerial skills. I agree with their assessment. You certainly have the ability to inspire people. Minutiae, on the other hand, might not be your forte. That being said, even if you are not the most organized person in the world, it would be a shame not to let everyone benefit from your experience and wisdom.
　　Can I ask how Mr. Couture is doing?

—You tell me. Last time I heard from him, he'd just gotten back to Montreal. That was also nine months ago. He's either not taking my calls or he's gone somewhere else. I guess he could be anywhere by now.

—He is still in Montreal. I take it this is not the high point of your relationship.

—I should have known it wouldn't last.

—Your relationship?

—No, your asking questions you don't already know the answer to. I thought something bad might have happened to him. It's nice to know he just doesn't want to talk to me. What's he doing now?

—That is a lot of cynicism to fit into just three sentences.

—I don't know what to tell you. He just left. After her death . . . It's all he could think about. It just ripped apart whatever was holding him together.

—I spoke to both of you after the incident. Unless you hid something important from me, it seems clear that neither of you are to blame for what happened.

—We didn't keep anything from you. But none of it would have happened if we'd listened to Dr. Franklin. Vincent chose not to. It's his legs that gave up, his hands that pushed those buttons. I know I'm as responsible as he is, maybe more. I was trained to listen to others. But I can't blame him for thinking he killed her. He did. I killed her too.

—Everyone knew there were risks involved, especially Dr. Franklin.

—It's one thing to risk your own life. It's fairly easy to rationalize the deaths of strangers. To shoulder the death of a friend, someone you know, that's a completely different thing.

—I would venture with some measure of certainty that she would not want either of you to blame yourself for her death.

—I know she wouldn't. There wasn't a mean bone in her body. Somehow, it doesn't make me feel any better about what happened. At least I know what to expect. I lost people that were close to me before. I lost family, I lost people on missions. I know how long I'll feel like this, I know what I'll be feeling later. Denial, grief, resentment. We're predictable little creatures. But I'm worried about Vincent. He doesn't know what's coming. I'd like to know how he's doing.

—I am not worried for his life, if that is what you are asking. He is . . . You are right. He is devastated by the passing of Dr. Franklin. That much is obvious. However, you can find some comfort in the fact that it is that obvious. He has no problems expressing his feeling of loss, his guilt, his anger over what happened. His emotions are well-defined, and he is coherent in expressing them. In time, he will come back.

—I'm not so sure. What does he do now?

—I am not certain he has a source of income. He was making model ships when I visited.

—Ships? Like . . . toys?

—Scaled model ships from World War II. I am not an expert, but some seemed quite elaborate.

— ˙. . .

—Some of them must have close to a thousand pieces. Building them requires a certain set of skills, a lot of patience, and attention to details.

— . . .

—Yes. You could call them toys.

—And that's all he does?

—For most of the day, yes. I realize it does not sound extremely encouraging, but it gives him something to focus on. I would rather see him work on a 1/200 scale USS *Arizona* than lie in bed all day.

—Does he eat? Does he bathe?

—I believe so. Although shaving seems to have made way for other, more important tasks in his daily routine. We keep talking about Mr. Couture but it is you I came to see. How do you feel?

—I feel . . . numb.

—What do you mean?

—After something this intense, everything else just . . . Things that would have had you up in arms before now seem so utterly trivial. Nothing really matters. You start to ignore little things, because they're little things. You compromise. You rationalize. Soon you look at yourself in the mirror and you don't recognize the person staring back at you.

But, you know. I'm alive. I'm OK. I wake up every day, and I get out of bed thinking today might be just a bit better than yesterday. Most of the time it is. Show must go on, as they say.

—Do you have any vacation time coming?

—I don't think a vacation is really what I need right now.

—I was not making conversation. I am inquiring as to whether or not you could take a short leave of absence, not about your predispositions.

—I don't know. Wasn't I just on extended leave for about two years? I never really thought about asking for more since I came back.

—Would it surprise you to know that you have accrued 22.5 days of leave since your reassignment at Fort Carson?

—I forgot who I was talking to. I suppose in a minute you'll tell me that I've already put in for some leave.

—You have. But I want you to feel perfectly comfortable, should you wish to reconsider.

—I'm free to reconsider taking the leave of absence I never asked for . . . Typical . . . I should have known you didn't come here just to see how I was doing.

—I did. I came here specifically to see how you were doing, and to ask for your help if you appeared capable.

—What is it you want me to do?

—I want you to locate someone for me.

—Can't you get any of your Special Forces friends to do it?

—The military are not involved in this operation. In fact, it is critical that no one working for the US government be involved in any way.

—Except for me . . .

—Except for you.

—So, where am I taking this much-needed vacation?

—Sarajevo.

—Really? This better be good.

—You will absolutely love Sarajevo. It is one of my favorite places in the world. By the time you leave, you will wish you did not have to.

—And what am I doing in lovely Bosnia?

—You should try and visit Mostar if time permits. But, aside from ancient cities and the usual tourist attractions, you are attending the Sarajevo Film Festival.

—Of course. I wouldn't miss it for the world.

—You will catch the premiere of *Oprosti mi, Mina*. It is a very small film by a young Serb cineaste named Goran Lukić. He is someone I know and trust. He will be your guide in Bosnia.

—What does *Oprosti Mina* mean?

—*Oprosti mi, Mina. Mina* is a name. *Oprosti mi* means "forgive me."

—Sounds like a nice guy . . .

—Goran is actually one of the kindest, most selfless people I have ever met.

—Coming from you, I'm not really sure what that means. When will he be expecting me?

—He will not be expecting anyone. He will, however, host a small party at Zlatna Ribica after the premiere. You will make an appearance and congratulate him on his movie. When no one else is around, you will remind him that he never paid for the plumber in Belgrade.

—What's that? Some sort of code?

—No, not a code. More like a subtle metaphor.

—Why don't you just contact him yourself? You seem to like him. He might enjoy talking to you again.

—I assure you he would not.

—How do you know him?

—I assisted in his interrogation during the war.

—You mean you helped torture him.

—It is, as most things are, a matter of personal and historical perspective. In CIA parlance, we were given an "alternative set of procedures." Suffice it to say that, however unpleasant the experience might have been, he is indebted to me.

You will procure some inconspicuous clothing and ask him to take you to Srebrenica. It is a small mountain town at the east end of Bosnia.

—Why does that ring a bell?

—Thousands of Bosnian Muslims were rounded up and slaughtered there in the mid-nineties. Once you reach Srebrenica, you will try and find a woman called Fata.

—Fata who?

—I do not know her last name. Nor do I know where she lives. I can tell you that she had three sons and one daughter. Her oldest son worked in the salt mines of Srebrenica with her husband. They might have come into town for work every day from one of the surrounding villages.

—Really? That's all you have? Do you know which village she might have come from?

—I do not have that information. Unfortunately, the Serbs also destroyed hundreds of villages during the war. Hers may no longer exist. She would be in her early fifties by now. I know she was well liked by everyone, and that she might have served as some sort of informal nurse.

—How will I know I found the right person? Unless I'm mistaken, Fata's short for Fatima. I'm gonna take a wild guess and say that's probably not the most unique name for a Muslim woman. Sounds a lot like: "Hey! Go find John in New York."

—You will know when you find her. Talk about the war. She will have stories to tell.

—How long do I have?

—You requested two weeks of vacation.

—When?

—The premiere is on the fifth. You leave Saturday.

—And let's assume I find this Fata of yours. What do I need her to do?

—Nothing. She needs to do nothing. I only need to know where to find her. I may need her in the future.

—For what?

—Nothing you should concern yourself with. Hopefully, it will never come to that, and you will have a worthwhile experience visiting the remote corners of Bosnia. Now, if you will excuse me, I have to be on a plane in one hour.

—Sir?

—What is it?

—Thank you.

FILE NO. 230

INTERVIEW WITH UNKNOWN SUBJECT
Location: New Dynasty Chinese Restaurant, Dupont Circle, Washington, DC

—Begin recording. It is almost noon. I am waiting for the man who contacted me this morning on a classified number. I am sitting by the window. There is a sniper across the street with a clear view of my table.

There is a short, stocky, old man entering the restaurant. He appears to be in his sixties or early seventies. He is wearing a tan trench coat, about two sizes too small, and a brim hat. He . . . He has no eyebrows . . . I sincerely hope he is not the man I am waiting for . . . Unfortunately, he is now approaching my table with a large smile on his face.

—Hello, sir! I'm so happy to finally meet you! I've heard so much about you.

—I seriously hope not, for your sake. Please be aware that this conversation is being recorded.

—I'm now perfectly aware. Thank you! Do you know who I am?

—I have absolutely no idea who you are, and I do not particularly care to find out. I want to hear what you know about *me*, who gave you that information, and what you intend to do with it.

—Oh . . . You're upset because I mentioned your son on the phone. I didn't mean to stir up bad memories. As I said, you have my deepest sympathies. I can't tell you how I know what I know, but you can trust me when I say you have nothing to fear from me. Your secret is perfectly safe.

—Listen to me very carefully for I will only say this once. If you value your life in any way, you will not mention my son to me, or to anyone else, ever again. You will tell me exactly what you know, and if I am satisfied with your answer, you will be allowed to leave this place unharmed.

—That's a bit rude, don't you think? What's the signal?

—What signal?

—The one for the sniper across the street?

— . . .

—It's OK, you can show me. He's sound asleep. By the way, get the man some food next time! Poor fellow would have had to watch us eat for an hour.

So . . . Let's start this again, shall we? Would you care to guess who I am?

—I would not.

—Please! Take a guess!

—You are a retired clown who lost his eyebrows in a tragic fire-juggling accident.

—OK. No guessing then. You can call me Mr. Burns.

—That is a horrible alias.

—It's my last name, thank you very much.

—What do you want?

—I'm here because we have a friend in common. You should try the Kung Pao chicken.

—Thank you, I am still looking at the menu. And who might that friend be?

—I don't believe you know her name. But she's a very special friend. Someone who had a very, very large place in your heart. Someone whom I understand you recently lost touch with.

— . . . I am listening.

—Ah! Finally! Now that I have your attention, it's *your* turn to listen very carefully to what I'm about to say . . .

Put the menu down and get the Kung Pao chicken. The Indonesian rice is also very good, but you have to try the chicken.

—I should warn you that I have little or no sense of humor, and very little patience.

—Don't be modest! You have a great sense of humor! You're a little phlegmatic, I agree, but it's there . . . I see it. OK, you look like you get grumpy when you're hungry so I'll just move right along.

Do you like stories? I hope you do. I'm going to tell you a story that I was told as a child. It has a bit of everything: love, war, betrayal. I'm sure you'll like it.

A very long time ago, there was a vast empire. I mean vast—it literally spanned thousands of colonies. It was ruled by extremely powerful people. They believed that each colony should evolve at its own pace and be free to rule itself. They would intervene as little as they could, only to preserve life or defend the interests of the empire. They were a very wise people, a race of artists and engineers that had an unmatched understanding of the makeup of the universe. They were able to build just about anything, to manipulate matter, and harness energy in ways that no one else could.

One of the colonies was ruled by a warrior race. What they lacked in sophistication and intelligence, they made up for with strength and grit. Their king, a legendary warrior, ruled over millions. Having mined most of the ore in his own land, he tried to conquer a neighboring people to exploit their natural resources. The empire sent several ships to intervene. The warrior king was captured, tried, and sentenced to a life of imprisonment.

Over time he was allowed to leave his gaol, and eventually he was permitted to live freely in the empire's metropolis, but he could never return home to his people. In the capital, he worked as a . . . there is no word for it—personal trainer is the closest thing I can think of, but that sounds silly. Anyway, this is how he met—Can you guess? Can you guess? A princess! The daughter of the Emperor himself.

He trained the princess for a few hours every day. Of course, it didn't take them long to fall for each other. They kept their relationship a secret for a while, but when the princess reached the age of marriage, she introduced the warrior king to her father. Let's just say that he did not approve. The fallen king was sent back to prison.

The princess was forbidden to see him but—you know, teenagers— she did. She did a lot more than that, actually. One night, she set a fire to lure the guards away and helped her lover escape. The warrior king wanted to run away, but the princess was stubborn as a mule and didn't want to leave her whole life and family behind. So instead of doing the sensible thing, she brought her lover to the palace to confront her father. Seems hard to imagine that he went along with that, but, like I said, his people were not known for their intelligence. And let's face it: We all do stupid things when it comes to women.

So, confront him she did. What started as a discussion soon turned into an argument. Words were exchanged, tempers were flaring. The Emperor's people are known for their calm demeanor, but family has a way of bringing out the worst in people. Every people.

The Emperor raised his hand to strike his daughter and the warrior king quickly got between them. The Emperor had never fought anyone, never yielded a sword, had never done any manual labor, so to say that he was overmatched would be an understatement. Within seconds, the Emperor was on his back with a sword to his throat. It was only the princess screaming for him to show mercy that stopped the warrior king from plunging his blade into the Emperor's heart. The royal guard eventually came in and the two lovers were arrested.

The Emperor was deeply wounded by his daughter's betrayal. He would never really be the same after that. But no matter how deep his sorrow, he could never bring himself to kill his own flesh and blood. Instead, his daughter would spend the rest of her life in the very cell her lover was jailed in.

He had a different fate in mind for the warrior king. Since he had spared his life in the palace, the Emperor would return the favor. Banishment would be his sentence, but not just for him—for his people as well. Massive ships were built in industrial colonies and the warrior king's entire people—tens of millions—were sent away, never to return.

—I am assuming there will be a point to this fable sometime in the near future.

—There will indeed, but the best part is the story. You should try to enjoy it.

The Emperor was no fool. He knew that he had just made a powerful enemy. It might be years, decades, centuries even, but someday these people would seek vengeance for their exile. This was not something one would forget. They would pass on the hatred from generation to generation until the day their honor was restored.

Preparing for an inevitable war, the Emperor had giant machines built in his people's image. Indestructible weapons so powerful they could level a village or kill ten thousand men in a matter of seconds. Thousands of these giants were built and sent to every corner of the empire.

There was one small colony at the far end of the realm. It was still in the early stages of its evolution and had received little attention from the empire in the past, but the Emperor insisted that they be protected as well. Twelve weapons were sent to the colony, along with a small detachment of soldiers to operate them. Six of them were built to resemble males, six were female. Technology was nearly nonexistent on the colony, and these giant machines that walked amongst men were instantly seen as gods and goddesses. They called them *tittah*.

Years passed, centuries went by, but the war never came. After more than two thousand years, the machines were removed from the colony. One was left behind, a female-looking giant the people called *dhehméys*. She was dismantled, and her parts were scattered across the colony. It was hoped that when the people had reached a certain stage in their evolution, they would rediscover the machine and use it to defend themselves should the war ever come.

—What of the soldiers that were sent with it?

—Excellent question. I see you're paying attention. They had a life expectancy about three times that of the colony's inhabitants, but this was still a multigenerational mission. When the machines were called back, the direct descendants of the soldiers, those whose blood was pure, were sent home as well. But over the centuries, some of the male soldiers had chosen women from the colony as spouses and eventually began to have children.

These "half-breeds," as they called them, were anatomically similar to the indigenous population but had the superior intellectual and physical abilities of their alien parent. They were left behind when the soldiers left. They assimilated with the colony's inhabitants. Because of their abilities and more advanced knowledge of science, many of them, and many of their descendants, rose to positions of power or fame.

—There were giants in the earth in those days; and also after that, when the sons of God came in unto the daughters of men, and they bore children to them, the same became mighty men which were of old, men of renown.

—So you know this story already?

—This is from the Bible. Genesis 6:4.

—Like I said, it's a good story. Many people have told it.

—How much of it is true?

—Maybe all of it. Maybe none of it is true. You have to decide for yourself. Stories are there to entertain, preserve history, or serve a societal purpose of some kind. I think this one does a bit of everything.

—You are one of them, are you not? You are one of their descendants.

—I'm just an old man who likes to tell stories.

—Can you help us? Can you help us control her?

—I can do no such thing. Even if I knew what you were talking about.

—Then why tell us? Why come to me?

—How about another story? I'm afraid this one does not have such a happy ending.

—By all means.

—Here we go. There was a man who lived in a small cabin in the woods with his two teenage boys. It was the middle of winter and there was a humongous storm coming. Soon, all the roads would be closed and they would be completely cut off from civilization . . .

—I am listening.

—I'm sorry. This sounds a little macabre already, and I haven't even mentioned the shotgun. Let's lighten things up a bit, shall we? I know you liked the other story, so let's make the man a king in this one as well. He was a powerful king in medieval times, a formidable warrior who inspired fear and respect. He was believed to have a magic sword that made him immortal and impossible to defeat. None of it was true, of course, he was just really good with a sword.

The king had two children, both teenage boys. One day, the king was asked to settle a dispute in a faraway village. His sons wanted to go with him, but the king feared there might be battle along the way.

When the sons argued that their enemies might see the king's absence as an opportunity to attack, he devised a plan to ensure everyone's safety. He would leave his sword with his children and spread the word across the realm. His enemies would think the sons as invincible as the father if they brandished the legendary blade.

The king went on his business and, upon his return, found his entire castle in mourning. An argument had arisen between the two brothers about which of them was the better warrior, and more worthy of yielding their father's sword. In their dispute, the oldest son struck his little brother with the blade. The cadet did not survive his injuries, but he did live long enough to see his father one last time. After holding his son through his last breaths, the king took the sword and threw it into the sea so that no one would ever have to suffer its curse.

That's it! That's how it ends.

—You will forgive me for asking what may seem obvious, but I prefer to deal in certainties. What was the moral of this story?

—Oh, I don't think there's a moral, nothing that deep. If you left a weapon with someone so they could defend themselves, and you found out they were killing each other with it, you'd probably want to take it back or get rid of it. It's just common sense, really. But then again, maybe I missed the point entirely. Maybe it's about something else.

Ahhh! Here's our waitress! I'm starving.

[Good evening gentlemen. Are you ready to order?]

—Oh yes, we're famished! I'll let my friend here order first.

—I will have the Kung Pao chicken.

—You're a wise man.

FILE NO. 233

INTERVIEW WITH INES TABIB, ASSISTANT TO THE PRESIDENT FOR NATIONAL SECURITY AFFAIRS

Location: White House, Washington, DC

—Thank you for seeing me, Ms. Tabib.

—I'm the one who called, so thank *you*. It's a pleasure to finally meet you. I hope you have no reservations about a woman's taking over this job.

—To which aspect of the situation are you referring? Do I have reservations about women working in general? About women holding positions of power? About women making decisions about sending men, or other women, to their deaths?

—I . . .

—My answer would be the same to all three questions: a resounding no. And if I had such reservations, I would probably be more focused on the fact that a woman is now the Commander in Chief of the United States Armed Forces than on the gender of her advisors. Speaking of the president, how is she?

—She's good. Still settling in. She wanted to thank you in person, but it'll have to wait a bit.

—**Thank me?**

—We had a good campaign, but it's no secret that we have your project to thank for such a landslide. You changed the world, starting with the president.

—**I did nothing of the sort. The former president could have handled things differently. He made his own bed.**

—That sounds an awful lot like: "Good for him! He got what he deserved." Would you have handled things differently?

—**I am not, was not, and will never be president of the United States. It does not really matter what I would have or would not have done in his place.**

—Fine. Don't tell me. I can tell you what I would have done differently. I wouldn't have hidden that . . . How do you call the alien device? Is it a "she" or an "it"?

—**To the people involved, it is "she."**

—Well, I wouldn't have hidden her. I would have parked her in front of the White House for everyone to see.

—**Your predecessor was concerned that other governments would react unfavorably to a show of strength.**

—I know. It never made sense to me. He would have had to take her out at some point, wouldn't he? Anyway, she's out now. I don't think there's a single person on the planet that hasn't heard about it. It's really a game changer, you know. The ramifications are just . . . endless.

—**I wish you were right. Unfortunately, I believe people will soon go back about their business as if nothing ever happened.**

—That's a little cynical, don't you think? Of course, people will more or less keep doing what they were doing. Aliens or not, they need to work, eat, sleep, send the children to school, take out the garbage. Most of their day's never gonna change, no matter what. I suppose that's why people are disenchanted with politics. They expect whoever they elect to change their lives. Anyway, that's not what matters.

Right now, all over the Earth, there are little children staring up at the stars, wondering if whoever built that robot is from there, or there, or there. They might grow up to be astronauts, engineers, anything that discovery inspires them to be. Twenty years from now, one of these kids might build a new kind of engine that allows us to travel outside our solar system, all because he saw that robot as a child.

Every major religion has to adjust to this revelation. Whatever god you believe in can't just be about humans anymore. He, or she, has to be a god for the whole universe. Heaven, Hell, Nirvana, whatever, all these things have to be rethought, reshaped. Fundamentalists are simply denying the whole thing ever happened, but for everyone else, the world is a different place than it was before that crater in Denver.

Even the president has to tweak her speeches to acknowledge the fact that there are other sentient life-forms in the universe. You'd be surprised how hard it is to fit God and aliens in the same sentence without sounding corny.

Most importantly, everyone, including world leaders, now knows there are beings out there capable of building formidable weapons so advanced that we probably would not stand a chance if they chose to attack us.

—They would eradicate us. They could probably do it from a distance.

—Exactly. It's a reality check for everyone, and it makes all our territorial or trade disputes seem just a little pettier. It wasn't a cataclysm, like an asteroid hitting the Earth or anything like that, but it was a traumatic moment, and traumatic moments have a way of bringing people together. I think this is changing the way we view ourselves. That change may be slow and imperceptible, but it's happening, I guarantee it.

—I sincerely hope you are correct. My deepest wish is for this discovery to redefine alterity for all of us.

—Alterity?

—The concept of "otherness." What I am is very much a function of what I am not. If the "other" is the Muslim world, then I am the Judeo-Christian world. If the other is from thousands of light-years away, I am simply human. Redefine alterity and you can erase boundaries.

—See, I knew you weren't that cynical. While you're here, the president wanted me to touch base with you, see what you thought a good timeline would be to get her back.

—When I told your predecessor it was not a permanent solution, I did not mean we could get it back whenever we wanted. It has only been four months.

—I know. I know. It's just . . . There's a lot happening right now. The president just wants to know what her options are.

—I am aware of no significant technological development in the last three months, none that pertain to our deep-sea-retrieval capabilities anyway. You can tell the president her options are exactly what they were yesterday, or four months ago, or before we ever heard of that giant hand in South Dakota.

—I told her you'd say that . . . Are you sure there's nothing we can do?

—Yes.

—Yes?

—Yes. I am sure there is nothing we can do.

—How about this: Are you sure there's nothing anyone else can do to get it back? Having lost the robot is one thing, but I'd hate to see her show up on television with a Chinese flag painted on her chest.

—Like I said, I am unaware of any such scientific or technological development. I would be surprised if the Chinese, or anyone else, had made any significant progress in that area without anyone else knowing about it. That being said, it is not entirely out of the realm of possibilities.

—How would you go about making sure someone else doesn't get it out first?

—You cannot stop anyone from grabbing it if you cannot reach that depth yourself. I would strongly suggest multiplying federal funding for research in deep-sea exploration by, shall we say, a thousandfold, if you have not already. I am absolutely certain other governments have done so before the first piece ever hit the bottom of the ocean.

—You make it sound like this is a race.

—I do. It is.

—So, you're saying this is the space race all over again. We're racing with the Russians, and God knows who else, to the far depths of the Earth, and whoever gets there first wins it all. Is that the gist of it?

—Unless you find a way to turn enemy into ally, that sums it up quite well.

—Are you suggesting we work with Russia on this thing?

—I cannot tell you if you should, only that you could. Most people forgot, but in 1963 Kennedy did offer to cooperate with Moscow to reach the moon. Had he not met with such an untimely death, the first lunar landing might have been a joint venture between the United States and the USSR.

—Somehow, I don't see that happening.

—I suppose that is what you meant by "slow and imperceptible change." Is there anything else I can help you with? I am on a fairly tight schedule.

—No. I guess not. Not unless you can get North Korea to shut down their nuclear program.

—What have they done this time?

—Third underground test this year. Only, this one looks like the real thing. In the past, they would just blow up a whole lot of explosives underground to make us think they had nukes. This time's different. Japan has detected radiation at the site.

　　With anyone else, we'd play the strength card and threaten to level the entire country . . . but they don't really seem to care. I'm not sure where that leaves us.

—A preemptive strike?

—As far as the president is concerned, that's what you call an "act of war" if you're the one making it.

—Then I am afraid I have nothing to offer. It pains me to say it, but I have always been thoroughly bewildered by North Korea. They cannot be threatened, as they feel themselves superior to the one making the threat. They cannot be reasoned with, and most importantly, they are 100 percent convinced of their righteousness, so they cannot be bought. Megalomaniacs with delusions of grandeur are notoriously difficult to handle, but how generations of them can follow one another is beyond me.

— . . . I'm sorry, my mind was drifting. I was thinking about racing the Russians to the trench. It's gonna be hard to make a good speech out of that. We choose to go to the . . . ocean. We choose to go to the bottom of the ocean in this decade and do the other things . . .

—Maybe you should leave the speechwriting to others.

FILE NO. 237

INTERVIEW WITH VINCENT COUTURE, UNEMPLOYED

Location: La Fontaine Park, Montreal, Canada

—Please sit down, Mr. Couture.

—We could have gone to my place. It's cold for a picnic.

—I have tried my best to hide the identity of everyone involved in our project, but after the incident I prefer to discuss this in a public location.

—You're worried someone bugged my apartment?

—I cannot discard the possibility. Besides, this park is lovely in the fall. Did you receive my message? .

—I'm not sure I'd call that a message, but yeah, I received the two words you sent me. It's pretty cool.

—Define *cool*.

—Cool is that at some point there might have been more of these giant robots on Earth, eleven more to be precise.

—How . . .

—How would I know? Well, the first word you sent, *tittah,* means "big" in Hattic. Hattic was spoken about five thousand years ago in Anatolia, that's more or less Turkey today. That word was borrowed by the folks living west of there, and in Greek you end up with the word *Titan.*

In Greek mythology, the Titans are children of Gaia and Uranus. That's also cool. Do you get it? They're children of the Earth and the Sky. They must have known where they came from, somehow.

There are twelve of them, six males and six females. I don't know all their names by heart, but I know which one we found. The other word you sent, *dhehméys,* looks a whole lot like what we call Proto-Indo-European, which we believe was spoken right around there at the time. If it is PIE, then that "d" will eventually turn into a "t," and by the time you get to Ancient Greek, you end up with Themis, one of the Titans.

—I am not familiar with the name.

—You've seen her a thousand times. She's blindfolded holding a scale in one hand and a sword in the other.

—Is that who we call Lady Justice?

—More or less. The statues in front of courthouses are fairly modern. They're usually a mixture of Themis and Iustitia, the Roman equivalent. What's the saying? Justice is blind. Well, now we know why; she doesn't have eyes.

I don't think *justice* is the right word, though. She represents something bigger, something like divine law. That's probably what *dhehméys* meant five thousand years ago already. I'm pretty sure that *dharma* in Sanskrit is from the same word, and it means cosmic order, what keeps the universe together. Her daughter, Dikē, is the Greek goddess of Justice.

—She had a daughter?

—Well, obviously, she doesn't have a "real" daughter. I don't think there's a minirobot buried somewhere either. Some mythology has got to be just that, mythology.

Can you imagine though? A dozen of these things walking around, all lit up in turquoise. Then again, maybe they glow in different colors. They didn't even have iron tools back then, let alone electricity. I wish I could go back in time just to see that for myself. One of these things is jaw-dropping today. Twelve of them, at a time when technology was more or less nonexistent? That would have been like coming face-to-face with gods.

I'd like to know why this one was left on Earth while all the other ones went back to wherever they came from.

—**What makes you think they went anywhere?**

—We pretty much searched the entire planet and we only found parts of this one. If there were eleven more spread around, surely we'd have a couple spare parts, extra hands, another foot, lying in a warehouse somewhere.

Are you gonna tell me what you know or do I have to guess everything?

—**I may not know anything.**

—Of course not. You just stumbled upon the words *tittah* and *dhehméys* while doing crosswords, and you called me for clues so you could finish the grid. What's a seven-letter word for "full of it"?

—**Caution.**

—At some point, you're gonna have to trust *someone*. If anything, you could get hit by a milk truck tomorrow and there'd be no one left who knows any of whatever it is you keep to yourself.

—**You do realize I am essentially a spectator in all of this. I do not come from outer space. I did not build a giant robot. I did not even play any significant part in finding it or understanding how it works.**

You can therefore assume that 100 percent of the knowledge that I possess was handed to me by other people. If anything were to happen to me, there would be someone left who knows what I know, a lot of someones. I trust that, in the event of my demise, the right information would find its way to the people who need it, as it found its way to me.

—Sure, but why not save us all a lot of time and tell us, so we can, you know, help a little!

—You are helping, tremendously. And part of the reason you are able to contribute so significantly to this project is that you are not burdened by unnecessary knowledge. Some of it might help you, I agree, but some of it would also narrow your options, steer your thoughts in one particular direction, prevent you from seeing all there is to see. Since I cannot know which information would hinder your thought processes, I find it best to provide you only with what you really need to know.

—Really? All this time I thought you were just the biggest micromanager the Earth had ever known. I never realized you were doing all of this for me. How can I ever thank you enough?

—You should leave the sarcasm to Ms. Resnik. She is infinitely better at it than you are. Are you ready to go back to work?

—What work? I've done two things so far, decipher some alien symbols on panels I accidentally dematerialized, and learn to pilot a robot you sent to the bottom of the ocean. As far as I can tell, there's nothing left for me to do.

—That was not my question. I was asking whether you felt ready or not.

—To do what?

—Anything. I am asking whether you feel ready to do anything.

—I don't understand.

—Unless there are aspects of your life I was not made aware of, all you have accomplished in the last five months is to grow a beard and build models of World War II naval ships. While those ships are admittedly highly detailed, and do testify to your patience and dexterity, they offer little in the way of reassuring anyone about your mental stability.

—I . . . I don't know what to say . . . I'm stable . . . mentally, and I can do . . . things, that you won't tell me about.

—What is the current state of your relationship with Ms. Resnik?

—My . . . I haven't spoken to her in quite some time.

—Precisely. How can you pretend to be strong enough to resume work if you cannot even pick up the phone and call a woman you obviously care for very deeply?

—I wanted to wait until I was sure.

—Sure of what?

—I'm almost there. I will call her soon, I promise. I wanted to wait until I was sure.

— . . .

—Until I was sure I'd never fall again.

— . . .

—I don't know how else to explain it. I wake up every morning hearing Rose screaming for me to stop. People keep telling me that it'll pass, that there'll come a day when I don't have to watch her die over and over again in my dreams. I don't think that day will come, but I've learned to live with it.

I mean, of course, I wish I could only remember the good parts. She gave me her trust, her friendship, and she opened the doors to a world I would never have dreamed of. I'll be in her debt until it's my turn to die. I wish I could only see that, but I can't. So, if waking up screaming every morning is part of remembering her, I'm fine with that.

I can't bring her back. It's too late for me to listen to her, and I can't promise I'll always do what anyone else asks me to do, but I swear to you, I swear on my life, I will never fall again. I will never let anything happen to someone I love because I wasn't strong enough, starting with Kara. That's why I'm waiting to call her.

—I do not question your resolve, I never have, but you cannot guarantee that your knees will not simply give again, as they did the last time.

—I climb stairs.

—What?

—I climb stairs with my knees in reverse.

—Perhaps there *are* aspects of your life I was not made aware of. Please go on.

—At night, in my apartment building. I set my alarm for 2:00 A.M., and I go up and down the back stairs. I go up four floors, then down, then up again, until I can't move anymore.

—How often do you do that?

—Every night since I came back here. My legs are too tired to work out during the day, so I drink protein shakes and work on my concentration. I build model ships while I do multiples in my head using alien math. It's a bit unorthodox, I know, and I'm sorry if it's not up to everyone's standards, but it's the closest thing I could find to working the console. So I don't know what you're really asking me to do, but if you're thinking of getting the band back together, I'm ready. I'm ten times more ready than I was the last time I set foot in the sphere.

—Getting the band back together might not be that easy.

— . . . I'm sorry. I'm not laughing at you. It's just, what you said, it's a quote from Jake in that movie, *The Blues Brothers*.

—I was citing you, from a moment ago . . .

—I know. I'm sorry. I didn't mean to . . .

— . . . and that line is from Elwood, not Jake. Congratulations.

—What did I do?

—You have convinced me that you are fit for duty. All you need to do now is to convince Ms. Resnik.

FILE NO. 239

INTERVIEW WITH ALYSSA PAPANTONIOU, CHIEF EXECUTIVE OFFICER AND CHIEF SCIENCE OFFICER, BVI COMPANY NUMBER 462753 INC.

Location: Undisclosed location, near San Juan, Puerto Rico

—Alas, Ms. Papantoniou, we meet again.

— Yes, it must be hard for you.

—Why would you say that? I was sorry to see you go.

— You had me de . . . deported.

—Yes. I meant afterward. I had underestimated your contribution to the team. I believe you lack the social skills and empathy that are necessary to lead people, but I realize that you are a uniquely talented individual and that we can greatly benefit from your presence.

—And now the board has ch . . . chosen me. I'm in charge this time.

—Indeed they have. You must have made quite an impression with the Russian government. I am curious, however, as to what you really offered them since you knew nothing of this facility. You must have convinced them that you could find a way to activate the controls for their pilots, were they able to retrieve the pieces from the bottom of the trench on their own. I am fairly certain the United States would not look kindly on your proposal to the Russians.

—I don't think they would look kindly on your setting up this consortium either.

—Exactly. As you can see, we have a lot in common. We are both deeply committed to this project, enough so that we must often choose between what is ethical, honorable, and what is important. I hope this shared commitment can serve as the foundation of our renewed relationship. I hope we can have a . . . fresh start.

—They dragged me out of my home . . . like a cri . . . criminal!

—They thought you were. But, as I said, water under the bridge. You do realize we have to find a way to work together? I am honestly willing to try if you are.

—I've always been professional. You're the one who made things pers . . . p . . .

—Personal. I would describe my actions as . . . decisive. I thought that was a quality you admired in others. Believe me, when I make things personal, it will leave no room for interpretation. So. Shall we begin? How is the construction progressing?

— . . .

—I will not leave before you talk to me. If you care for this project as much as you claim to, you will not let a . . . temporary relocation get in the way of its success.

—We're ahead of schedule by almost a month. Cons . . . Construction of the lab is almost complete, and we're laying track much faster than we thought possible. You should get the pilots here now.

—It was my understanding that you would not be ready for training until Christmas. Even with the good news you just presented me with, I fail to see what the pilots could possibly do here now.

—Nothing. They'd have nothing to do. They could go to the b . . . beach, have a few drinks, have some fun. Let the resentment dissipate slowly for a few weeks.

—Do you believe they resent me for ending the program?

—No, I don't think so. But they'll certainly resent *me*. They'll be useless to me for at least a . . . at least a month. They didn't like me before, but they'll ha . . . hate me now.

—This line of thinking seems somewhat irrational to me. You have spent only a short time with them. They do not know you well enough to hate you.

—Irrational's the ri . . . right word. They won't know why, but they'll resent me for not being her. They'll resent me just for . . . for being alive.

—Dr. Franklin?

—Yes. They probably won't realize it, but the thought of anyone but Dr. . . . anyone but her being in charge will make their stomachs turn. They'll hate me for not being exactly like her, and they'll hate me when I remind them of her. They'll hate me for making them relive her d . . . death over and over. Trust me, they'll hate me. So I'm asking you to get them here now, give them a chance to get over it. I can't do my job if they want me dead, even if it is sub . . . consciously.

—I will see what can be done. They might need some time to work out their own differences. Let us leave these psychological concerns aside for a moment and go back to the work you have accomplished. You said that construction of the lab was almost complete. Will it be as large as the room we used in Denver?

—Almost. It's about forty feet smaller lengthwise. The ground was more unstable toward the ocean than what the . . . geological surveys had shown. Don't worry—there'll still be enough room for it to move around, but you wouldn't want the roof to collapse. It's a lot . . . deeper than Denver. There'll be millions of tons of rock and water above our heads.

—How many men do you have laying tracks?

—Zero. I didn't like the security risk to begin with, people can't keep a secret. Divers could only have done the first few hundred feet anyway. Our German friends managed to build the train so it can lay its own track. It's more of a shaft, really. A good portion of the path is on a near-vertical slope, so the weight doesn't push on the track like a regular train. What we built looks like a steel I-beam with a series of holes in the middle. The train drive has geared wheels on both sides of the beam to move along the shaft.

It's a nice piece of engineering. It goes to the end of the path, lays a new section of the track, and comes back to get the n . . . next one. When we started, it would come back every couple hours or so, now it's gone for almost a day at a time. It's really slow, but it's . . . steady.

—How will you collect the pieces once you reach the target area?

—We have an unmanned submarine with a robotic arm. When we get to the bottom of the trench, we'll attach . . . buoys to the pieces to reduce the weight, and we'll hoist them on the train platform with cables. Then we bring the pieces in . . . one by one.

—Is the train powerful enough to pull the pieces out of the trench?

—No, it's not. With enough buoys, it could probably handle the smaller pieces on its own, the hands or the feet, but not the thighs or torso. When it's done laying track, we'll put a cable on the train and help it up. We have a winch the size of a four-story building.

I . . . I know you're keeping things from me, and there's probably a good reason for that, but I'm assuming you wouldn't k . . . keep this to yourself. Why is it taking so long to find the propulsion system? You found the rest of the pieces in a relatively short period, and you must have covered most of the Earth's surface by now.

—We have not found the propulsion system, as you call it, because we have not been searching for one. In fact, all search efforts were abandoned once we recovered the head. What makes you think there is such a thing?

—Well, I'm sure there's a lot I don't know, but . . .

—This is the second time you allude to the notion that crucial information is being withheld from you. I assure you it is not.

—It doesn't matter. I knew that when . . . when I signed on.

—I . . .

—Just let me finish. As I understand, this device, this robot, it was built by advanced beings from . . . outer space, in the hopes of defending our planet against some other aliens, is that correct?

—Yes.

—I mean, are you certain it was designed for p . . . planetary defense?

—That is my understanding.

—Then how could there not be? This thing, the way you describe it, is extremely powerful, and I'm certain it could defend a neighborhood really well, perhaps a city, against just about anything. But what's it gonna do if the enemy attacks in another country, let alone another . . . continent? Is it just gonna walk there? It's not like it can hail a cab.

Without a propulsion system, its mobility would be so limited, it would be com . . . completely useless. All the enemy would have to do is land more than a few miles away. By the time this thing gets there walking, it would already be over. This would be the s . . . stupidest planetary defense system ever—not that I know of another one—if it can't cross an ocean.

—That is a sound argument. One I am surprised no one, including myself, has made in the past. I will endeavor to resume our search efforts as soon as possible. However, as you pointed out, we have covered a significant percentage of all the continents except Antarctica. If such a propulsion system does exist, and we do not find it there, it would most likely be submerged.

The surface we will need to cover is much larger than what we have searched to date, and we currently do not have a reliable underwater-delivery mechanism for the compound Dr. Franklin developed.

—We'll need to hire someone. I'm a geneticist, not a chemist or an engineer.

—Neither was Dr. Franklin.

—Well, maybe she was a bit of a Renaissance woman . . . but she's dead. Your pilots killed her. So we're gonna have to d . . . deal with that as best we can. Like I said, I'm a geneticist. I'm already managing . . . steelworkers and engineers, and I don't understand half of what they're saying. With the money we're s . . . spending building this place, I don't think one more salary will make much of a difference. If we need a chemist, we'll hire a chemist. If the engineers who thought this place up can't come up with a delivery system for that compound, we'll hire one more.

Speaking of genetics, that's another reason I'd like to get the pilots here as soon as possible. If I'm gonna figure out what it is about these two that makes this machine tick, I'll need access to their . . . to their bodies. I'll need samples.

—I can have them send blood samples here by courier.

—I might need a lot of samples, and not just blood. Please just get them here as soon as possible.

—They might object to a lot of physical probing.

—It'll be real difficult for me to do my job if they don't co . . . coo . . . perate. They're an uncontrollable variable in this equation. It makes the board real uneasy that a project this big is at the mercy of two people. You and I have already had this conversation. Let's not have it again. I'd like to get these tests started as fast as we can.

—All I am asking is for you to make these tests as nonintrusive and painless as you can without sacrificing the results. As for the board of directors, you let me worry about them. Your job is to get us back on track, as soon as possible. When we are fully operational, we can work on a contingency plan, should anything happen to either of our pilots. But for now, we have pilots. You should focus on what we do not have, and as of this moment, we do not have a robot, nor do we have a viable work environment to continue training.

—I understand. But I can't just ignore the b . . . board of directors. They're the ones who named me CEO. I understand your implication in this project, but there is an administrative structure in place here, and as far as I know, you're not p . . . you're not a part of it. I have all the respect in the world for what you did for this project, but my obligation is to the board.

—I admire your loyalty and your desire to fulfill your duties as CEO as best you can.

—Thank you.

—If I may offer a suggestion. It would be wise, for a woman in your position, to take some time to get a better understanding of your surroundings, perhaps to revisit some assumptions you may have made early on. Understanding the true nature of the power structure in such a complex enterprise is not something one can achieve instantly.

—Thank you for your concern. It's very nice of you.

FILE NO. 249

INTERVIEW WITH VINCENT COUTURE, CONSULTANT, BVI COMPANY NUMBER 462753 INC.

Location: Undisclosed location, near San Juan, Puerto Rico

—I hope you are enjoying yourself in this new setting.

—How could I not? I live on the beach! I don't know where you're from, but for someone who's lived in Quebec all his life, this is pretty awesome.

—I am happy that the beach house is to your liking. I was actually referring to this facility.

—I've only been here twice. I met with Alyssa—did you know they brought her back?—the day I arrived, and I met her again when I came in for a physical a few days later.

—You have been here for nearly two weeks if I am not mistaken. What have you been doing with your time if you do not spend it here?

—I'm learning to surf! Well, I'm trying to learn to surf. I'm horrible at it, but it's *so . . . much . . . fun*! I know I can't, but I keep thinking it might be a lot easier with my knees flipped. You should come! I'm easy to spot, I'm the glowing white guy with really bad sunburns.

—I . . . Is it really necessary for me to state that I do not surf? Can we talk about work?

—Sure!

—What do you think of the new base?

—I'm sure you know a lot more about this place than I do. Like I said, I've only been here twice. I thought our room in Denver was impressive, but this thing is completely insane. Do you know we're almost a mile deep underground?

The door behind us leads to a large room roughly the size of the one we trained in, back in Denver. There are also half a dozen laboratories on this floor, and a huge bay—I mean gigantic—that leads into the Atlantic. I've only been on this floor, though, I don't know what else there is.

—There is only one floor. There is also a twenty-thousand-square-foot machine shop, medical facilities, crew quarters, and a power plant.

—Can I ask a stupid question?

—No. You cannot.

—Then, can I ask a really smart question?

—As you wish.

—How do we get the robot out of here? The only door I've seen that might be large enough leads straight into the ocean.

—Once assembled, the device cannot leave this facility on the ground. She must be disassembled and hoisted to the surface near

the shore. There, we can load the pieces onto cargo ships. She does, however, fit into the sea-lock chamber, so, in theory, she could simply walk her way out of the ocean along the more moderate slopes of the coastline.

—You think she can work underwater? That'd be cool.

—We do not know. I certainly intend to find out. And, yes, it would.

—Who runs this place? Is this an American base?

—Not quite. These facilities belong to a consortium of four nations: Japan, Russia, South Korea, and the United Arab Emirates, as well as four corporations: two from Germany, one from the United States, and one from Japan.

—That seems like a completely random list of countries. Did you pick the names out of a hat?

—Russia had to be involved in some manner. The situation was simply too volatile after two of their officers were shot during one of our missions.

—We shot two Russian officers?

—We did not shoot anyone. Tuvan peasants did . . . It is a long story. Suffice it to say that any attempt by the United States to keep the robot would have had catastrophic consequences. I had to offer Moscow some assurances. Unfortunately, they do not have the financial resources necessary to fund a project of this magnitude. The Emirates did. Japan was an acceptable partner for both of them, and South Korea is the most obvious client for our product. Our private partners bring specific technologies to the table.

—Did you just say "our product"?

—Our goal is to provide close-range defensive capabilities for member nations.

—How about offensive capabilities?

—No. It is part of our charter. It can only be used to defend against an enemy strike or invasion, never as an offensive weapon, and never against another consortium member.

—I'm sorry, I'm still trying to wrap my head around this. You can do that? Just grab the robot and say you own it?

—It is open to interpretation. Ownership could perhaps be contested. We do, however, own over seven thousand patents on the technology. It would be legally perilous for anyone else to use it.

—What do the private companies get out of it?

—The cost of membership is . . . significant. As more nations join our group, those who provided seed funding could enjoy a considerable return on their investment.

—So we went from the greatest discovery in history, for the betterment of all mankind, blah blah blah, to a weapon for profit? Is that it?

—I will concede that this situation is far from what I had envisioned, but it is one that allows us to continue our research and avoid a global conflict.

—What's it called?

—What is what called?

—The consortium. Oh, that'd be a good name, just that: "The Consortium . . ."

—It does not have a name at this point. It is a numbered International Business Company incorporated in the British Virgin Islands.

—How romantic. You didn't want to call it the Themis Consortium? It's got a good ring to it.

—I have not shared information pertaining to her history or identity with anyone else at this time.

—Why?

—I have my reasons. However, I do admit that a numbered company is less than ideal from a motivational point of view. Perhaps you can suggest a good name for our group. I would like our personnel to feel a certain sense of belonging. Given the security restrictions and personal life limitations that come with working in our facility, strengthening morale will be of the essence.

—Well, if you don't want to use Themis . . . She's a daughter of Gaia and Uranus. You're not dealing with teenagers, but I would still avoid having Uranus in the name. Gaia's not bad. The Gaia Consortium.

—I will suggest it to the board of directors.

—There's a board?

—It is a corporation.

—I guess so. Anyway, I'm not gonna complain. Buying this place must have cost a fortune. Who was here before us?

—I do not understand.

—I mean, what was this place before we came in? Was it a mine?

—There was nothing here. We are below a national park. We had to excavate from the sea.

—You're kidding. There's absolutely no way you can build something this size in just a few months. It would take years to dig this much, this deep.

—It took approximately two years.

—Did you just say two years?

—Yes, we built this facility in less than two years. The costs were, unfortunately, inversely proportional to the speed.

—That makes no sense. Two years ago, we hadn't even put all the pieces together. We didn't even have a head.

—I rarely do anything without planning for contingencies.

—Aren't you a little worried about how the US government's going to react to all this? They weren't on that list of countries you mentioned.

—Indeed, they are not. They are, however, immune to any attack since one of our members is an American company.

—I'm sure that'll be a great comfort to them . . . I must be missing something. The US paid for all the research. We retrieved all the pieces with their Army, and now you're giving it to Russia? I don't know about you, but I'd be a little ticked off.

—You are correct in assuming there will be some fences to mend at some point.

—OK then. Who am I to complain anyway? I'm from Canada. When do you think we'll be able to start training again?

—If Ms. Papantoniou is correct, we should have retrieved all the pieces within a month.

—We're also missing a pilot. I thought Kara would be here by now.

—She should be here soon. She may have been involved in an accident.

—What happened? Is she OK?

—She is fine. She may not have had the accident yet. You may have forgotten that she is US Army personnel. Without direct involvement from the United States, I cannot simply ask the government for her services. There is nothing I am officially, or unofficially, involved with at this point that would require a helicopter pilot.

—So?

—So sometime soon, if it has not happened already, she will be involved in a routine traffic accident. She will suffer a concussion, whiplash. Her physician will diagnose her with postconcussive syndrome and cervical radiculopathy and declare her unfit for duty. He will recommend that she be placed on medical leave for at least six months.

When she arrives, you will have some fences of your own to mend. She was deeply hurt by your disappearing act. While I sincerely hope that your relationship can be restored to its former status, I will gladly settle for peaceful coexistence at this point. It is imperative that the two of you learn to work together again and communicate in the most efficient manner, just as you did in the past. Furthermore, you must learn to do this very quickly. Recent events have forced me to increase the number of players involved. There are now too many people, with too much vested in this project, to see it set back because of personal issues, even if it is only by a few days.

—I don't think you need to worry about Kara. She may hate my guts now, but she'll do her job.

—You are absolutely correct. Ms. Resnik is a professional, and she will perform her duties to the best of her abilities, despite whatever feelings she may have. It is you I am worried about.

—I've never . . .

—There is no need to be on the defensive. I have no doubts about your determination to perform your duties well, but you lack the military experience Ms. Resnik possesses. You have mentioned several times, and so has Ms. Resnik, that working in the sphere has a unique psychological effect on people. I am concerned that, should one of you not find his or her feelings reciprocated, the sphere will quickly become a toxic environment. I do not believe you could cope with this much added stress and be efficient.

—We'll be fine.

—You need to be more than fine. You need to be in sync. Your minds need to work in unison.

—Kara and I had absolutely no business being together in the first place. She has more issues than the *New York Times,* and I'm about as charming as a root canal, and yet, we found each other. It took about—what? twenty minutes?—after I kissed her the first time for some yahoo to run me into a cement wall with a pickup truck. We stuck together through that. We destroyed an airport together, killed our best friend, and brought the world to the brink of World War III, all in a day's work.

Don't you see? The two of us ending up together is either the biggest cosmic joke ever, or it was somehow meant to be. The real funny thing is, I don't believe in fate. Like I said, Kara and I will be fine. If I were you, I'd be more worried about the next mess we're gonna make.

FILE NO. 250

INTERVIEW WITH CW4 KARA RESNIK, UNITED STATES ARMY

Location: Undisclosed location, near San Juan, Puerto Rico

—Mr. Couture has been through a lot.

—You think it's been a walk in the park for me? I was there too, remember! He abandoned me! Didn't call, didn't write. It's not like I have really high standards for relationships. If you need some time alone, fine, but if you're gonna just bail on me, at least let me know that you're OK, and—I don't know—maybe tell me if you're coming back or not. Is that too much to ask?

—I am increasingly uncomfortable with the direction in which this conversation is heading.

—Just tell me! Am I being unreasonable?

—A modicum of communication would seem like a sensible requisite.

—Thank you!

—Your sudden gratitude worries me, deeply. Please do not take anything I have said to mean that I am taking "your side."

—What would you have done?

—I will pretend you did not just ask me that. The truth is: Neither you nor I can understand what went through the mind of Mr. Couture, as he bears the better part of the responsibility for the death of Dr. Franklin.

—That's a horrible thing to say. I'm just as responsible as he is for what happened.

—That is very generous of you. However, both of us know it to be inaccurate. The hands that pressed the buttons that caused the energy burst belonged to Mr. Couture, not to you.

—That's not fair! The robot tripped!

—Yes, the robot tripped while Mr. Couture was controlling the legs. Had Dr. Franklin been crushed under a giant thumb, I might point . . . blame the person who was controlling the hands. You should talk to him.

—We talked.

—I do not mean exchanging pleasantries. I mean talk. When I last visited him, I had serious doubts about his mental status, about his willingness to continue, and yes, about the nature of his feelings for you. I no longer have these doubts. While it may be difficult to understand, his prolonged absence, and what he did during that time, is a validation of his commitment to this project and, to an even greater extent, of his devotion to you.

—You said he played with toys.

—That is not exactly what I said. I may also have been more affected by the accident than I wished to believe when I first visited Mr. Couture, enough to miss certain things that, in retrospect, should have been obvious. I realize now that my rendition of the event may have compounded an already difficult situation, and I sincerely apologize for my shortsightedness.

—You're right about one thing for sure. Whatever he did in Montreal, it sure as hell made him better up there in the sphere. We had our first trial this morning.

—In the simulator?

—No, the real thing. They retrieved the last part during the night. She was fully assembled and ready to roll by the time we woke up. I don't know if I like this private-business thing, but we sure have more staff.

—Has the water caused any damage?

—The chamber was as dry as the day we left it. Anyway, we were a bit rusty at first, but after about a half hour, Vincent had us running in circles in the room. Running! Last time we strapped ourselves in, he could barely take a few steps. Now he's running . . . He's even able to work the console while walking. I just didn't think he had enough muscle left to do this.

—It is amazing what someone can accomplish once they really set their heart to something. I am very interested in the fact that the sphere remained sealed after being subjected to such incredible pressure. I would like to know if we can operate the robot underwater.

—Alyssa's one step ahead of you on this one. We're supposed to have a trial run in the sea-lock room on Friday. If it works, we can put some distance between us and dry land and try a few things while submerged. She'd like us to find out how to focus the energy release. It's not a bad idea. If anything bad happens, we might kill some fish, but we won't vaporize anyone and destroy the base . . . again.

—She did not mention anything to me.

—I'm not surprised. I don't like her. She's driven, I'll give her that. But there's something about her that just doesn't feel right. It didn't feel right in Denver. It doesn't feel right now.

—She said you would not like her.

—I didn't like her before.

—She said you would not like her because she is not Dr. Franklin.

—Oh, that explains it then. And here I was thinking it might have something to do with her.

—Feelings aside, has she done anything to earn your disfavor?

—Well, for one thing, she keeps sticking needles in me. The needles are getting bigger too. I've been here three days, and I've been asked— told—to report to med bay four times.

She took some blood the day I came in, and a few swabs. I guess those are for DNA.

—She is a geneticist.

—She's a bit of a mad scientist if you ask me. The next morning, I was called back in for more blood samples. She had me spend a good half hour inside an MRI. I'm not claustrophobic, but I gotta say I really don't like that machine. She treats me like a guinea pig. She doesn't explain anything, doesn't tell me what any of this is for. She probably thinks I'm too dumb to understand.

After dinner, I was getting ready for a bath—it had been a really long day and I wanted to go to bed early—when I heard my name in the intercom. "Kara Resnik, please report to med bay one." . . . I get there, and she sticks an IV in my arm to get me ready for a CT scan. I'm still burning up from the iodine shot when she tells me she needs to do a spinal tap. Do you know how big the needle is for a spinal tap?

—Did it hurt?

—I don't know, I just ripped the IV out of my arm and went back to my room. I'm sure it would have hurt.

—You said you were called into the medical bay four times. That makes three.

—Yep. I was asked to report to med bay again this morning.

—I will take the lack of details to mean that you did not comply. That may have been ill-advised. She might not take no for an answer.

—She's just gonna have to learn to live with disappointment. I mean, what's she gonna do? Drag me there?

—I would not discount the possibility.

—I'd like to see her try. Why does she need all this anyway? Dr. Franklin already determined there's nothing out of the ordinary in our DNA.

—I do not know precisely. She wants to understand why the helmets only activate for you and Mr. Couture and to remove these limitations if at all possible.

—Oh yeah, she's open about it. She wants to have a "B team." She says her first priority is to get the helmets to work for anyone. She's gonna have a hard time finding someone with legs like Vincent, but if she gets her way with the helmets, she might be able to replace me.

—I do not believe she wants to replace you, but she is evidently uncomfortable having this entire project depend on the health, or the will, of a single person. I would be lying if I said I did not share the sentiment. It would be incredibly easy for anyone to remove the robot as a threat by simply having either of you killed.

—I understand. I just hope it takes her a while to do it. I don't think she'll keep me around if she doesn't have to.

—What makes you think she would prefer to see you go?

—Oh, trust me, she'd love to get rid of me. If you fall in love with someone, there's a good chance the person won't love you back. Hatred, though, is usually mutual. If you despise someone, it's pretty much a given they're also not your biggest fan.

—I did not realize you disliked her this much.

—Maybe I'm exaggerating a bit. I don't really hate her. I just don't like her, a lot. I think she loathes me.

—I wish I could be more helpful. Unfortunately, my relationship with her is not all it could be. She is a strong-willed woman, perhaps too assertive at times. Her determination is commendable, but she is somewhat . . . defiant.

—You mean she doesn't agree with everything you say? Now, I'm beginning to like her . . .

—I meant to say that I fear it will become increasingly more difficult for me to help you.

—I'm just thankful she's stuck with me for the time being.

—Speaking of thankfulness, I realize I may not have properly expressed my gratitude for what you did in Bosnia.

—You don't need to. You were right. I didn't really notice it until I was on my way to the airport, but I didn't want to leave. The people there are so . . . They're so strong, and they're so vulnerable at the same time. Everything there just feels more . . .

—Real.

—Yes. Thank you for sending me.

—Thank you for finding Fata.

—You're welcome. I won't forget her either. That poor woman. What she had to endure, it's . . . I can't find the words. It's inhuman. What kind of monster would do such a thing to another person?

—War brings out the worst, and sometimes the best, in people.

—Speaking of war, I'm worried about what we're doing here. We started this as a research project. I don't have a degree in physics or anything, but it felt somewhat like science. This is not. It's not a research project anymore, and I'm starting to feel like a soldier again.

There's just too much money riding on this thing not to use it. At some point, we're gonna take her out, and we're gonna kill people, a hundred, a thousand . . . ten thousand. It's hard to see it for what it is, because it looks like a person, a woman, but what we have is a weapon, at least that's the way we're treating it. If we had found a bomb, a giant missile . . .

—Would you be a part of this project if we had?

—Maybe. Probably. Somehow it would be easier if I weren't the one driving this thing. I mean there's no one else. Well, there's one other person. But they'll send us out there, and we won't have a choice but to kill whoever comes at us.

You know they'll have absolutely no idea what they're up against, no clue that they don't stand a chance. I guess what I'm saying is: It's easier to be just one more soldier in a giant army than being the whole army by yourself.

—It does not matter whether you are all alone or one in an army of thousands. You have a choice. You have always had a choice. You should be grateful to be in a position to make it when the stakes are so clear. They rarely are.

—I'm not sure I understand.

—You are in control of a formidable weapon, but one that is designed for close combat. This means that you will always see whomever you choose to kill. That is a clear choice. Destroying a bridge in a night incursion is a much harder decision to make. You just never took the time to think about it. Removing it could prevent enemy reinforcements from reaching the front line. That bridge could also be the only escape route for civilians. How many peo-

ple will you save? How many will you send to their deaths? That is a complicated decision to make, especially without all—

—Is that your phone or mine?

—Yours, I believe . . .

—Then that must be yours.

—Indeed it is. We seem to be popular at the moment.

—What does yours say?

—North Korea just sank a South Korean ship in the Yellow Sea. They are moving troops toward the DMZ. I believe you . . .

—Yep. We're being deployed.

PART FIVE

UP IN ARMS

FILE NO. 251

MISSION LOG—CW4 KARA RESNIK, UNITED STATES ARMY

Location: Paju, near the demilitarized zone, South Korea

—Can you hear me, Ms. Resnik? Please cough if you can hear me.

—Cough? How about I just tell you? I hear you loud and clear. I muted my comms with Alyssa. She can't hear us.

—Good. Where are you now?

—We're in Paju. We're walking along the highway toward the border. We took a nice stroll in the river before that.

—Is the South Korean Army following you?

—No. There are some troops behind us across the river, but they're not moving. This is our show now. Oh, except for that tiny jeep riding next to us on the highway. I think it's escorting us, silly as it sounds.

—How are you feeling?

—Stiff. I'm sore all over the place.

—Has there been an incident I have not been made aware of?

—No, nothing happened. Absolutely nothing. Do you know how long it took for us to get here? Eleven days! Eleven days in a container ship, sleeping in that sorry excuse for a bunk they gave us.

We really have to do something about transport, or we need to find really patient enemies. It did give Vincent and me a chance to talk, though.

—Have you made any progress toward reconciliation?

—Eh . . . Can we do this another time? I'm sort of in the middle of something. Where are you calling me from anyway?

—Beijing. I still have a few friends here. I tried to win you a few extra days.

—I doubt you have any friends, anywhere.

—People who owe me favors are called friends. I asked them to stall Pyongyang for as long as they could.

—Seems to have worked. You know, I never knew it was this pretty.

—What is?

—Here. I'd never been to Korea, let alone to the border. I always imagined the demilitarized zone as something—I don't know—rugged. Some half-plowed mine-filled dirt field with crooked barbed wire all over the place. This looks like a national park. There's grass everywhere. It's insanely green. Everything is really pretty, very well kept. I'm sure it would all explode if we walked over it, but still, pretty.

Can you hold on for a minute? I have to report in . . .

Yes, Alyssa. We're entering the DMZ. We're a little over a mile from the—what do they call it?—the MDL. I can see a checkpoint from here. I'll go out on a limb and say they've seen us by now . . . No, nothing's happening . . . Yep. I'll let you know in a minute when we reach the border . . .

Are you there? I can't keep turning my mic off. I can still hear you, but I won't be able to respond.

—**Very well. Just keep this channel open so I can hear you.**

—All right. Here goes nothing . . .

Alyssa, I'm back. Yes, I was talking to Vincent . . . Things that don't concern you. I thought you'd like to know we're almost at the border. I can see troops about a mile away . . . I don't know, I see a lot of tanks, maybe two hundred. I'm guessing that's a brigade. Lots of infantry . . .

How am I supposed to know? They're in tents. I can tell you there are no more than fifty thousand men here. They sure didn't bring everyone. If they're getting ready to march in, I don't think this is where it's happening. My guess is they're just showing off . . .

You did ask for my opinion. You wanted to know how many troops there were. And since we're supposed to be here to stop an invasion, I thought the fact that there just aren't enough soldiers here to invade anything would be, you know, relevant.

Sure. We can walk to the border, but they can see us just fine from where we are if that's what you're worried about . . . We're going. We're going . . .

Vincent, that's far enough. OK. We're there. We're right at the fence. There are about a hundred men, a couple trucks about two hundred feet from us . . . No, Alyssa. No one's doing anything. They're just staring at us . . . I'm telling you! No one's shooting at us! . . . Where?

Oh, yeah. I see him. There's one guy about a thousand feet to the side taking potshots at us with an AK . . . What do you want me to do? Yell at him? HEY YOU DOWN THERE! STOP SHOOTING AT OUR FEET! How's that?

You're kidding, right? I'm not walking into North Korea because of some kid with a peashooter. He's probably just scared shitless . . . We can't shoot back, Alyssa. We could squish him if he gets closer, but we can't reach him from over here. No, Alyssa, we're not under attack. I don't care how much you wanna show off your new toy, there's no imminent threat here . . .

Do you have bad reception over there? I said no. We're not gonna pick a fight with fifty thousand men and an armored division for the fun of it . . .

—Do not cross that border. I do not care what Ms. Papantoniou is telling you. Do not cross.

—An order . . . Are you sure, Alyssa? It sounded more like a suggestion to me . . .

Fire me then! We were sent here to prevent something. Now we know it's not happening. We need to pack our bags and go home . . . Vincent, turn us around. We're out of here. Vincent?

—You cannot cross that border, do you hear me?!

—We're not crossing that border! Vincent! Move! I'm not gonna say . . . What was that? . . .

Yes, I hear you, Alyssa. I think we've been shot at, for real this time . . . I don't know, an RPG I think. Don't you have cameras up there? You tell me what hit us . . . I don't know where it came from—close, I think. I just saw something in the corner of my eye . . .

In the shoulder . . . No, we didn't feel an explosion, more like a hum. My suit tensed up for a second but that's about . . . Wait . . . INCOMING!!!

—Ms. Resnik? What is happening? Ms. Resnik!? . . .

— . . . We've been hit! We've been hit! . . . An antitank missile. It came from a launching vehicle on the west side . . . I felt that one. I don't think it did any damage, but my suit is giving me some sort of feedback. That felt like an electric shock. Vincent, did you feel that too? . . .

Yeah. Vincent felt the same thing. Vincent, we better turn on the shield. I don't know how many of these we can take before we discharge . . . Oh, and can someone tell that idiot in the jeep to get the hell away from us?

Of course, they're shooting at us, Alyssa. They have a twenty-story alien robot on their doorstep. They have no idea what . . . There's another one! INCOMING!

Turn on the shield! GO! GO! GO! . . . To the left, Vincent! To the left! . . . GOT IT!

Did you guys see that?

—I assume that is a rhetorical question? I am on the phone in China.

—No, Alyssa, that was another missile, probably an AT-5. I meant, did you see the light? I raised my arm just in time to catch it on the edge of the shield. It was weird—the shield went flat, and it turned bright, and I mean bright. We couldn't see through it at all for a second. I wonder why it changes shape like that.

All right. This is a whole lot of fun, but what do you say we get out of here before this gets out of hand? . . . Yep, take us back the way we came in. Alyssa, we're heading back . . .

You gotta be kidding me. How long? OK.

Vincent, there are two MIGs under way. ETA three minutes . . . Yeah, I say we wait here. Turn us around. If they fire, I'd rather not get hit in the back. Alyssa, we're about a thousand feet from where we were. We're gonna sit tight until the MIGs get here. I'm turning my coms off for a minute . . .

Can you stop this?

—Are you addressing me?

—Yes, Alyssa can't hear me. Any chance you can get those MIGs to turn around?

—It pains me to say it, but that is beyond my reach.

—OK . . . So, any good stories to tell? I got three minutes.

—What would you like to hear?

—Anything that'll get my mind off two MIG 21s.

—I do not believe they can destroy you.

—You're welcome to come here and take my place.

—I will have to take a rain check on that one.

—Tell me about Beijing.

—I am the wrong person to ask. This city is filled with bad memories. I can no longer see it for what it is.

—Fine. Tell me about your childhood. Talk about dogs.

—You have just disobeyed a direct order from your superior.

—Oh, that . . . Yeah, if by "disobey," you mean not do what she asked, I might have done that.

—We talked about this before. You were trained not to question orders.

—Apparently, I wasn't trained that well.

— . . .

—I don't know what to tell you. This isn't the Army.

—Would your response have been the same had Dr. Franklin given the order?

—Probably not. Look, I'm sorry! I won't do it again. I won't have a chance. I don't think Alyssa'll send me anywhere anytime soon.

—She may not have a choice. Perhaps this is not the right time, but I fear I may not get a chance to talk to you before you get back to Puerto Rico. There has been a development, and I believe you deserve better than to find out after the fact . . .

—Well, can you tell me in under a minute and a half?

—Alyssa has found replacement pilots. She will want you and Vincent to start training them as soon as you get back. The person who is slated to take your station is an Israeli pilot.

—Is he any good?

—*She* is the best they have. I have never met her, but I have read her file, I believe you two will get along. I am more concerned with whom they found to substitute for Mr. Couture.

—Who is it?

—Ms. Papantoniou has been—shall I say—less than forthcoming on the matter, but I have learned that a certain Army pilot has just received an early release from the confinement facility at Fort Carson.

—An Army pi . . . Ryan? You're joking . . .

—I wish I were. Unless you can think of another reason for Mr. Mitchell to book a flight to San Juan the day of his release. I am sorry. I know this must be upsetting.

—You think?! How do you think Vincent's gonna react? . . . No, Vincent, it's nothing! Well, it's not nothing. I'll tell you later, OK? . . .

She's just nuts if she thinks he's gonna train him . . . You were right, though. You picked one heck of a time to tell me . . .

—I know.

—Oh, shit, they're here. Gotta go.

—Good luck . . .

— . . .

—Ms. Resnik?

— . . .

—Ms. Resnik. Are you there?

FILE NO. 252

INTERVIEW WITH ALYSSA PAPANTONIOU, CHIEF EXECUTIVE OFFICER AND CHIEF SCIENCE OFFICER, GAIA CONSORTIUM

Location: Undisclosed location, near San Juan, Puerto Rico

—She's gone. Ka . . . Kara's gone.

—That is not true.

—She's gone! Get it thr . . . through your head!

—You have resented her from the very beginning. It must be frustrating for you.

—Don't tell me you agree w . . . with what she did? She disobeyed a di . . . a direct order! If this had been the Army, she'd have been . . . court-martialed. She'd already be in jail. You know that.

—Indeed. Were this the United States Army, she would most likely be dishonorably discharged after serving her sentence . . . unless, of course, her orders were illegal. You had no right to ask her to walk into North Korea. I was very clear about this. No offensive action. I think we can all agree that a direct strike inside the borders of a sovereign state qualifies as offensive action. I would give Ms. Resnik a medal for standing her ground. I am much more concerned with your complete disregard for my directives.

—I don't report to you. She does to me. I gave her an order! She d . . . didn't just refuse, she made a fool out of me!

—You are being paranoid.

—She defied me!

—You were trying to start a war! Are you so egotistical to believe this was all about you?

—She won't get away with this.

—You do realize that you need her a lot more than she needs you?

—Not for long. We're close. We're really close. Believe me, she'll never s . . . set foot in that thing again. Ever.

—Are you saying you have found a way to unlock the helmets?

—Yes . . . Well, no. Not exactly. I still need her head to get it working, but I think I've found a way to make the helmet believe she's still . . . still in it, even if she's not. I'm also pursuing more permanent solutions.

—Could you keep it on indefinitely? I am only asking because she might be less enthusiastic about helping if you take her pilot station away from her.

—I hope so. I need more samples to find out.

—You may not have noticed, but Ms. Resnik does not like to be probed.

—She doesn't have a say anymore. I'll g . . . I'll get what I need one way or another.

—I am more than willing to talk to her. I can probably persuade her to undergo more testing, but you will not subject her to anything that she has not volunteered for. I hope this much is clear.

There are very few certainties in this world. One of them is that you are replaceable, in this project or any other, and she is not. There is a line you cannot cross. It is very well defined. You are welcome to call me for clarification, should that line become ever so slightly blurred.

—I'll run this project as I see fit. I d . . . didn't wanna do this now, but it'll have to do. I spoke to the board, and it is my . . . my duty to inform you that your services will no longer be needed, as of today. We appreciate everything you've done for this project. We realize we couldn't have gone this far without you and we'll always be g . . . grateful for all your help. Security will ask you to leave your ID on your way out.

—You spoke to the board?

—Yes.

—The "board," you realize, is a low-level officer from Russian Intelligence, a retired South Korean general, the son of an Arab prince, and four lawyers who represent private companies but are not allowed to tell them anything they see. If you were to write down a list of all the people who are ill equipped to deal with the current situation, the "board" would undoubtedly have its name somewhere on the first page. Granted, yours would certainly appear farther down the list, but you are, nonetheless, incapable of facing what is bound to come very soon.

—W . . . What are you talking about?

—You really have no grasp of the situation, do you?

—Enlighten me.

—Approximately twelve days ago, you unveiled to the world, for the second time, an alien device powerful enough to tip the balance of power in any ground conflict. You marched it to the North Korean border against my specific instructions and effectively taunted the North Korean Army to attack you so you could demonstrate just how destructive that machine can be. In doing so, you have not only considerably raised tensions amongst Asian nations, but you have also antagonized the United States, and perhaps—pardon the pun—alienated forces infinitely more powerful.

—We didn't do anything against the US. North K . . . Korea isn't exactly a friendly state.

—The government of the United States spared no expense to locate and secure the pieces of that alien device. Staggering amounts of money and resources were allocated to this project. After the robot was revealed to the world, they also went to great lengths to avoid an international conflict and to ensure that, if they could not have it, no one else would. You essentially stole it from them, took it out for everyone to see, and left a hole the size of a small town along the Korean DMZ.

—I didn't steal anything! It was your idea to get it from the bottom of the . . . trench. You brought me on board long after the construction work had begun.

—Since, as you emphasized, I am no longer a part of this project, it would appear that the responsibility now rests solely on your shoulders.

—I only did what the board . . . what the board sanctioned. We had to show the world what it can do if it's going to be effective as a deterrent. Don't wo . . . worry about me. I know what I'm doing.

—You unfortunately do not. That much is obvious. If you had even the most basic understanding of the situation, you would not have taken her out before you knew more of what she can do, and you certainly would not have been reckless enough to bring her back here.

—Where was I supposed to take it?

—Perhaps the base in Russia. Anywhere but here.

—The . . . the base in Russia isn't finished yet.

—That is something you might have considered before you took her out for a stroll. That is definitely something you should have thought of before you took her back into United States territory, on a boat. It took over a week to get back here. There is not a government on the planet that does not know exactly where the robot is.

There are three countries that are part of this consortium, one of which you were already in. Yet, you chose to bring the robot back into the one country that has a legitimate claim on it. One thing is certain, you will never get it out of Puerto Rico again. I would also expect the board to react, shall we say, unfavorably to this decision, as you have effectively turned over their investment to the US.

I spoke to the Office of the President several times since the event. They were ready to declare a blockade when they realized where you were going. The only reason US Marines have not already stormed this place is because they have not yet figured out why you would do something so stupid.

They have, however, deployed half the Atlantic Fleet around the island. The seaward boundaries of Puerto Rico extend nine nautical miles from the shore. Believe me when I say that no one, especially Russia, will ever cross that line. Neither will you.

—What about the other nations in the consortium?

—The Emirates do not have boats that could come this far. If they did, they would not use them. You can also assume that South Korea will not enter US coastal waters uninvited.

—So what are we supposed to do?

—You can either trust Russian diplomats to work out a compromise, or you can let me handle it. Either way, I hope you brought a few good books. You will be inside this compound for a while.

—I can't make that kind of decision without running it by . . .

—The board. Yes. You do that. By now, Russia and Korea will have realized what you have done, but your private partners will be glad someone is there to explain to them why they are out of business.

—You're loving this. Aren't you?

—I take no pleasure in your misfortune, Ms. Papantoniou.

—Sure you do. You cou . . . could have warned me.

—Would you have listened if I had? I have explained to you, several times, that you could only use this weapon when absolutely necessary, and only for defensive purposes. In fact, I specifically told you to ensure that your actions could never be misconstrued as offensive. That did not stop you from marching right into the Korean demilitarized zone before anyone threw so much as a rock at South Korea.

—There was an immediate threat.

—North Korean troops gathering . . . inside North Korea. That is unheard of.

—They were massing very close to the border.

—North Korea is the size of Ohio. It would be geographically challenging for them to gather very far from the border.

—Say what you will. You could have warned me on the way back. As you were happy to point out, we weren't exactly traveling at super . . . sonic speed. You had more than a week to tell me to turn around.

—Indeed. I chose not to.

—Like I said. I don't know you very well. I know you don't like me, but I have a hard time thinking you'd purposely s . . . s . . . sabotage this entire project just for the pleasure of watching me fail.

I assume this was all part of some great master plan. So how does it work? You swoop in, save the day, and you get to run this project yourself?

—Rest assured, Ms. Papantoniou, I have no desire to take your place. Nor do I wish to see this project fail. I do have a vested interest in the people I recruited, and their well-being is very important to me. I would like you to make peace with Ms. Resnik.

—I can't help it if she won't cooperate.

—She still lives in the compound, comes to work every day. She spent more than a week on a cargo ship to go to Korea on a mission that should never have happened. She has, as I understand it, set limits on the type of procedures she will allow you to perform on her body. That seems within her rights even under these special circumstances.

—You didn't always have a problem messing with another person's . . . body against their will.

—I could say the same about you.

—I don't know what you're talking about.

— . . . Perhaps. Were you referring to Mr. Couture's legs?

—I was.

—The doctor performed the surgery against his will. Mr. Couture had no reservations about the operation.

—Did he even know what you were gonna do to him?

—He knew the alternative was to lose his legs. However painful the experience may have been for him, I believe he would choose to undergo the procedure again.

In any case, if Ms. Resnik will not consent to more invasive procedures, I suggest you find a way to work with what she *will* consent to. In the meantime, I will go back to Washington and see if I can find a solution to your current predicament.

—Thank you. I'll talk to . . .

—To the board, yes.

—I'll talk to the board about keeping you on as a consultant, but I can't . . . can't promise anything.

—That is very generous of you.

FILE NO. 253

TRANSCRIPT—GEOINT SURVEILLANCE— KH-9 SATELLITE (BIG BIRD)

National Reconnaissance Office, Chantilly, VA

[11:30] Movement alert. Big Bird is geostat over Puerto Rico. Now leaving Watch Mode. Manual tracking enabled.

[11:31] Male, female, designated Alpha, Bravo, spotted outside compound. Heading west on foot along access road.

[11:39] Several people exiting compound. Eight men total, all armed, wearing tactical gear. Designation: Charlie 1 through 8.

[11:42] Charlie 1–8 entering two vehicles, pickup trucks, parked outside compound. Vehicles heading west.

[11:46] Tracking. Vehicles approaching Alpha and Bravo. Male and female leaving access road, heading north through wooded area.

[11:47] Vehicles stopped. Charlie in pursuit on foot.

[11:52] Bravo down.

[11:53] Alpha heading North. Bravo still down.

[11:54] Charlie 1–4 stopping near Bravo. Charlie 5–8 still in pursuit heading north.

[11:56] Charlie 1–4 carrying Bravo, possibly dead, back to vehicle.

[12:01] Lost track of Alpha. Charlie 5–8 slowing down, splitting up into two groups.

[12:08] Charlie 5–8 abandoning pursuit. Heading back to vehicles.

[12:17] Vehicles heading back to compound.

[12:24] Vehicles back at compound. All occupants entering.

[12:32] No further activity. Big Bird resuming Watch Mode.

FILE NO. 254

INTERVIEW WITH VINCENT COUTURE, CONSULTANT, GAIA CONSORTIUM

Location: Bar El Batey, San Juan, Puerto Rico

—Where is Ms. Resnik? I was expecting both of you.

—She didn't make it.

—You left her behind?

—There was nothing I could do. She got hit in the back with a Taser gun. I tried to help her up, but they got me in the shoulder and I fell backward down the hillside. When I came to, I was a few hundred feet from the water.

—They did not chase you?

—I don't know. I didn't see anyone, but I didn't really stick around to find out. Maybe they were too busy restraining Kara, maybe they don't care so much about me.

—Believe me, they care very much about you. Even if Ms. Papantoniou managed to get the helmets to accept other people, she would need someone to operate the legs and the console. You are the only one with a sufficient understanding of the math involved.

—It's not that hard. It can be learned.

—I am certain it can, but you are also the only person whose anatomy is compatible with the controls. Anyone else would have to stand backward and face away from the console. They could use a third pilot on the other side of it, but coordinating the actions of three people when one of them is facing away does not seem like a viable solution. If they had been able to catch you, you would have been recaptured before her. She is easier to replace than you are.

How did you get to San Juan?

—There was a small fishing boat near the shore. I swam to it, told them I was snorkeling and the boat I came on left without me. At least, I think that's what I said. You know how good my Spanish is. Anyway, they took me to Playa Sardinera. I took a bus to get here.

—Very astute of you. How did things get so bad? What happened at the compound?

—We escaped.

—I meant what happened before. When did you decide to escape?

—Yesterday. Well, today, but it all started yesterday.

—Please take me through it.

—I woke up late. I didn't take a shower, I just ran downstairs for breakfast. They called her on the intercom about halfway through.

—Ms. Resnik?

—Yes. She said she'd be right back. She told me to make sure no one took her coffee.

—Then?

—Then nothing. I waited for a half hour. I went to her room, to med bay. The door was locked. I started knocking. After about five minutes, the door opened. Did you know that piece of shit Ryan was there?

—I did.

—And you didn't think that was something I might wanna know?

—Can we do this at another time? Ms. Resnik was in the medical bay . . .

—Yeah. I tried to get to her. She was lying unconscious on a metal table. Her arms and legs were strapped. She must have put up one hell of a fight. Ryan's brow was cut. He must have helped to restrain her because I don't think the two guards that were there could have handled her on their own. Alyssa certainly couldn't.

Ryan grabbed me. He said no one would hurt her. I didn't believe him so I kept on fighting, but he's a lot stronger than I am. Alyssa was there, and she picked up something in one of the drawers and she stabbed me in the neck with it. Next thing I know, I was in my room.

—What did they do to you?

—I don't know. I woke up with one hell of a headache, but not much else.

—Did your back hurt?

—No, not really. Why?

—What kind of tests did Alyssa perform on you before the mission to Korea?

—She sent me to San Juan for some X-rays. She took a bunch of samples.

—What kind of samples?

—Everything, I guess. Blood. A lot of blood. Saliva, sperm, hair. Why? What do you think she's doing?

—I do not know. How did you manage to free Ms. Resnik?

—I didn't free her. I think they were done with her so they let her go. She knocked at my door.

—How was she?

—Pretty banged up. She was still hammered from whatever Alyssa had given her. She grabbed my hand, and we lay down in bed until morning. When I woke up, she was already dressed. She looked really nervous. We both knew we had to get out of there.

—What was your plan?

—We didn't have a plan. We just tried walking out the front door. The guards had orders not to let us through. I could tell Kara was thinking about fighting her way out. I wasn't really up to fighting four armed men. I put my hand on her shoulder to stop her. It took a few seconds, but I eventually felt her relax. Once she'd given up on the idea, we went back to my room to whip up some sort of plan.

—What did you come up with?

—Nothing at first. There's only one elevator shaft, and it's heavily guarded. That left only the underwater hatch and the air shafts. Neither of us knew how to ride a sub, so we gave up on that one rather quickly, and we couldn't come up with a way to climb the shafts. They're about a mile long. Then I thought: Han Solo.

— . . .

—Han Solo, you know. "If they follow standard imperial procedure, they'll dump their garbage before they go to light speed, and then we just float away."

—Is that supposed to help?

—Today's garbage day. They take out the Dumpsters once a week, whatever they couldn't incinerate—metal, all kinds of scraps, and then a truck picks it up. We snuck into one of the containers, and they carried us out, with the rest of the trash.

—I am surprised Ms. Resnik went along with that plan.

—I was too. I can't say I was too confident about it myself. The one thing we knew is that we didn't wanna spend another day in there. It was just better than not trying anything at all.

We got out of the Dumpsters when we heard the door close and we started walking. We weren't even half a mile away when we heard the trucks they sent after us. We cut through the woods and ran as fast as we could. They caught up to us real fast. I told you the rest already.

We can't leave Kara in there with that psycho.

—I agree.

—OK, so what's the plan?

—I have absolutely no idea.

—Can't you storm the place with a platoon of Marines?

—No.

—Delta Force, anything?

—I wish I could. I no longer have access to military personnel. As far as the United States government is concerned, I am in the proverbial doghouse for the time being.

—You must have friends somewhere else.

—I have connections in several countries, but if by "friends," you mean military-trained people who will foray into US territory for a rescue mission in a hostile environment, then no, I do not have friends at the moment. I do have access to substantial amounts of money. Given enough time, I can probably assemble a team of mercenaries, but it is not something that can be done in a matter of hours, even days.

—How long?

—Two or three weeks at best.

—She can't stay in there for two weeks. She could die today, tomorrow. She might be dead already.

—There is time. They will not kill her. This might sound insensitive, but she is too valuable an asset to risk permanently damaging her. Her stay will involve some unpleasantries, I am sure. Ms. Papantoniou will do everything in her power to discover what makes her . . . special, but she will not kill her.

—I know Alyssa won't kill her on purpose, but you know Kara. She can get a rise out of anyone. I'm worried she might do something stupid. I'm sure the guards were told not to harm her, but they won't just stand there while she beats the crap out of them. There are a lot of guns in there, people on edge. A lot of things can go wrong.

—I suggest you accompany me back to the United States. We may be able to convince the Office of the President that it is in their best interest to help.

—What do you need me for?

—I will be arrested the minute I step through the White House gate. If they decide to let me sit in a cell for a few days, you can deliver the message yourself.

—They won't lock you up before they hear what you have to say. You go. You convince them we need their help. I'll stay behind and see what I can do from here.

—What could you possibly do? You do not know anyone and you do not speak the language. Where will you hide?

—Nowhere. You're right. I'd have a hard time ordering coffee out here. I'll go back. I think they'll let me in.

—They will lock you in a room and never let you out.

—I don't think so. I'll tell them I realized that this project is all I have, that I have nowhere to go. They probably won't trust me at first—I mean, it's too obvious—but if I keep it up, they'll want to trust me. It would be too convenient for them if I really wanted back in. It'll be impossible to resist. I'm pretty sure they'll give it a shot.

—If they do fall for this rather patent subterfuge, what will you do then?

—Wait for the cavalry. Make sure nothing happens to Kara.

—And if I were to be unsuccessful? You will have risked your life and lost your freedom again, for nothing.

—I'll find a way, maybe. I'll try to come up with something better than hiding in the trash. I'll try to find out what Alyssa has up her sleeve. I mean, if she's willing to treat us like prisoners, she can't really expect us to cooperate that much. She must be really close. Maybe she has something working already.

—Before she evicted me from the premises, she suggested she might have found a way to keep the helmets working after you had turned them on. She made it sound more like a project than something functional.

—I doubt that. She has a big ego, but if you were that close, wouldn't you step on your pride for a few more days rather than risk everything on a bet? And that can't be all of it. She couldn't keep the helmets turned on forever. She'd still need us to start her up from time to time. It would need to be something we don't have to do voluntarily. It's hard enough to get up there as it is, I can't imagine trying to bring up someone who doesn't want to go.

—Please forget about the investigation and focus on finding a way to escape again. I am worried that Alyssa may not be the only imminent threat to your life and that of Ms. Resnik. The cavalry, as you called it, might do more harm than good.

—Do I wanna know?

—There are a lot of moving parts to this plan. The United States government might simply decide to cut its losses and neutralize the threat.

—You mean blow us all to pieces?

—Nothing so dramatic. The public might frown upon the United States carpet bombing a national park in Puerto Rico.

—That's reassuring. You had me worried there for a second.

—I would surmise that a few well-placed torpedoes near the sea-lock chamber would prove just as effective.

—Nice. If it breached, we'd all drown within seconds, and no one would have to know.

—Do you wish to reconsider your decision to return?

—I can't leave Kara down there. Besides, just in case there is an afterlife, I don't wanna spend eternity hearing how I let her drown alone in Puerto Rico.

FILE NO. 255

INTERVIEW WITH MR. BURNS
OCCUPATION UNKNOWN

Location: New Dynasty Chinese Restaurant, Dupont Circle, Washington, DC

—I am on my way to the White House.

—I know. That's exciting! And yet you wanted to have lunch. You must be famished.

—Time is of the essence so I will not waste it with pleasantries. I need your help.

—You, asking for help? You really can't think straight on an empty stomach and you haven't eaten since you left San Juan.

—Do I dare ask how you know so much about my whereabouts?

—Funny, isn't it?

—What?

—How strange this must be for you. You're usually the one who knows things he shouldn't about other people.

—Perhaps. But everyone can guess as to how I am privy to such information. It seems logical to assume that you and I do not frequent the same circles, which would suggest a vast network of information that no one is aware of.

—I'll take that as a compliment, coming from someone who specializes in vast networks of information no one is aware of . . . Did I ever tell you the story of the fisherman and . . .

—No, you have not, and you will not. I do not have time for stories or colorful metaphors. What I require of you now are facts, and expediency. If you are unable or unwilling to oblige, please do not delay me any further.

—No stories then, but it's your loss, it was a good one. I should be on my way.

—Please stay. If you are concerned by recent events in North Korea, I can assure you I did everything in my power to prevent them.

—Me, concerned? If you knew what I've seen in the last . . . in the last years, you'd know it takes a lot more than that to worry me. Please don't take this as a personal insult, it's not, but I may have overestimated you. I really thought you understood. I wouldn't have come forward otherwise. I'm sorry.

—What exactly have I so miserably failed to grasp?

—I don't know where to start . . . Oh, yes I do. First, it's not about you, you arrogant prick! In the grand scheme of things, no one gives a damn what you approve of, don't approve of, what you try to prevent or what you have for breakfast. This is a grand scheme of things . . . thing.

Second, it's not about me either. I'm flattered if you're looking for my personal approval, but it doesn't matter much in the end. *They* are worried. *That's* your problem.

—I fully realize the extent of my insignificance in history, believe me. I have yet to form an opinion on the extent of yours. I suspect your place in it is more considerable than you would like me to believe.

Before you judge me, and by extension, all of us, you must understand that while I would do everything I can not to antagonize technologically superior beings and risk a conflict of apocalyptic proportions in a near or distant future, my first duty is to ensure that this discovery does not lead to pandemonium in the here and now.

—Of course! You have a job to do. You don't need to justify yourself to me.

[Good evening gentlemen. Are you ready to order?]

—I will have the Kung Pao chicken, and a cooling tea.

—I'll have the same . . . Maybe there's hope for you after all.

—Will you help me?

—I would love to help you, with something fun, but you don't like fun. You want to talk about things like doomsday, humanity's final judgment. Those are not fun. Why don't we do something that will help you relax? Have you ever built a shed? It's like building a tiny house. We can build one in a day, and you'll feel this incredible sense of pride when we're done.

—I feel the situation slipping from my control.

—You know what your problem is, don't you? You place the fate of an entire planet squarely on your shoulders. Do you have any idea what that'll do to your health?

—Please.

—Would it make you feel any better if I told you that you're not responsible for what happens in the end?

—Do you *know* what happens? Do not make me beg.

—I know how hard this must be for you, but you have to work on your facial expression. You can't say something like that with a poker face. How about this? I have absolutely no idea—honestly—what you can do to prevent all-powerful aliens from coming to this planet. I do not know that they are either. Beyond that, you should, by now, have begun to realize that I've already told you a lot more than I should have. What I really want you to understand—and that part may be a little more difficult to grasp—is that I can only make things worse by telling you more.

—Is there not a chance that they have simply forgotten about us?

—Not one. If there's one thing they're good at, it's record keeping. You're also very interesting at the moment. From an evolutionary perspective, most of the systems they are overseeing are either close enough to them to appear mundane, or at the earliest stages of their development, often without any sentient life or even complex organisms. Your "coming of age" is a rare event, a very exciting and important one. You can take my word when I say they are keeping a close eye on you.

—Our coming of age?

—Yes. This, all that's happening now, this is your bat mitzvah. You can play with atoms, you can sit with the grown-ups.

—What does that mean for us?

—That means you won't be forgiven for childhood mistakes anymore.

—How can we be accountable for our actions if we do not know what is expected of us?

—Nothing is expected of you. As I said, they're not colonizers. The last thing they want is to interfere.

—I do not understand. They do not want us to kill one another using the weapon they left for us, yet we have been doing it for millennia using our own weaponry, and they did not raise an eyebrow.

—They don't have eyebrows, a very resilient genetic trait as you can see.

—Nonetheless, can you tell me where the distinction lies?

—There's no distinction. They don't care whether you kill one another with a stick or with something they built. They don't even care whether or not you kill one another. They will be perfectly content to watch humanity destroy itself completely. Your extinction is not the issue.

—So we need to demonstrate that we can be responsible with this newly acquired power, or they will come and take it away. Is that correct?

—If they decide that you're not ready, yes. They'll either take it back or they'll send you back to the Stone Age and let you mature for a few millennia.

—How many robots would they send, should they decide to annihilate us?

—They don't need to send any robots, they could wipe you out from orbit. But I suppose if they did, half a dozen would suffice, a hundred would be quicker, a thousand . . . you get the picture.

—Would we stand a chance in combat with our robot?

—I don't think so. You have to remember, the one you have is six thousand years old. It's an antique.

You never know, though, you might get lucky. Their weapons might have evolved considerably, but they're still fundamentally the same—focused energy. What they have now will do more or less the same thing yours can, just more of it.

—So the safest course of action would be to do nothing and hope for mercy, is that it?

—I hope not! I think you should fight your heart out. If they decide to get rid of all humans and start over, they'll do it no matter what you do. If it were me, I'd rather go out swinging.

—I do not believe our robot could be victorious in a sword fight, not with our pilots.

—You're probably right. I would fight from a distance.

—How can we when all we have is a sword?

—A sword? You didn't destroy Denver International with a sword!

—So the energy burst is a weapon. We believed it might be a by-product of the material used to construct the device. It may be my underdeveloped cerebrum, but I fail to see how an omnidirectional burst of energy with a very limited range could allow us to fight from a distance.

—Nice try. You'll have to figure that one out yourself. I've really said all that I can. You should go to your meeting. I'll get the check.

—If I may ask, why are you helping us? Is that not against the rules?

—I'm just an old man who likes to tell stories. I can't help it if you're crazy enough to believe them.

—But why? Why not let them deal with us as they see fit?

—I live here. I know people, good people. I don't want anything bad to happen to them.

—I am well aware that you were born here and that you are human for the most part. You won't tell us how to fight them, but you tell us we should. You speak of them as "they," not as "we," which suggests some ambivalence, but there is something more. I sense an emotion I am familiar with when you speak of your ancestry. I cannot quite put my finger on it. Anger perhaps . . . Resentment?

—That's a lot to read into the choice of a pronoun.

—They abandoned you here, did they not?

—I was born in Michigan.

—Your ancestors. They left your ancestors here with no instructions other than to blend in as much as possible. They left highly evolved people—they would have been some sort of scientists, the elite—alone with primitive, half-clothed people who probably had not even invented the wheel. Centuries spent longing for what must have seemed like the most basic necessities. Having children, but knowing they will never be all that they can, because you will teach them to be . . . ordinary. I can only imagine what I might feel, but rancor does come to mind.

—Nice speech! You're right about one thing: You have no idea what these people went through or what they could possibly have felt. I will say one more thing before you go. Stop worrying so much! Are you doing your best?

—I fear my best may not be enough.

—Then you should come to peace with whatever comes. All you can do is try your best. Go now. Next time, you're the one buying lunch, and you *have* to hear that story about the fisherman and the seagull. By the way, you owe me a favor. A big one.

—For your advice?

—No.

—Then I do not see how I am indebted?

—You'll see . . . But you definitely owe me. Remember that.

FILE NO. 256

MISSION LOG—CW2 RYAN MITCHELL, UNITED STATES ARMY

Location: Undisclosed location, near San Juan, Puerto Rico

—Where are you now, Mr. Mitchell?

—In Alyssa's office. I broke in to get her sat phone and her keys. You have to help me, sir. Please! I have to get her out of there. Can you help me?

—I assume you are referring to Ms. Resnik. Is she in imminent danger?

—She's in med bay one with Alyssa. She's . . . They're doing things to her, sir.

—Who is?

—Alyssa. She's . . . Look, there's no time to explain everything. I need to get her out of there now. Can you send in troops?

—There is already a platoon of Marines on-site, but they will not breach. They will not risk it without knowing what they are up against.

—I can tell you! Just tell them to breach! I'll tell you everything they need to know. They need to hurry!

—Mr. Mitchell, the Marines are not there at my request, and they are not there to help you. They are there to arrest you, you and everyone in that base.

—Wh . . . I . . . I don't care! Tell them to breach. Tell them to arrest us. We need to get to Kara now!

—I am wanted for treason. You, Ms. Resnik, Mr. Couture, we are all traitors in the eyes of the United States government.

—Then why not breach and arrest us all?

—I can only speculate, Mr. Mitchell, but if I were in charge, I would not risk the life of my men by walking into a possibly hostile environment with a single point of entry, especially when you have no way out.

—What are you saying, sir?

—I am saying that if you want the Marines to come in, you will need to open the door for them.

—I can do that.

—I was being facetious! There are over a dozen armed men protecting that base. Most of them are ex-military. They will not hesitate to shoot you.

—I'm telling you, sir. I can do it. I can secure the base.

—Do you have the key to the armory?

—I'm on my way there now . . . Sir?

—Yes, Mr. Mitchell.

—I know that if you had your way, I'd still be rotting at Fort Carson . . . I'm sorry, sir. I know it doesn't mean anything, but I'm sorry for what I did. I just wanted to say it.

—...

—I'm at the armory. Looking for the key. This has gotta be it . . .

—**Have you ever fired at anyone?**

—Not with a gun, sir, but I'm not gonna kill anyone.

—**You will not be able to simply disarm a dozen men on your own.**

—Look sir, I got myself into this mess because I almost killed Vincent. I'm not gonna try and fix this by killing a bunch of people.

—**Mr. Mitchell, listen to me . . .**

—It's OK, sir, I found what I was looking for. I remembered they keep XREP rounds to get rid of trespassers on the surface.

—**I know very little about firearms. What is an XREP?**

—They're less-than-lethal bullets that deliver an electric shock. They're mini-Tasers you can fire with a shotgun. Very expensive little things. Anyway, there must be more somewhere, but I found three boxes of these and two shotguns. I'll just grab a few stun grenades and a lot of tie-wraps.

—**Tie-wraps? Mr. Mitchell, I strongly urge you . . .**

—You're right, sir. I can't do this alone.

—**Where are you going?**

—Living quarters, there should be no more than one guard at the door. I just hope I can do this quietly. I need to stop talking now.

—**. . . Mr. Mitchell?**

—. . .

—**Are you there?**

—I am. I tried to knock the guard out, but I caught him in the back of the neck. I had to hit him again. Now if I can just find the right key . . . Unless . . . Yes! Good man. He had it around his neck.

—The key to what?

—Now, this guy's not gonna be happy to see me . . .

Hi! I need your hel . . . Don't . . . Stop . . . Would you . . . *Stop fighting*!

I need your help! Kara's in trouble! Kara's in trouble and I need your help to get her out. You can either trust me and help me or go back to your room, but I'll need to knock you out too if you keep making this much noise.

—Who are you talking to? Mr. Couture? Tell him I was unsuccessful. Tell him the cavalry is not coming.

—He says the cavalry isn't coming . . . You know who. Him! Now can you shut the hell up for a minute? OK. Help me drag this guy in here. Now take this key and lock every door in this corridor. They lock from the outside. There are twelve more guards on base. If we're lucky, a couple of them are still in their rooms . . .

—Is Mr. Couture unharmed?

—Yeah, he's fine. Well, he seems fine to me. He's a lot stronger than I remember him to be . . . Are you done?

—Are you talking to me?

—Now here's what we're gonna do. Take these and put them in your pocket. I know they're tie-wraps. Take this gun . . .

No, I don't want you to shoot anyone. I want you to give it to me when I run out of shells and reload the one I give you. This is a Mossberg 500. It holds five shells in the magazine tube. You put them in like this . . . There's room for one more in the chamber here . . .

No, Vincent, we're not gonna kill anyone. These are nonlethal bullets. Are you good? Can you do this? Good. Now load yours.

—Mr. Couture has received no military training. He may get you both captured or killed.

—He'll be fine . . . No, Vincent, you're doing great. One more . . . That's it.

The machine shop is locked at this hour. Sea lock and the power plant are closed. That means all the guards should be at the entrance or in the main hallway. Look in the bag. These are stun grenades. When we get to the hallway, I'll need you to grab two of these, remove the pin here, count to three, and throw them as far as you can away from us. That should disorient however many guards are there for a few seconds. Hopefully, that'll be long enough for me to shoot them. Then you follow me in and you tie the guards' hands together with tie-wrap . . .

No, that's not it. I wish it were. Those grenades will make a lot of noise, the shotgun too. Whoever isn't in that hallway, and the guards at the entrance, they'll either wait for us or they'll come for us. Whatever happens, we'll have to improvise a bit. If you need to, you just shoot, then pump, then shoot, then pump—just like in the movies.

—Mr. Mitchell. I could not help but overhear your plan, or lack thereof. Are you sure you do not wish to reconsider your choice of weapon? Need I remind you that the guards you are so intent on keeping alive are using live ammunition?

—I'm well aware of that part. Vincent, are you ready for this? Cool! Just stay behind me . . .

We're at the corner to the main hallway. I see two men talking along the wall, two more sitting at a table. No, make that three . . . Take the stun grenades out of the bag. Remember, count to three, then throw them away. Try to throw one as far right as you can. Oh, and don't look. On my count, three . . . two . . . one . . . now!

. . .

One guard.

. . .

Two.

Vincent, come on!

Three!

Four!

. . .

Five. No! Come on, stop moving. *Five!*

OK, Vincent, tie them up . . . No, not like that, hands behind the back. Like that, don't be afraid to pull. You want this to be tight!

Five guards down, plus one at Vincent's door. There's one guard with Alyssa in med bay; that leaves anywhere from zero to five guards at the main entrance. Vincent, give me your shotgun and reloa . . . *Get down!* . . .

—**Mr. Mitchell, are you hit?**

—There was a guard in the bathroom. He went back in when he heard me scream. Vincent, give me the gun and grab a grenade from the bag . . . Whenever you're ready . . . Five, four, three . . .

Hi there! You probably can't hear me, but my friend here's gonna tie your hands behind your back. If you move, I'll have to shoot you, so . . . don't move. Tie him up, Vincent! Go! Go! . . .

We're done here. That leaves the main entrance. Vincent, get a grenade from the bag. Let's go!

Chances are they'll start shooting at us as soon as I open this door. Get the grenade ready. And . . . here . . . goes . . . Vincent, don't pull the pin! Shit, quick, throw it in the bathroom! Go! Go!

—**What is happening, Mr. Mitchell? Talk to me.**

—There are only two guards at the main entrance. They have their guns on the floor and their hands up in the air. I guess a few of them were still in their rooms. Hi, guys! . . . Yeah, I didn't sign up for this either. Would you mind putting your hands behind your back so my friend here can restrain you? It's only for a few minutes, then the Marines will storm in, and they'll cuff you all over again. Vincent, hurry!

We're a few steps from med bay. There should be one guard with Alyssa. Vincent, do you want to do the honors? . . . Just throw your grenade in there and disarm the guard . . .

Kara's sedated and strapped on a table, I don't think you can disorient her any more than she is . . . Here you go. Get in there!

I told you he'd be fine, sir. You should know the kid was smiling through most of it. I think he might have taken a little pride in improving his tie-wrap technique. I just hope he doesn't figure out what was going on in there.

—Are you referring to the tissue samples Ms. Papantoniou was collecting?

—She's not collecting tissue, sir. That's why I called you. I swear, I had no idea what she was doing when I signed up. I just thought I could help.

—I believe you. Now tell me what you witnessed.

—Well, you know Alyssa's been collecting samples from Kara and Vincent: blood, skin, bodily fluids. When I went to see her this morning, she had Kara in a . . . She didn't have any pants on . . . I asked what was going on, and she told me she was removing eggs from Kara's ovaries.

—Is that what prompted your rebellion?

—I wasn't finished. She told me she'd attempt in vitro fertilization the next day. Could she do that, sir?

—My understanding of IVF is very limited, but I do not believe she has the necessary equipment. She does have access to cryogenic material, however. She could freeze the ova and semen samples from Mr. Couture. She would need to take them to a clinic outside the compound. The eggs and semen would then be thawed. Those that survive the process could be fertilized and left to develop for a few days. Most clinics will now perform what is known as blastocyst transfer.

—I don't . . .

—A blastocyst is an embryo in which cell division has occurred enough times in the first few days. The embryos that have reached that stage can be transferred into a host after five days with a reasonable chance of success.

—You mean into another woman?

—That is correct.

—That's insane!

—Indeed. Your decision to intervene was timely.

—I would never have agreed to help her if I'd known. You know that, sir. Don't you?

—I do, and you have told me already.

—Vincent's back with Kara . . . Hello, Sleeping Beauty! What do you mean she's not there?

—Ms. Resnik is gone?

—No, Alyssa is . . . Are you sure you checked everywhere? . . . I know it's a small room. Look, Kara can barely stand, why don't you guys go sit over there? . . .

I don't know what to say, sir. We've been pretty much everywhere. She was here twenty minutes ago. Unless she went in one of the guards' room, we should have run into her. It's not like she can get out.

—Perhaps she can. She did supervise the construction of that complex.

—I gotta look for her.

—Let the Marines do it. Ms. Resnik may need immediate medical attention. You should let the Marines in now.

—I will in a minute. I gotta tell them about what Alyssa's doing.

—You will do no such thing. Both of them have been through enough already. You will not add to their ordeal by telling them about a situation they can do nothing about.

—Sir! They could have a child a year from now and not know about it.

—They could have a dozen. You will say nothing to them, Mr. Mitchell. Do you understand?

—Sir! They have a right to know.

—**They do. I will tell them when the time comes.**

—Do I have your word on that?

—**You do. Now open the door and let the Marines in.**

—OK. I'm getting on the elevator now. What'll happen to us when they come in?

—**They will cuff you. They will most likely separate you until you all have been debriefed. I suspect it will be a . . . thorough debriefing. After that, I do not know. At best, you will go back to Fort Carson to finish your sentence. At worst, we will all receive a lethal injection.**

—What should I tell them?

—**Unfortunately, there is very little the United States government does not know at this point. What you say, or do not say, will be of no consequence. Make this easy on yourself and tell them what they want to hear.**

—OK. Thank you, sir, for everything. I've unlocked the main door. Here goes nothing . . .

Hi, guys! Welcome to Puerto Rico! OUCH! Come on! I just secured the whole place for you, shithead! Does it have to be so tight?! Come on, man! That hurts! . . .

FILE NO. 257

INTERVIEW WITH INES TABIB, ASSISTANT TO THE PRESIDENT FOR NATIONAL SECURITY AFFAIRS
Location: White House, Washington, DC

—Do you have anything to say before I have you arrested and tried for treason?

—I fail to see the point, but I am happy to let you posture for a short while. How are Ms. Resnik and Mr. Couture doing?

—Your pilots are still in Puerto Rico being debriefed. They're fine. You can all stand trial as a happy family.

—You and I both know I will not stand trial. Justice is usually much swifter for someone in my trade. It comes unannounced, usually from behind, and, as far as I know, it is never prefaced by a meeting at the White House. What happened? Did the president stop you herself, or did someone else intervene when you tried to have me arrested? You are relatively new to this line of work so I would presume that having me killed would not be your first choice.

—She said she would handle it personally. How did you know?

—I did not. It seemed like a logical explanation.

—You find this logical? You use US funds to finance this project, US helicopters, drones, American troops to locate and retrieve all the pieces of this machine from all over the world—illegally, I might add—killing several American citizens and foreign nationals in the process. You assemble it on US soil, use American scientists on the US government payroll to figure out how it works, in an American base, of course, a base that you later destroy, bringing this country to the brink of war.

At your suggestion, the president of the United States then agrees to drop this machine into the ocean, a measure you yourself described as temporary. Then you turn around and give it to Russia and the UAE. Does that about sum it up? What part of this does *not* constitute treason from your perspective?

—Which question should I answer first?

—Answer whichever you like.

—No.

—No, you don't want to answer?

—No is the answer to your first question.

—Which was?

—"Does that about sum it up?" It does not.

—What did I miss?

—The first part of your statement, however redundant and melodramatic, was generally accurate. Aside from the individuals who were directly involved in this project, the United States is mostly responsible for its success. As for the latter, you forgot South Korea. Most importantly, I did not "give" anything to anyone. First, it was not mine to give. Second, it was not free, far from it.

—I'm not really interested in hearing anything you have to say.

—You did ask. Your plan, as we have established, was to have me arrested and tried for treason. We now both know that this particular plan will not come to fruition. I am offering you an alternative, one that will greatly benefit the United States. It also does not involve my having a sudden heart attack or a fatal reaction to a bee sting.

—Why, though? Why would the president not want to arrest you?

—You will have to ask her.

—She knew. Didn't she? She knew all along. Did the former president know?

—I . . .

—Don't answer that. I know you won't tell me. So that's it, isn't it? That was the plan all along.

—You just told me not to answer.

—I don't get it.

—That was not a joke.

—I don't understand how any of this is good for us.

—Perhaps your feeling of impotence regarding my arrest is clouding your judgment. Let me repeat what I said earlier. I did not give anything to anyone. First, it was not mine to give. It was not yours either. The reason the former president agreed to drop it in the ocean is precisely because for the United States to insist on keeping the device for itself would have precipitated a global conflict. Do you agree?

—Does it matter? Let's say that I do, for the sake of argument.

—Why would it precipitate a global conflict?

—Because Russia wouldn't let us keep it.

—Correct. Russia would not have let the balance of power tip so far in your favor. They would not have been alone. It would have left the Middle East in even more turmoil. They know you would eventually use it there. Asia would have been upset as well.

—Your point?

—Having established that the device was not yours to keep, I presume I will not have to convince you that it did not belong to Russia either.

—I thought that was *my* point.

—Indeed. Moscow is well aware of that. Now that they have had their hand caught in the cookie jar, so to speak, do you believe they are in a position to play the moral card as they did in the past with the robot now in US custody?

—I'm pretty sure you want me to answer no here.

—How about the Middle East? Perhaps if, say, the Emirates had been involved ... How about Europe? Asia? Would a German company being part of the consortium be helpful? Japan, Korea . . . Do you believe any of them, now faced with the likely prospect of losing everything, will try to prevent the United States from participating in this venture?

—OK, it's clever; I get it. So we share it with Russia, now that they'll let us . . .

—More or less. But you are missing the real beauty of this situation. As I said before, I did not give anything away. It was not free. The nations involved spent in the neighborhood of $200 billion to retrieve the device and construct the Puerto Rico base. Had the US attempted to do the same, it would have had to disburse that amount on its own. To do it clandestinely would have been impossible, as you could not appropriate $200 billion, for anything, without anyone's noticing.

—OK, it's clever *and* we saved a bunch of money. What do you want from me, a medal?

—A simple thank-you would suffice.

—I still don't get it. If the president knew, and it sure looks that way, why not let me in on that clever plan of yours?

—I cannot tell you what the president knew or did not know, I do not handle these briefings. As I mentioned several times to your predecessor, there are a great many things that require an attention span greater than eight years. Consequently, there are also a great many things that never reach this office. As for the plan, you must realize that, if it existed at all, it would never have been that well-defined. The device was causing too much turmoil, in part owing to the manner in which the pieces were acquired. Hypothetically speaking, the former president might have agreed that other nations should share some of the burden, and some of the cost. I would then have assembled a group of interested parties and begun construction on the Puerto Rico facility.

—You mean you got them to build a base in Puerto Rico *before* we dropped the robot anywhere near it?

—I like to believe I have a reputation for keeping my word.

—Not sure I'd bet $200 billion on that.

—It would have been the only way for the project not to come to a halt for a year or two. We would have needed a head start on the construction while our team continued to work. If, hypothetically, I had promised to get the device to the bottom of the trench at the first occasion, the accident in Denver would have provided the perfect opportunity.

That being said, it baffles me that they would be so hasty to show it publicly, let alone that they would bring it back to Puerto Rico afterward.

—Hypothetically . . .

—No. That part is fact. I suppose I could take some of the credit for unwittingly recruiting morons. Without their sheer stupidity, it could have been years, decades, before you and I had this conversation.

—So how does that work? We come to an agreement with South Korea, Russia, the Emirates, and we get to parade it three months a year? You know we'll never be able to use it against anyone with that list of partners.

—I suppose now is as good a time as any to break the bad news. You will not like what comes next.

—I'm not exactly ecstatic so far . . .

—You will not share it with 3 countries, you will share it with 192.

—You want to give it to the UN?

—No, you do.

—Why would I want that?

—It has to be this way, so I suggest you find a good reason. If you are at a loss, I can suggest a few, world peace being one of them. The point is that it has to come from you. The consortium must be absolutely convinced that you will never agree to release the device otherwise.

—Now we'll really never be able to use it.

—You never could. This much should be clear by now. Neither you nor anyone else can ever use this device to attack another human being. That means you cannot blow up the Vatican, even if they are not part of the UN. But instead of sobbing about all the great wars that might have been, I suggest you pray to whatever god you worship and ask that we never have to use it at all, because if we do, it will likely mean the end of everything.

On the positive side, I am certain the UN will be willing to erase a good portion of your debt for this. You owe them quite a bit of money. And, yes, you will get to parade it every now and then, though perhaps not three months a year.

You once told me that this discovery would forever change the way we view ourselves, melt away some of our differences. I sincerely hope you meant what you said, because today, you and the president get to do something good for all mankind, not something some CIA analyst said might help stabilize the Middle East or lower oil prices. You get to do something undeniably good, for everyone. Tell me: How often does that happen?

—What if I said no?

—I have the utmost respect for freedom of choice. In fact, most of what I do is aimed at preserving it. This, however, is not one of those moments. Feel free to take a few days before you say yes. I would also like Ms. Resnik and Mr. Couture released immediately.

—The president said nothing about your pilots. They'll have to stand trial.

—Trials seem to be an obsession of yours. You can have the guards tried if you wish. I strongly urge you to prosecute Ms. Papantoniou if you find her.

—You mean the psychopath you chose to run your program, the one who took everyone hostage to run some insane experiments.

—Yes. That one. I would be very grateful if you were able to apprehend her promptly. The pilots, however, have to go.

—I may not have the power to arrest you, but I don't have to do *everything* you say.

—You certainly do not. You should speak to the president and make your decision without considering me at all. You know that she will want to spin what comes next to her advantage. The United States giving the alien device to the world, creating the first planetary armed force. A gift of hope, from the president of the United States to humanity. I would imagine a parade, fireworks, and a very long and inspiring speech. That speech will be much easier to write if the pilots are not on death row for treason. The parade will also look better if you do not have to tow the robot.

— . . .

—Will that be all? I have a plane to catch.

FILE NO. 263

INTERVIEW WITH CW4 KARA RESNIK, UNITED STATES ARMY

Location: United States Army Garrison Fort Buchanan, Puerto Rico

—Can't believe Ryan had to be the hero. How typical.

—He did help you and Mr. Couture escape.

—He helped me escape all right. He got me out of the very bed he helped strapped me on . . . twice. He's a dick. But he *loves* a grand gesture.

—He does have a flair for the dramatic, but you should make room for the possibility that his actions were not entirely selfish.

—He just wanted to feel better about himself. Ryan doesn't deal well with guilt.

—Redemption is not the worst motive I can think of. I doubt he fully realized what he was signing on for when Ms. Papantoniou contacted him.

—He sure took his sweet time to catch on. Why are you defending Ryan all of a sudden? You're the one who threw him in jail.

—And I will send him back, after I express my gratitude for saving both of your lives. I am merely pointing out that Mr. Mitchell is not all evil. He did risk his life and disarm a dozen men to save you.

—Less-than-total-evilness . . . OK. I'll give you that. What will happen to them? The guards?

—Nothing, I assume. They were all legally employed by a legitimate corporation, and most of them have done nothing illegal.

—What about Alyssa?

—Will she be punished for what she did to you?

—To me? Yeah. To me, to Vincent. Whoever else she hurt.

—Probably not. She would argue that her actions were sanctioned, if not ordered, by the governments involved. It would be . . . messy, for lack of a better word.

—So they just let her go?

—No one even saw her. She must have found a way to escape the compound before Mr. Mitchell took action.

—Where would she go?

—I do not know. The Marines looked for her at the airport. There were no women by that name on any of the passenger manifests for the day. They have calculated some possible routes. The most likely scenario is that she took a short flight to one of the neighboring islands. She may have hopped between a few islands before taking a flight to America or Europe.

—So she gets away and we forget about the whole thing? I'm not that forgiving.

—Me neither. I contacted the government of Bosnia and Herze-govina this morning. I provided them with some evidence. It might be enough for Sarajevo to ask for her extradition when she is found.

—Evidence of what? What'd she do in Bosnia?

—She was born there.

—Papantoniou?

—It is not her name. She never went back to her maiden name after her husband died.

—So what's the evidence?

—There is a thirteen-month gap in her employment history. Yet, her financial records show little or no change in her spending patterns during that period.

—Wow. Let me get this straight: you think she's a criminal because she kept spending the same even though she had no job. Maybe she had enough savings. Maybe Mom and Dad helped.

—Both her parents were dead. More to the point, that thirteen-month gap occurred right around the time of the Srebrenica mas-sacre.

—Srebren . . . You think she's the doctor who tortured those poor people? Who forced Muslim women to . . . I . . . I can't speak . . .

—Take your time.

—Is that why you sent me to find Fata?

—I sent you there to find a potential witness. As I said, I have no hard evidence. She has a medical background. Her previous employment was in a hospital only ninety miles from Srebrenica, and she cannot account for her income during the time of the massacre.

I did find a sympathetic ear with the Bosnian government. It would be a significant political victory to bring the Butcher of Srebrenica to justice, so they will look into the matter further. They will send an investigator to the village where you found Fata and show her some pictures.

—Are you sure it was her? I mean, "really" sure?

—I am about 98 percent certain that she had absolutely nothing to do with the events that occurred in Srebrenica. In all honesty, it is a terribly far-fetched interpretation of the facts. But, I have been proven wrong before. The Bosnian government might be able to build a case against her, whether or not she is guilty of that particular crime.

—Remind me never to get on your bad side. When will we know?

—I would say in about ten years.

—Ten years! How long can it take to show a woman one picture? Or is that how long you think a trial would take?

—I do not know how rapidly the wheels of justice move in Bosnia. What I do know is that a trial could not start until she is extradited, and she could not be extradited if she is serving a prison sentence for another crime.

—What other crime? What else could she have done? Kill Kennedy?

—She has done nothing yet. But if she lands in one of the major airports I have contacts in, she will be found in possession of several kilos of heroin, or some other illegal narcotic. That should considerably extend her stay, wherever that is. I would say for approximately ten years, based on the average sentence for drug trafficking.

—You don't mess around, do you?

—I like to be thorough.

—I don't like to think of myself as vindictive, but . . .

—But you are.

—Exactly. So, thank you. She deserves it. How the hell did you end up picking Eva Braun to run this place anyway? Don't answer that, I don't really wanna know.

—I can answer that very easily. She is the only person I did not choose myself. And people ask me why I micromanage every-thing . . .

—So, can we go home now?

—There is another matter I am afraid we must discuss before we depart. It concerns you and Mr. Couture personally.

—Should I be worried?

—How would you like to make history?

—Whoa. Cheesy. Isn't that what we've been doing all along?

—Well, how would you like to serve in the Earth Defense Corps?

—What the heck is that?

—An armed branch of the United Nations dedicated to planetary defense. It will be the first ever military force maintained directly by the UN.

—An army with soldiers from all over the world?

—For now, personnel would mostly come from the United States and Canada.

—It would just be me and Vincent . . .

—Yes. The preliminary plan calls for a command and research center to be created within two years. It will need to be staffed. When that happens, you are correct: personnel will come from everywhere.

—What will we do?

—The primary focus of the organization will be research: exploring the capabilities of the device and using it as a springboard for the development of new technologies with planetary-defense applications.

—I meant what will Vincent and I do?

—Parades and photo opportunities, for the most part. Unless, of course, Earth is attacked by alien forces, in which case you will most likely die a quick and meaningless death at the hands of a superior enemy with overwhelming numbers.

—You make everything sound so exciting. I'm psyched. And who will run this Earth Defense thing?

—I do not know. I have been tasked with finding a suitable team leader. I promise to stay away from any candidate exhibiting sociopathic tendencies. What matters for now is that this project cannot go forward without you, and I would like to tell the UN that they can count on your continued involvement.

—You want my answer now?

—There is no time like the present.

— . . . Sure. What am I gonna say? No, I don't want to drive that awesome alien thing? I know Vincent wouldn't give this up for the world. I sure won't be the one to take it away from him.

—I am very pleased to hear you say it. I felt it necessary to ask, given all that you have been through recently.

—I know, you big softy. You act all tough, but really you're all mush inside.

—That reminds me, your mother would like to see you.

—Mom? Where is she?

—Guantanamo.

— . . . Come on! Really? You put my mother in a cell to use her as leverage in case I said no?

—While it is not unfathomable that I would use the presence of your loved ones as a means of persuasion, you should know I would never put your mother in a cell. I am, after all, all mush inside. She is at the base in Guantanamo, not the prison. Her plane had to drop some Marines along the way. She should be here within the hour. You can fly back to the United States together.

—You're an asshole. Vincent said you'd pull something like that.

—How is Mr. Couture doing? I have not had the chance to see him yet.

—He's fine. He's more than fine. He really likes that hero stuff. It's scary.

—Is that a bad thing?

—I don't know. I'm still mad at him.

—What has he done now to deserve your ire? He has been, as you pointed out, fairly heroic these past few days.

—Exactly. How could he be stupid enough to come back for me?

—Do you believe he had an ulterior motive?

—No, he just cared. That's the thing. You know how I don't easily trust other people.

—Is there anyone that does not know?

—Well, how could I possibly not trust him now? You know what'll happen, don't you? I'll let my guard down, I'll say stupid things I'll regret later, I'll turn into a fifteen-year-old. At some point, he'll ask me to marry him, and I'll be too gaga to get myself out of it.

—Mr. Couture does not seem like the marriage type to me.

—Did you know he's been shopping for a ring?

—...

—Yep, I was speechless too when I found out. I've been acting as caustic as I can under the circumstances. So far, I've managed to look ambivalent enough about my feelings to keep him from popping the question.

—Perhaps, deep down inside that rugged shell of yours, there is a little girl desperately waiting for her Prince Charming to propose.

—Of course there is. Only until now, I'd been pretty successful at keeping that little brat's mouth shut.

—What will your answer be if he asks?

—You're funny. He can't ask. I'll find a way to be bitchy enough for the next forty years so that perfect moment never comes.

—You seem to have a good handle on that little girl after all. Goodbye, Ms. Resnik.

EPILOGUE

FILE NO. 360

INTERVIEW WITH UNKNOWN SUBJECT

Location: Embassy of the United States, Dublin, Ireland

—How are you feeling physically? Do you require medical attention?

—I'm OK. Thank you.

—Is there anything I can get you to make you more comfortable? You were exposed to the cold for quite some time.

—I'm fine, really. They let me take a shower and gave me some warm clothes. Thank you.

—Do you know who I am?

—No, I'm sorry. I don't know anyone in Ireland.

—What are you doing in this country?

—I've been kidnapped! Look, I've told you people a dozen times already. I don't know how I ended up in Europe. A truck driver found me on the side of the road this morning—naked, for God's sake.

—You say you have been kidnapped. Can you tell me how it happened?

—I was driving home from work when this van hit the brakes right in front of me. I crashed into it pretty hard. Someone dragged me out of my car. I must have fainted afterward.

—Where is home?

—I'm an American. I live in Chicago.

—You fainted and you woke up on the side of the road near Dublin.

—Yes . . . I . . . Yes, I did.

—What is it?

—I'm not sure. I think I was awake for a few seconds in between. I couldn't see anything, but I heard some voices.

—How many voices did you hear?

—Four or five. I don't know. I'm not even sure I didn't dream the whole thing.

—What were they saying?

—I couldn't tell. I don't know what language they were speaking. It sounded like . . . I don't know what it sounded like. Maybe Swedish, Lakota with a heavy German accent. I really don't know. Something I've never heard before.

—How do you know what Lakota sounds like?

—I don't really. *Dances with Wolves?* It's the only Native American language I can think of. I was born in South Dakota. There are a few reservations around. Actually, the whole area where we lived used to be Lakota territory.

—You have no papers, no identification of any kind. Is that correct?

—I told you. I was completely naked when I woke up. I don't know what happened to my bag.

—You should know that the doctors who examined you found no signs of sexual activity.

—Thank you. That's a relief.

—Can you think of anything that would help us confirm your identity?

—No, not in Ireland. That's not a crime, is it? If you get me home, you can talk to my friends, people I work with.

—I would like to show you some photos.

—Go ahead.

—Do you recognize the woman in this picture?

—No, I don't know who that is. She's pretty.

—How about this man?

—I don't know him either. Who is he?

—A linguist from Canada.

—A lin . . . Do you think these are the people who abducted me?

—I do not. In fact, I can tell you without hesitation that they are not.

—Then why show me their pictures?

—To see whether or not you recognized them.

—Is there a reason I should? I can tell you I don't have amnesia. Aside from the few hours I was unconscious, I remember everything very clearly.

—Can I ask you one more personal question? How old are you?

—I'm twenty-seven.

—For the record, could you please state your name and occupation one more time?

—My name is Rose Franklin. I'm a researcher at the University of Chicago.

—Your DNA profile is indeed a match to that of Dr. Franklin.

—You seem surprised. I know who I am. Can I please go home now? I haven't fed my cat since I left for work yesterday.

—. . . Ms. Franklin, from what I understand, that was more than four years ago.

—Wh . . . That makes no sense. I was kidnapped. I wasn't in a coma. It's not like I slept for four years.

—I believe you. Strange as it may seem, there is no accurate scientific method for determining the age of a living person. However, the results of your physical examination and dental X-rays are consistent with your being twenty-seven.

—I know, I told you my age.

—What I meant is that you are missing recent scars and some dental work that was done to Dr. Franklin after the age of twenty-seven.

—I . . . I don't understand.

—Dr. Rose Franklin would be thirty-one years old by now.

—What exactly do you mean by "would be"?

—Please come with me, there is much we need to discuss . . .

ACKNOWLEDGMENTS

(IN REVERSE CHRONOLOGICAL ORDER)

A giant-robot-sized thank-you to my editor, Mark Tavani and everyone at Del Rey. Thank you, Mark, for giving this book a home, for your enthusiasm and guidance, and for coping with my semicolon addiction. Thank you, Seth Fishman, my winged agent; and Rebecca Gardner and Will Roberts at The Gernert Co. Seth, you rule. Thank you for putting me out of business as a publisher.

I wouldn't be writing any of this without my movie agent, Jon Cassir at CAA (I also couldn't say things like "my movie agent"). Thank you Jon. That brings me to Josh Bratman. Josh, you know what you did. Thank you for changing my life.

Many thanks to my beta readers, especially to Toby and Andrew. You guys are definitely alphas. Thank you, Barbara, for letting me ignore you for a few hours every night, though I strongly suspect you were just happy to have more time to read.

Thank you, Theodore. You asked so many questions when I offered to make you a toy robot, I had to write a book about it. Thank you, Jean, for passing your love of language on to me. Thank you, Thérèse, for giving me the guts to try just about anything.

ABOUT THE AUTHOR

SYLVAIN NEUVEL dropped out of high school at age fifteen. Along the way, he has been a journalist, worked in soil decontamination, sold ice cream in California, and peddled furniture across Canada. He received a Ph.D. in linguistics from the University of Chicago. He taught linguistics in India and worked as a software engineer in Montreal. He is also a certified translator though he wishes he were an astronaut. He likes to tinker, dabbles in robotics, and is somewhat obsessed with Halloween. He absolutely loves toys; his girlfriend would have him believe that he has too many, so he writes about aliens and giant robots as a blatant excuse to build action figures (for his son, of course).

neuvel.net
Facebook.com/sylvainneuvel
@neuvel

ABOUT THE TYPE

This book was set in Sabon, a typeface designed by the well-known German typographer Jan Tschichold (1902–74). Sabon's design is based upon the original letter forms of sixteenth-century French type designer Claude Garamond and was created specifically to be used for three sources: foundry type for hand composition, Linotype, and Monotype. Tschichold named his typeface for the famous Frankfurt typefounder Jacques Sabon (c. 1520–80).